About the Author

Jaime Grookett studied Creative Writing at Drexel University. She is a professor of Teacher Education. Her work appears in various publications, such as *Typehouse* Literary Magazine, *Quail Bell* Magazine and *Valiant Scribe*. She was awarded Best of Fiction 2020 at Across the Margin. She lives in New Jersey, with her husband, two children, and two rescue dogs. This is her first novel.

The Invisible Ones

Jaime Grookett

The Invisible Ones

To Sue,
It was great meeting
you at the Fortnightly.
I hope you enjoy Kiara's
story. Jamie Grookett

Vanguard Press

VANGUARD PAPERBACK

© Copyright 2024
Jaime Grookett

The right of Jaime Grookett to be identified as author of
this work has been asserted by her in accordance with the
Copyright, Designs and Patents Act 1988.

A CIP catalogue record for this title is
available from the British Library.

ISBN 978 1 83794 010 3

Vanguard Press is an imprint of
Pegasus Elliot Mackenzie Publishers Ltd.
www.pegasuspublishers.com

First Published in 2024

Vanguard Press
Sheraton House Castle Park
Cambridge England

Printed & Bound in Great Britain

To my mom, Dianna, who bought me Smarty Bear for Christmas instead of the Cricket doll I wanted. Whatever you were going for worked.

Although this book is a work of fiction, my grandmother's and great-grandmother's stories inspired me to create the tale of Anna Wilson. They drove me to learn more about the treatment of women in American history and led me to discover the story of Carrie Buck and countless other women who lost their identities, many of whom remain nameless. I want to thank my mother, Dianna, for sharing their history with me. American eugenics is often misunderstood and forgotten, yet it impacts the heritage of so many of us. These women's voices went unheard for enough years. Thank you to those who read earlier versions of this story, which I wrote during the first months of the pandemic. Jessica Lucas, Heather Kreismer, Jenn Sangillo, Ashley McGuire, and Colleen Bianco Bezich, have stood by me throughout this process and supported me in far more ways than simply reading my words. Thank you to Doug Raschenburger and the Haddonfield Historical Society for your guidance, as I created Anna's world. Also, thank you to Patricia Martinelli and the Vineland Historical Society for sharing a wealth of information on the Vineland Training School. I learned that the practices in this school in New Jersey were more humane than many similar institutions. So I decided to place Anna's story in Pennsylvania, where my grandmother and great-grandmother lived. My research in

American eugenics and the treatment of those labeled as feeble-minded or undesirable led me to many interesting and surprising parts of American history, such as the Pennsylvania Training School for Feeble-Minded Children, Pennhurst State School and Hospital, the Vineland Training School, and the story of Carrie Buck and her mother, Emma Buck. Thank you to the incredible Nomi Eve for your excellent advice and support throughout the writing process and beyond. And thank you to Ann Garvin, Harriet Levin Millan, Heather Webb, Sadeqa Johnson, and Brandi Megan Granett, and the entire Drexel MFA, for the community you've created and the minds you've inspired. Your impact on the creative world is immeasurable. A special thank you to two friends who have been by my side since I started this journey, Juliet Del Rio and Leah Mele-Bazaz. I treasure your friendship, writing critiques, and constant encouragement. Without you, writing, for me, would be a solitary endeavor. I'm grateful to have you by my side. Thank you to my husband, Tom, and my children, Ava and Tommy. Your encouragement made this book possible. You listened to hours of my reading and rereading lines, and you gave me the space to become absorbed in my writing, knowing you were happy because I was doing what made me happy. Your love and support mean everything to me.

Chapter One

If you listen closely enough, when the cicadas quit their chitter-chatter and the wind hushes, the stars whisper everything you need to know. That day, as dawn threatened to erase them from the sky, the stars warned me I won't be invisible anymore. All my life, we moved about like ghosts, not caring a lick about the world outside our measly farm. It didn't care much for us, our hungry bellies and thin-soled boots, so why would we care much for it? I never imagined anyone paid us, the Wilsons out in a shack on Shaker Street, any mind at all. But they did. Turns out, they were hunting us. Dreamed of ridding the world of the likes of us. And in our solitude, our happiness with what little we had in life, we never saw it coming. But the stars? The stars saw it all.

#

The winter of 1928 was a brutal one, freezing our only horse to death, right there in his own stall. We found him as a frozen bag of bones mid-February, after we cleared the snow enough to trek through the icy grounds to check on him. I called Helen, who was fifteen—two years younger than me but whip-smart—to help haul the carcass. But even when we got little John and Alice to pitch in and push, we couldn't move that sucker a lick.

That day, though, I had a shock of hope while staring at the stars, as I felt the temperature tip above freezing. Even the clouds rolling in made my heart grow warm. We'd get this farm back to good once the weather turned. It was all about the weather.

The rain pecked my head. I looked up to see the storm clouds rolling in over a mess of vines that covered our fields like a swarm of timber rattlesnakes. I raced to the house. "Buckets!" I shouted.

The lot of us ran to the back corner of the kitchen, where we stored tin pails, then we spread them throughout the house to catch the water that would soon seep through the busted roof.

The rain came fast. We hardly heard the rumbling of the gravel driveway until Alice shouted, "A Lizzie, a Lizzie!"

I looked out the wide front window to see a rusted, black car pulling towards the house. Alice, ten years old and always falling in love with things she'd never have— fancy automobiles, tame dogs, family dinners—knew a Tin Lizzie when she saw one. I didn't know any of that. But I had a knack for knowing trouble when it found me.

"Get yourselves in the cellar. Hurry!" I shouted.

We tore down the shaky wooden steps to the root cellar and hid amid the dwindling supply of russet potatoes and parsnips, breathing in the fresh rot of the ones about to turn.

"Anna, what's going on? Why are they here?" asked Alice. She crouched her scrawny frame into the back corner by a wooden shelf littered with empty baskets. She almost disappeared.

"Hush, Alice," I said.

"Anna, what's happening? Why we hiding?" Helen asked.

You'd never know Helen was my sister, with her pretty hair, sharp chin, and bold eyes. She knew me too well not to pick up on my panic.

She huddled next to John, her knees tucked to her chest. "What's going on?"

I crept from the corner of the cellar, towards the bottom of the steps, listening for the creak of the front door. Then I watched Helen's lips part wide to howl, so I raced back and clasped my hand over her mouth. "Hush up!"

Helen squeezed my wrist until I let up. "Why are we hiding?"

She looked back at six-year-old John, skinnier than a stalk of corn, cowering behind her. He didn't know enough about anything, so I imagined his skin wasn't prickling with fear. He followed our lead but with a smirk, saying he thought we might be play pretending.

Helen's words shot out so fast that they tripped over one another. "Are they going to want Mama? What we going to tell them about Mama?"

"Do you think I know what to tell them?" I shouted too loud for someone who was supposed to be hiding.

The broken front door thumped open, and the rickety floor above us creaked. My throat closed.

A chipper voice shot through the thin walls. "Hello. Children's Aid Society of Pennsylvania. Anyone home?"

Helen snatched my arm. "You said she was coming back. Why are these people here?" Helen's voice shook, as the floorboards cracked with the sound of heeled shoes.

We all looked up with gaping mouths.

I gazed at John. His eyes grew as big as a raccoons'. He knew this wasn't pretend. Alice, who could smash the bruised apples from Mr. Herbert's old tree into the sweetest applesauce, had tears welling up in her blue eyes and spilling over like twin waterfalls.

"Shhh—" My heart beat in my ears so loud that I couldn't hear the floorboards anymore. I whispered, "Mama never said she was leaving. So how am I supposed to know when she's coming back?"

"But you said—" John stammered. His ragged hair and dirt-crusted face would give away all our secrets.

The stench of mildew filled my lungs as I took a deep breath, trying to keep back the tears. For the first time, the three of them looked like corpses—sunken cheeks, bones poking out like they had nothing to hold them back.

"What did you expect? You wouldn't have believed the truth, so I gave you a lie." The footsteps drew closer. "Been half a year. You only believed because you wanted to. Wasn't fair of Mama to leave the truth-telling to me."

"Hello," a sugary voice called from the top of the steps.

A clap of thunder sounded, and we all jumped. The rain began to plink into the buckets.

"Are you down there?" Sharp heels clanked on the wooden steps, in time with the pelting rain.

Each tap of her heel snapped us further into the cellar corner, cowering like scared kittens. We crowded on top of one another now.

"There you are," she said, crouching down, resting her hands on her thick knees. "The Wilson children, I presume?" Her voice rose like a question, but she wasn't really asking. "I'm Miss Atkinson from the Children's Aid Society."

A gentleman with thin, long limbs and a rounded cap followed behind her.

"This here is Mr. Williams."

He swept his derby hat off his bald head and bowed to greet us, like we were some kind of royalty. I was no fool. They didn't come here to help us.

Alice opened her mouth to speak, but I shot her a dagger stare before she had a chance—*Don't say a word.* Blood rushed to my ears as I stood in front of my siblings. I raised my hands wide as if I could hide them and willed my scrawny self to look bigger. Another thunder rumbled. I didn't flinch this time.

Miss Atkinson stared me right in the eye. "We understand you children are living here alone, no?"

"No, ma'am. We aren't alone. We're with each other." My voice cracked a little, but I said it loud, like I was right.

"I'm sorry, dear. You're all going to come with us."

She reached for my wrist, but I flung it away, whacking Helen in the face. I took a step back and spread my arms out wider. "No, ma'am. We're not going anywhere."

"Anna," John yelled, gripping the back of my apron strings.

"Hush up, John," I scolded.

He wrapped his pale arms around my waist.

"Get him, Helen," I yelled. We couldn't be coming undone in front of the authorities. They didn't need more reason to take us. I turned back to Miss Atkinson. "With all due respect, ma'am, we aren't going anywhere. This here is our home."

"You cannot stay here without a guardian, Miss Wilson. Anna, is it?"

The sound of my name on her tongue made my ears feel like they were about to blow fire.

"You cannot stay here. You are children."

Rain pounding on the roof echoed in the dank cellar. The splashing into the tin buckets upstairs grew louder.

The lady snatched my arm and pulled me towards her, but little John hung tight. She dragged me towards the steps, John's arms still wrapped around my waist and his bare feet sliding across the cold, cement floor.

The man shuffled behind us, grabbing ahold of Helen and Alice's shoulders.

"Run!" I shouted to Helen and Alice, but the man dropped their shoulders and snatched them each by an arm. Their fight wasn't enough to free them.

I screamed to the lady as she towed me and John upstairs. "We're not going! We're not leaving our farm! This here is our home."

When we reached the living room, we waited while Mr. Williams struggled with my sisters. I looked at the buckets. Plenty of space left to catch the rain. We needn't worry about the floors.

Right as Mr. Williams glanced back at Alice and Helen, I turned to Miss Atkinson and stood tall, smiled my best smile, and leaned towards her. As her lips parted to return my smile, I spat in her face then stomped on her pretty high-heeled shoes with my old boot.

"I'll have none of that," she said, squeezing me tighter then reaching down to grab ahold of John to yank him off my waist. She shoved him to the other side of the living room, where he stood, his mouth open like a fish, by the torn sofa. Leaning down towards my ear, she whispered, "This foolishness will undo you, my dear. A girl in your lot cannot carry such rage. You'll find yourself locked away forever."

Behind me, Helen and Alice whimpered. John had dropped to the floor, hugging his knees. Already, there was no fight left in him.

"We ain't going, Miss Atkinson. This farm is all we know. This here's our home." The words caught in my throat.

"We aren't asking, Miss Wilson. We're telling. Get yourself out that door and into that car, or you might never see them again." She eyed my sisters, then my baby brother. They looked a feral lot. Thunder clapped again. "You have five minutes to gather any necessary personal belongings and get yourself into that car."

I did all the gathering, afraid that if I didn't listen, things might go from bad to worse. We piled into that Lizzie and hugged each other tight, as the rain washed over the clean windows. We flipped around to stare out the back as we pulled out the dirt drive, watching our sagging home disappear as we drove down muddy Shaker Street, finding ourselves no longer invisible.

Chapter Two

We drove down muddy, winding roads flanked with rain-soaked farmland until we reached the paved streets of a town I didn't know. It took about three of Alice's stories and one singing of 'Let Me Call You Sweetheart' from John to get there.

Alice shouted, "Eastwood!" as we passed a bright-blue sign surrounded by prickly winterberry hollies.

Right then I was wishing I'd taken Alice up on the reading lessons she always offered afternoons when she got home from the consolidated school, but I always had hens to tend to or laundry to beat, so all I knew of reading was the little I learned in school before Mama had John and made me stay home to help with the chores.

As we drove, we entered a world I'd never seen. Orderly houses were lined with wintergreen-filled, white window boxes and tar, black streets, each one with a motorcar in the drive. My stomach cartwheeled as we slowed to the front of the powder-blue one with a wide front porch and two rocking chairs teetering in the wind. As we parked in front, I could tell the rain had already passed through, because the steppingstones to the porch sparkled clean.

Miss Atkinson stepped out of the passenger side door and opened the back door. "Anna, this is you," she said, and handed me an envelope with my name written in curly letters: 'Anna Wilson'.

"No!" I shouted, clinging to Helen, but she was a waif of a girl and didn't give me much to grab on to. My heart beat so hard that it felt like it burst. I had never been off my farm before, not without my family. I didn't know how to do life without them.

Miss Atkinson got me by the arm and snapped me right out of the car. Her lips sealed a red line, like a freshly sown row of berries. *Best do what she said, or I might make things worse for the others,* so I clutched my pillowcase filled with my few things and followed.

"I'll find you," I shouted to the others, right before Miss Atkinson slammed the door.

My boots splashed into puddles as we walked around the car towards the house. I took one last look back at the car and watched tears streak the window as they pressed their faces against the pane. I couldn't believe they were separating us. They never knew life without me darning their socks.

"Come with me," Miss Atkinson said.

The house had neat square windows with boxes in a perfect line. On the farm, we had replaced our broken windows years ago with some we found along Old Mill Road, so they tilted like they had too much whiskey. But these windows sat ramrod. These were definitely not going to be my kind of people.

Miss Atkinson balled her fist and pounded on the wooden door. "Mrs. Lucille Monroe. Your new charge is here."

The door swung open, and the thick scent of burning wood smacked me in the face. A woman with gray, wild hair filled the doorway. "About time," she said, her voice husky and deep. "I'll see her in."

"She has few things, Mrs. Monroe. She'll need the basics."

Miss Atkinson turned to leave, and my throat closed. I wanted to call after her, ask her to stay or take me with her, but my dumb mouth wouldn't see to it. I stayed mum while I watched Miss Atkinson get in that car and drive away with my life.

"You'll call me Ma," Mrs. Monroe said, clipping her voice, so I knew best not to question her.

The living room was cozy, crowded with odds and ends in need of dusting. There was no snowy fluff poking through the arms of the sofa. Even the floorboards gave way differently than ours at home, little creaking or shifting as I walked down the long hall, past the kitchen and towards a door at the far end.

"This here is where you'll stay," Ma said. She swung the door open to reveal a tiny room with a single bed, an end table, and a long dresser against the wall, with an oval mirror set above it.

For a second my heart jumped. I had never had my own room before. I scolded myself for even feeling a hint of excitement. No room was worth my family. "This is all mine?" I asked.

"Yours while you're here. The church dropped off some clothes for you this morning. Might be a bit big. Didn't realize you'd be such a scrawny thing. But you'll make do."

"Yes, ma'am," I whispered. I stepped towards the bed, set down my pillowcase and the letter, then opened the bag of worn nun clothes.

"You'll earn your keep here. Miss Atkinson told me you haven't been to school for some time." She stood by the doorway, her thick hands leaning against the frame.

I held a threadbare dress against my chest to see if it might fit. "No, ma'am. I left school when my brother John was born six years ago. Mama needed help on the farm since Papa left."

Before she turned to leave, she said, "No sense starting now. Nearly grown as you are. There's plenty to do around here. I'll have a list waiting for you in the kitchen, so settle in quick."

Ma closed the door behind her. I sat on the edge of the bed, rubbing the soft quilt between my fingers, my head growing dizzier and dizzier.

After I had a moment to take in the room, I set the folded clothes in a musty drawer of the dresser. In the mirror, I caught my reflection but didn't recognize the eyes staring back. The same matted, brown hair crowned my head, but those eyes. It was like staring at someone I hadn't met yet.

I opened my pillowcase to find the few things I brought from home: a fine-tooth comb, the crocheted doll that Alice made me, and a pair of tights and placed them into the top drawer. Underneath them, I hid my letter. But first, I opened it to see if I could make out a few words. Only my siblings' names. I recognized them like the lines on my palm. I traced their names as if I somehow could feel them tucked in the loops of the writing.

In the closet, dangled three worn leather belts from a rusty metal hanger. Next to them, I hung the last thing I brought from home—a blue apron I wore every day on the farm. It lolled there in the near-empty closet, looking as out of place in this home as I was.

#

That first afternoon, head bowed and shoulders caved like I'd been gut-punched, I swept the porch with a straw broom and dusted all those knickknacks in the parlor with an old pair of hose. When Ma handed me the chores written on lined paper, she whined about how 'my kind' had no sense, her voice dropping to a whisper like we should keep it secret, so I thought best to hide my not being able to read her lists. The words looked like scribbles to me, so I asked her to read it aloud, blaming her chicken scratch for my not being able to read. She did, but her eyes narrowed and got the butterflies in my belly started up again.

By suppertime, I completed almost every job but sweeping the parlor. I peered through the large kitchen window, as the lazy sun set along the horizon of pointed roofs and bare trees, with specks of green here or there, the first signs of spring bleeding into late winter. The thought of time passing, seasons fading in and out before I saw my family again, made my knees wobble. I breathed a deep breath that hurt my lungs. The savory scent of garlic and onions on the stove warmed me, reminding me of the days before Mama left, but I shook the memory loose. I had a plan to hatch. No comfort could come without home.

By the dim light of the kitchen-table lamp, I hunched over a plate of lukewarm pink beans and soupy rice. To my right, Ma slumped over an enormous plate piled high with the meal, her eyes poised on me like she was waiting for me to forget my manners. I thought back to Miss Atkinson's warning and swore to myself I wouldn't give her reason to scorn me. Although she seemed to hate me just fine already. I figured she wanted me for a housemaid, so I just had to do my work until I learned to read that letter. That letter held the key to finding my family. I just knew it. Knowing that letter was tucked safe in my drawer gave me hope as bright as those green sprouts poking through the winter grass.

To my left sat Randolph, a tall boy with bad skin and a penchant for snorting whenever Ma gave an order. Across from me rested Randolph's dad, who Ma said I should call Pa. His grizzly beard and black eye patch made him look gruff, but between each bite he'd gaze up at me and smile, as if I was handing him a sucker. It made me miss the days before Papa turned to whiskey. Back then, he had a smile that warmed my insides, too.

While we hadn't had many family dinners since Mama left, the sight of the four of us made tears bloom in my eyes and settle right on the edge of my lower lids. I tried to hold those buggers in, but my breath—my breath would not be contained. It escaped without warning. A heaving sigh fanned crumbs of burnt bread across the narrow kitchen table, each one plinking as it struck a glass, a bowl, a fork. I watched them scatter like dandelion fluff.

"Stop that, now. You're making a mess of things." Ma teetered on the small chair, her weight bowing the crane seat. She slurped a considerable spoonful of beans and looked at Pa.

He gazed at me then busied himself with the business of eating, paying no mind to Ma's howling.

"You won't last long here if you keep carrying on like that," Ma said, shaking her fork at me, spewing white flecks of rice into my knotted hair.

My mouth dropped open to speak before my brain had a chance to stop it. "I don't much want to be long for this place." I picked the sticky rice from my hair as anger rushed me. "I hate it here."

The paneled walls inhaled my muted voice. I stared at my plate overflowing with beans and rice and bread, a hefty meal. Even before Mama left, before Papa fell in love with whiskey and out of love with us, we never had full plates like this. For years we kids fended for ourselves, and I made sure the younger ones always had bellies as full as I could get them. Even if that meant my own belly rumbled that night. Still, I couldn't find it in me to be grateful for the feast or the warm house.

"What are you saying?" Ma's thick voice bellowed.

"I'm saying I hate it here." This time, my voice and my eyes raised to meet hers.

Randolph piped in with a mouthful of beans. "That all you can say? I hate it here. I hate it here. You're just a dumb appleknocker. You've said nothing else since you got here. Right, Pa?" He looked at his father, but his father never met his gaze. "Think she's slow. Just like the rest of them." He snorted then shoveled his remaining beans into his gaping mouth, scraping the fork sideways along the length of the plate and using his finger to scoop up the last bits of rice. He shook his head at me, his long, straggly hair lobbing in front of his wild eyes.

I stopped chewing and stared at him with pursed lips but said nothing.

Pa grunted and gnawed on a slab of crusty bread. Crumbs flecked his graying beard. His good eye squeezed closed for a second longer than a blink. Was he winking at me? "Leave the girl alone, Randy. You be nice." Pa's soft voice didn't budge the smirk off Randolph's face.

"Oh, I'll be nice, Pa." Randolph, who stood a foot taller than my five-foot frame, puffed his scrawny chest and wiped his nose with the back of his hand.

He and I were both seventeen, but adulthood hadn't flowered in either of us.

Pa said, "She just got here this morning. She isn't used to life off the farm. Isn't that right, Anna?"

The way he said my name made my tummy swirl. "Yes, sir. I only ever lived on the farm. It's a good farm, though. Have ourselves a full-on henhouse and five acres for crops."

"Well," he said, "sounds like you're a mighty hard worker to keep up with all that." He watched Ma straighten the shade of the lamp. "How you liking it here?"

The truth would push me further into trouble, so I said the only thing I thought of. "I like electric. We don't have electricity on the farm."

"How you see?" asked Randolph.

I twisted my napkin in my lap. "We get by."

"You have one of those, I bet," Pa said, nodding towards a cast-iron potbelly stove.

"Sure do. Heat the whole house if we got enough coal," I said. We never had enough coal.

The Monroes weren't rich, I could tell. They had a radio and a sturdy kitchen table, but everything in that house showed wear. But compared to our farm, I might as well be in the President's house.

"I bet you took good care of your farm," said Pa, smiling.

"Nothing on a farm but manure and stinky cows," said Randolph, as he sopped up the drippings on his plate with his bread.

"Cows ran off years ago," I said, wishing to take back the words, but my heart felt full when I talked of my farm, even if it was about the bad parts.

Pa ripped off a hunk of bread and passed it to me. I smiled and took it. The doughy insides warmed my tongue. I smelled the sweet butter across the table.

"May I have the butter, please?" I asked.

Pa passed it, and I lathered it on. Wasn't often we had butter at home. I didn't want to lose that lightness in my heart, so I kept talking. "Lots of fields, we had. Grew corn, tomatoes, anything that'd grow. Aside from my brother and sisters, the hens are what I loved most about my home." I thought to how it would fare without us. The crops that survived the winter would sprout to wilt. No one would be there to tend them.

"Hush up, now," Ma said, scraping her chair across the floor as she stood up from the table. "That godforsaken place isn't your home now. I don't want to hear another word about it." She began clearing the table. "Got ourselves a market up the street. Plenty of eggs and vegetables there. No need for farms."

"Only appleknockers live on farms," chuckled Randolph. His eyes met mine, and I held his stare until he turned to Pa. "Isn't that right? She just a dumb appleknocker."

"I love my land," I snapped. "And I'm not dumb." They had no idea how that land had nestled into my heart. No matter where I went, that land stayed a part of me, and I'd do anything to get back there.

"You sure are dumb," he said. "Bet you never been to a city."

"Don't mean I'm dumb. I bet you can't sow and reap a crop of turnips."

"You watch your tongue, young lady. You're our guest." Ma dropped the tin plates into the sink with a clang. "Know your place."

I thought back to Miss Atkinson's warning about making more trouble for myself, but trouble kept finding me. After taking one last look into Randolph's icy-blue eyes, too pretty for his pocked face and sharp nose, I searched Pa's face for a smile and noticed a definite wink. I swallowed hard and stood up to help Ma clear the table. This place, I knew, would try to tear me away from who I was, my land, my family, but I'd fight it the whole way, no matter what Miss Atkinson said.

#

I ended the night's work inside where it'd be warmer. By nightfall, any signs of spring from earlier in the day disappeared, and a chill set in that made my bones ache.

For all my talk of not wanting to be at the Monroe's, the thought of finding myself in more trouble made my breath catch. As bad as the Monroe's was, I knew things could get worse for me. After the stink Randolph made about my being dumb, I knew I'd have to get mighty clever to trick someone into reading me my chore list until I learned all those words. I pushed the idea aside as I started sweeping the parlor.

I was all hard work and spitfire. I loved my family fierce and did what I had to. I was proud of what I gave up for them. Alice, at ten, could almost read *The Story of Doctor Dolittle*. She even tried to teach me to read every now and again. Showed me the letters and their sounds and how you jumbled them up to make words. Helen, at only fifteen, could weave a story so tight it'd hold water. Only thing I ever weaved was an apple basket out of honeysuckle vines. And my John, a wee thing, had a mind to fix anything broken on the farm. He'd rig the old well each time the connecting rod slipped loose from the handle. Only one who figured it out. Every one of them fit in my life like a jigsaw. Who was I without them?

I took the tall straw broom from the closet and turned on the electric table lamp in the hall. I worked my way towards the door, forming little piles of dust and dirt to scoop up later. The house sat so quietly that I heard the soft winter wind breathing outside the door. At home, I always saved sweeping for last, because it was my favorite. Although never much of a dancer—that talent fell to Alice—when I swept, I'd sashay back and forth across the porch, pretending that chipped-up porch was my stage.

All of a sudden, tears started coming, so I let myself pretend to be back on that porch, dancing and singing like I used to. Closing my eyes and spinning with my broom, I sang 'Sweet Georgia Brown' in a soft voice, like we did at our neighbor's, the Joneses, when we listened to the Ben

Bernie album blare through the horn. The Joneses had no electricity or icebox, like everyone else on Shaker Street, but they had a phonograph and one album. They'd crank the handle and play for anyone who'd listen. That sweet jazz song was the only one I knew.

The memory pulled me in so far, I never heard the creaking of the floorboard until a heaviness came over me, as if those stars dropped a blanket on me from the sky. I looked up to see a yawning silhouette stretch across the parlor. My voice went mute as I raised the broom to shield myself.

Chapter Three

The looming threat in the heart of the parlor moved in like storm clouds. By the glow of the table lamp, I watched Ma's trunk of an arm raise up over my head. I stumbled back, still shielding myself with the broom. My eyes sprung wide as her angry fist thrashed down on me, slamming the side of my face into the front door. Steadying myself, I toppled towards the corner. Ma snatched the collar of my nightdress and yanked me so close I could smell the supper onions on her breath. Fear wove a knot thick in my throat.

"Are you singing, child? You're singing at this hour when you should be working?"

"No, ma'am. I wasn't. I was—"

"Do you think I don't know singing? Are you calling me a liar?" Her eyes spread as wide as those of a cat who had caught sight of a rat. "You're singing that Negro music in my house?"

"No, ma'am. No—" My voice stammered as I searched for words to calm Ma down.

Fisting my cotton collar, Ma heaved me up off the floor, until we met eyes. My stocking toes dangled above the swept floor. The entire day ran through my head as I hung there, feet a hair off the wood, no ground to stand on. My mind let loose. Miss Atkinson. Mr. Williams. Ma. Randolph. My own Mama having run off without sending a word. All the anger balled up in my hand as I held a grip on the broom. With one hand, I swung it like an axe to wood at Ma, slamming the side of her face. She hardly moved, just opened her palm and let me thud to the floor. She leaned over me, her shaking body blocking the light. Ma grabbed the broomstick, tore it from my hand then hurled it across the parlor into the living room. I watched it thud against the brick fireplace and clank to the hearth.

"Do you think you can fight your way out of your lot in life?" Ma laughed. "I'll see to it you end up where you belong."

I scooted to the corner by the door and curled up as tight as I could, hoping I'd disappear, burying my face in my hands and closing my eyes.

She whispered my name, "Anna," as soft as lamb's wool. It sounded like a song.

I looked up to see Ma's hand raised high overhead, and before I had a chance to cover my face again, she unleashed her fist across my cheek. Huffing, Ma turned her back to me, swinging the long end of her flannel nightgown, exposing her slippered feet, and strutted back down the hall.

After Ma left, I breathed again. Shallow little puffs, not enough to undizzy my head. I sat, curled up against that wall for a moment, remembering the nights when whiskey got the best of Papa. I always found myself the target for the rage, no matter how much I hid. Ma was no match for me. I'd been here before; I'd seen worse. Papa's rage equaled his love, and I got used to never knowing which one I'd get. Ma would not win this.

I thrust myself up from the floor, walked over to the fireplace to take back my broom, and finished sweeping. Under my breath, I went right back to singing 'Sweet Georgia Brown.' In my head, I belted the song as loud as my lungs would let me.

#

A week passed as the bruise on my face faded from the color of eggplant to parsnip. While that lightened, the heaviness in my chest gained weight. Nights, I'd wake gasping for air, swearing something was crushing my guts.

Each morning, I'd dress in the nuns' clothes, inhaling the sharp scent of mothballs, and make my way to the kitchen for my list of chores. Tricking Ma into reading the list proved easy. I had dust in my eye. Her writing curled too much. The pencil smeared into a gray cloud. She'd huff and her eyes risked rolling right out of her head onto the swept floor, but she read them, giving me the chance to study the words all day while I tidied or dusted or scrubbed. And study I did. Within my first week, I learned a few new words and started to figure out the voice of some letters. I needed to do more, though, if I wanted to find my brother and sisters. The chore list would never be enough for me to learn to read on my own. And if I didn't learn to read Miss Atkinson's letter, I had no chance of finding my way home.

That day, I found Ma crocheting a blue scarf, looping stitches one after the other like she was weaving a basket with yarn. I thought I could do that. I could crochet myself a scarf someday. A red one.

"Morning, Ma. My chores for today?"

"The shed. It needs a good cleaning before spring comes. See to it you don't take all day. Pa and I are out tonight, and I might need you to fix supper for Randolph."

It was Saturday. No school for Randolph. No work for Pa. For me, it felt like any other day but more people to work around. Not much different from the farm, really. I always saw to it that Helen got herself and the younger ones to school. They didn't even miss when the snow hit knee-deep. They'd load themselves up on the sled and take turns hauling each other down Shaker Street to the schoolhouse on the county road. When one grew tired, she'd hop on the sled and let another pull the weight. On weekends, I'd set them to cleaning out the henhouse or harvesting the crops, when we were lucky enough to have a harvest. I'd have to mind them, though. They always needed minding.

In the rear of the yard, a few feet in front of an ailing picket fence, stood a crooked, wooden shed painted white to match the house. I rubbed sawdust from a windowpane with the sleeve of the worn coat Ma had given me and peered in. Though it was dark inside, I could tell the job would take the day. I stepped around a frozen patch of mud and onto a small, chipped cement stoop. I rattled the knob, and the door creaked open. The musty smell reminded me of our cellar, and the last time I set foot in it.

The tilting of the shed's walls made it feel like they were closing in on me.

Figuring the sweeping would be last, I set aside a few brooms that lay across the cement floor. I made swift work of straightening up the tools on a workbench and hung up some hoes and rakes on nails across the side wall. For a moment, a shadow passed along the back window. When I looked, there was nothing but the backyards of neighbors' houses and bare, red oaks.

A loud clack cut through the stillness, knocking me loose for a moment. I peered out the open door and watched Pa, sporting overalls and a wool coat, hacking at thick wood with an axe. Towards the back of the shed, I sensed someone watching me. But I was alone.

Full corrugated boxes sat scattered in the far corners, and I thought to put them up onto a shelf above the back window. It was high, and it would take a lot of stretching and heaving for me to get those suckers up there, but it'd keep the mice from nesting in them and make space to store the wash buckets Ma kept on the back porch.

I decided to move all the boxes into one place on the floor by the shelf, to get them out of the way. I kicked them into place, sliding them across the dusty floor, breathing in the thick scent of old books. Fumbling to pick up the first box, it slipped then thudded to the floor, the fall crushing its sides. I tried again, this time hoisting it from the bottom.

As I raised the box onto the shelf, it teetered between the wood and my fingertips. I thought about how much there was to do. None of it for me, or for my family. All of it for the godforsaken Monroes. It wasn't fair. I didn't even know where my sisters and brother were. Who was protecting them? Was anyone? Or were they trapped, like me, in a world that didn't give a lick about them? Before I knew it, the box tumbled from above my head and smashed onto the floor.

The crash echoed in the small shed. Pa darted in. I lay on the cold concrete, the innards of the box scattered about me.

"I see you found our library," Pa said, as he walked into the shed. "If you wanted to know what was in the box, you could have just opened it," he chuckled, his belly bouncing up and down. He took off his winter hat and rubbed a tuft of gray hair in the center of his balding head. He wiped away sawdust from his eye patch then squatted next to me and began stacking books.

It was a small room, and Pa seemed to take up so much space.

"Sorry, sir. I was just trying to—" Sweat dripped down my back, despite the coldness of the shed. "I was trying to put the boxes on the shelf."

He smiled and patted the pile of books. "That's a high shelf for a small girl. Like some help?"

The softness of his voice made my breath catch. A tingling scattered around my temples. I was smiling. I hadn't smiled since the night before the Children's Aid

37

Society came, when Alice danced by the fire, kicking her legs and swinging her apron to the rhythm of a song she made up.

"I've got it. I don't need any help." I stood up and began creating my own stack with the few remaining scattered books.

"Here's an idea. You hand me the boxes, and I'll place them on the shelf," Pa said.

I looked around the shed to find a replacement for the broken box. "Thanks, but I can handle it. Did lots of chores back home." In the group of boxes, I found one half full and began putting more books in it.

"Have any family that misses you?" Pa asked.

"Got three siblings. Helen, Alice and John." Their names were honey on my tongue. I thought of including my mama and my papa among those that'd miss me, but they wouldn't know I was gone. They'd left long before. I wondered if they had missed us. Do they miss us now? When Papa first left, we noticed right away. By the time Mama walked out, I knew our hearts couldn't take more leaving, so I pretended she'd be back. Had every one of them convinced. Even convinced myself.

"I bet they're missing you." His voice trailed off at the end. "Are they being cared for together, in the same home?"

"I don't know where they are," I said, snatching a book from his hand and placing it into the box. When I leaned down to pick it up, it slipped and dropped back to the floor. "Ugh," I shouted, as I hauled back and kicked the box over. The books tumbled onto the floor.

"Hold on. That's too much weight in there. You try to pick up too much at once, and you end up not being able to pick up anything at all." He took a few of the bigger books from the box and spread them out among the other boxes.

I clenched my fists, trying to keep my rage inside. I glanced at the open door and wondered why my legs didn't just run me right out of here, as far as I could get. That anger I felt, I realized, was for me now. I cursed myself under my breath for never putting more time into reading. For never having imagined someday I'd be anyplace but Shaker Street. Now here I was, and I didn't have the stomach or the brains for it.

What I wanted to do was haul off and kick another box, figure out how far I could send it, but instead I picked up a box and handed it to Pa, who positioned himself under the shelf.

"Here's a light one," I said, but words taste bitter when they're not the ones you want to say.

He took the box and placed it on the shelf. "So no Ma or Pa back home? How'd you kids come to be alone?"

I thought back to Mama's last day home. I'd never felt so alone. It was late spring when Mama had packed up a few shifts, a comb, and some knickers in a carpetbag, while the other children had played pick-up sticks in the sunny garden, having no idea their lives were changing. I had just made them peanut butter sandwiches for lunch, and Mama had helped them make iced tea. As soon as they'd gone out back to play, she'd rushed around the house, shoving the stuff in her bag. She never even went to her room to gather pictures or money. We didn't have much, but what we had, she kept stored in her chest by the foot of her bed. She left it.

"I've got scraps set to spread onto the tomatoes. Should have a mighty crop this year," I had said, as I watched Mama gather a pen and a scratchpad from the kitchen drawers. I poured fresh iced tea into a jelly jar and gave it to her. She took a long sip. Mama never did use the pen or scratchpad to write home.

"Right. You'll be set through fall with the coming harvest. Best be sure to get the tomatoes out onto the roadside early, before the Hatcher's setup." Mama had set her dusty bag on the kitchen counter. She had pumped water into the sink, then poured in a scoop of soap to scour a tin cake pan with one of John's old shirts. "You know if those Hatchers get a jump on you, they'll keep it goin' all season."

"Yes, Mama. I know."

She placed her hands on the counter and took two heaving breaths.

"Looks like the weather will cooperate, too. According to the butcher, the Farmer's Almanac is calling for sun this summer. Lots of it," I had said. I stood inches away from Mama in the narrow kitchen. Through the dusty window, I had watched the little ones playing.

"Yes, Anna. Weather'll cooperate. And you be sure corn's sown early, ya hear? Nothing worse than a too-late planting." She had set the clean tin onto the drying towel and had grabbed her bag. Although hardly a stitch in it, her body had bowed from the weight of it. She had walked past me. I was taller than her by a few inches, but gazing down at her, I felt even taller than that. I'd been taking care of all of us for so long. She barely looked like my mama anymore. She had pushed through the swinging kitchen doors, into the sun-lit living room. Specks of dust had floated through the bright rays.

I had moved around her and reclined on the worn chair by the front door, resting my feet on the fraying crocheted footstool. I had wiped stray hairs from my tired eyes, fixed my loosening braid then peered at Mama, but she had never looked back.

Still not looking at me, she had said, "You be a good girl, now. You watch out for the others," in a voice hardly audible over the creaking screen door. Then she had stepped outside, shaking her head as if feeling the air for the first time.

"I will, Mama. I will," I had said. But I didn't think she heard me.

The memory faded as I dropped a book on my foot. "Oww!" I said, bending to retrieve it. As I rubbed my sore foot, I told him what he wanted to know, though it made my stomach hurt to say it out loud. "I have a mama and papa, but they didn't want us no more."

"When did your daddy leave?" Pa asked.

I wasn't looking for a friend in Pa, but I answered anyway. "Papa took off a while back. Few years, I think."

I saw his good eye looking down at the floor, then right back at me. "And your mama?"

"Mama? She left a half a year ago this May." I lined the boxes up and quickened my pace. I wanted no more talk about family. That was my business. I handed him another box.

"How were you kids getting by with no help?" He placed the box on the shelf and turned back towards me.

"I made sure everyone got enough. Never needed help." I paused and bit my tongue. Then I spoke again. "We were fine to stay where we were. They had no right to come take us."

"Well, I can't comment on that," he said, placing his hand on my shoulder. "But we're glad to have you."

In my head, I heard, *Anna, bite your tongue.* But I kept going. "I don't need help from anyone. I am just fine to do it all by myself." The words slipped from my mouth, and I knew, for the first time, they were a lie. We barely survived this past winter. Our water froze up. The chickens we didn't sell all died off from cold or Coccidiosis. I couldn't seem to oil that water-pump windmill enough to get it turning last summer, and all the crops died by late August. But I wasn't a stranger to a lie, and so I kept this one to myself.

I handed him the last box and changed the subject to him. "What happened to your eye? Does it hurt?"

He hoisted the box onto the shelf then wiped his hands on his overalls. "This old thing?" he said, pointing to the patch. "Ain't a story worth telling." His good eye grew misty.

"Is it hard to see with only one eye?" I asked, catching his gaze. Randolph got his beautiful eyes from him.

"Naw. Just changed the way I see things. No better. No worse. Just different. Sometimes you have to learn to look at things differently, or else you never know what you're missing."

Pa turned to leave but bent down to pick up a book that had been tucked behind the door. "*Peter and Wendy*," he said. "One of my favorites." He tossed it on top of the worktable and turned to leave.

After I was sure he was gone, I slipped the book into the pocket of my coat, picked up the broom, and started sweeping. Out of the corner of my eye, I watched Randolph duck past the back window. I put my hand over my pocket and pressed the book close to my side. Again, rustling came from behind the shed, and I knew it was Randolph up to no good. I didn't know why he kept nosing around me, but it sure did give me the willies.

Chapter Four

Two weeks had passed, and the Monroe's home still held a mighty chill, although the crocuses sprang to life in the patch by the lamppost in the front yard. As I teetered on a pine kitchen chair, wiping cobwebs from corners of the ceiling with a feather duster, I stared out the window as dusk painted the sky orange. Long days of chore after chore gave me too much time to think of how much I missed my kin. Too much time was passing, and the worrying over whether I'd ever see them again formed a lump in my throat so thick that I struggled to swallow.

The houses on the Monroe's street sat one next to the other, like eggs in a carton. Neighbors strolled the paved streets and drove motorcars to the market. On Shaker Street, tiny houses dotted acres of land, and we swapped turnips for potatoes or eggs for stew meat, because we didn't have money for the grocer. When pickings got slim, I sold our broiler chickens to the Joneses, so we could pay the tax man. They had plenty of their own, but you can never have enough broilers, Mr. Jones said. Those fowls saved our farm last year.

"Supper's on the table," Ma said, snapping me from memory.

Ham and cabbage. The sharp scent of rotten eggs gave it away. I hated boiled cabbage more than I hated rotten eggs. "Yes, ma'am." I stepped down from the chair and dragged it to the table.

Randolph, caked with dirt from fishing at the creek with his friend, walked into the kitchen, served himself an overflowing plate, then plopped down at his seat.

"It's too cold for fishing, Randy. Why do you bother?" Ma asked.

Randolph snorted. "Can't know unless you try." He shot me a look then shoveled a forkful into his mouth.

"Pa is at his Lion's Club meeting tonight, down at the VFW. Mrs. Rossor is driving me out to the Castle building for a meeting of the Child Conservation League," Ma said, stretching the name Ro-ss-or long like taffy. She held up a macaroni casserole like she'd won it. "You two will be eating alone."

I followed her as she walked towards the front door and took her blue dress coat with the metal buttons off the coat rack.

"Mrs. Rossor and I may be late. There's a speaker, Dr. Birch or Birsch, something or other, speaking on the betterment of society. After, I'm sure they'll serve cookies."

I watched her swing her beaded evening bag over her shoulder, wondering who this Mrs. Rossor was. Ma never wore rouge or eye shadow, but tonight she looked like someone I'd never seen before.

After she left, I swept the brick hearth and straightened the lace doilies on the pair of end tables. I skipped dinner, not wanting to spend time alone with Randolph or eat ham and cabbage.

I shut the door to my bedroom and slipped into my cotton nightdress. It was the one piece of new clothing that smelled like soap and felt soft on my tired body. I began piling log after log into the tiny fireplace by my bed, rolled up a piece of newsprint for kindling and struck a match. The paper sizzled as I tossed it on the logs, igniting flames across the wood. I jabbed kindling with the metal poker to spread the fire, then set it against the wooden mantle.

I crept to my closet and slipped the stolen book from the pocket of my apron. Butterflies filled my belly as I thought about the possibility of reading it, any of it. I sat cross-legged on the woven, brown rug in front of the hearth, the fire behind me shining light on the pages as I began reading. A gust of wind whipped through the trees outside, sending a draft through the house. I slid back a little further, to feel the heat of flames warm my back. The scent of burning wood reminded me of home, when we'd light a fire and tell stories into the night.

I stared at the cover. *Peter and Wendy*, Pa had said. Flickering of the fire brought the words in and out of view. I opened the cover. The stiff spine cracked. I touched the smooth pages, the brittle paper delicate on my fingertips, as I scanned them for familiar words. Up. The. In. A. I had little to go on, only what I had learned from watching Alice soar through books I never imagined reading. But I understood that reading unlocked the message in the letter that would get me back home.

My mind raced. If I could read, I could write. If I found out where my siblings were, I could write them letters, tell them I'd been searching for them, promise them I'd bring them home. The weight of want threatened to bury me, so I started digging.

Each word seemed heavier than the last, longer and stranger. Some letters translated to sound, budding into a few words here or there. With each one I pieced together, I'd learn the sounds of new letters. I kept at it, word after word, learning their shapes, their angles, their curves. Focusing on the few I could read, I returned to them again and again. They rebuilt my confidence when I wanted to give up. Which was often. Every word seemed a mystery, and even when I believed I had cracked it, I couldn't be sure. The struggle made me long for Alice in a way I hadn't before. I doubted I'd ever be able to match her brains.

I studied the small words like a puzzle, choosing those with sounds I recognized from my name or my kin's names. "A-n-d." I sounded it out as quietly as a seed sprouting in soil. "A-n-d." With each repetition, the butterflies settled a bit in the pit of my belly. A, the ahh sound of Alice. N, the nah sound from John. D, the duh sound from Dottie, my Mama's name. They were teaching me to read, and they had no idea.

A shuffle outside the door broke my focus. I tucked the book between the folds of my nightdress and waited for silence. When all I could hear was a skittering beetle, I slipped the book back out and held it up so that the fire's light brought the words to life again. The sweet scent of burning oak filled my lungs. I gripped the edge of a page, thumb to forefinger, and stroked it. The secret of having stolen the book excited me, like a story whose ending only I knew. I focused on each sound as if our future depended on it. Because it did.

I heard a creak again by the door and spotted a shadow creeping. Darkness swallowed the thin ray of light that the moon cast into the hallway through the back porch. I held my breath until it passed, then tried a few more words. Exhausted and frustrated, I gave in to my tired eyes and fed the fire two more logs to get me through the night. Using the iron poker to spread the flames, the fire blazed.

I returned the book to my apron pocket then cracked open the door to peek down the hall. Nothing. I closed my door and climbed into bed, burying myself under the warm quilt. At home, we'd be piled four on top of a single bed, with all the blankets we had, trying to keep warm. Still, we'd wake stiff and frozen, our frigid bodies pressed to one another. I never dreamed of having my own bed, a fireplace, a warm quilt. And even so, I'd trade it all for home.

The moonlight shined through my window. I opened the lace curtain to watch the stars twinkle. I placed the palm of my hand against my beating heart; it pulsed against the palm of my hand. The beating of my heart made me feel closer to my family, as if our hearts always beat together, no matter where we were. I drifted to sleep and dreamed first of all of us, even Mama and Papa, standing in a circle under a full moon in a patch of primrose on the farm, holding hands, then of an angry ghost strolling the hall outside my door, with pockets full of stars that shined so brightly, they blinded me. The flat of my palm, still pressed against my chest, pulsed stronger and stronger, until the pounding grew so fierce that it woke me.

My eyes shot wide open, and my body tensed so tight that I thought I might snap. The door creaked open wider and wider, but I couldn't move. Soft, gleaming light from the fire cast a faint glow towards the door. I saw him, his eyes sparkling even in the low light. And I braced myself.

Chapter Five

I pulled the quilt up to my neck but otherwise played opossum, as Randolph crept towards me to stand at the side of my bed. I held my breath as he pulled off his white T-shirt, dropped his drawers and stepped out of them so slowly that I thought he might be sleepwalking.

When he yanked the cover from me, my stubborn mouth did not scream. I jumped back before he had a chance to pin me down, and a measly puff wheezed from my lungs. Pressing my back against the headboard, I kicked my legs. I was never strong enough when I needed to be. If I had been, maybe I'd have done enough to keep Mama from feeling like she had to run. Maybe I'd have held that farm together like glue, so the Children's Aid Society wouldn't have known we were on our own. Maybe I'd be able to fight off Randolph as he forced himself on me. But if I was learning anything these days, I wasn't enough of anything to hold my life together.

I got tangled up in the edges of the blanket, so his long limbs had to fish under it for me. He fingered the edges of my socks, so I pulled my knees up towards my chest. Then I froze, my body tucked like a ball against the back of the bed. *Get away, Anna,* I heard a voice say. *Get away.*

A log cracked in the fire, then dropped. A gust of wind blew outside, shaking the trees and snapping limbs. He turned towards the sound, and I smashed my hand to his face, trying to pull myself out from under him. He quickly returned his attention to me, his empty eyes staring at me as if I were an animal he caught in a trap.

My breath drew inward to scream, so he covered my mouth with his broad hand. I clenched down on his palm. When I tasted salty blood, I bit harder. He yanked his hand from my mouth and smacked my face. My body went rigid, arms straight, legs pressed together. He looked at his bitten hand and shook it. Droplets of red speckled my white nightdress.

His fingers pressed deep into my wrists as he lay his chest on me, his heavy shoulders pinning me. I couldn't move. He forced a knee between my closed legs, shifted, then pressed the other in the small gap. Before I knew it, he thrust his legs apart, splintering mine.

I watched out the window, as Orion's Belt stretched across the sky overtop the red oaks. Years ago, when I was a few years older than John, Papa gifted each of us a constellation. It was the only gift he ever gave me. But stars meant something, Papa said. He learned that from his papa. Mine was Orion's Belt. That was perfect for me, he said, because I held our family together. Through Randolph's grunting, the voice of the stars broke through. *You won't be invisible forever.*

Randolph climbed off me and stood at the base of the bed. He pulled on his drawers and shook his head of wild hair at me. "No good appleknocker." Rubbing his bitten hand, he turned towards the door then turned back to take one more look at me. The fire faded to a dim glow. He opened his mouth to speak but snapped it shut, as if he needn't bother with it.

As he left, I realized I couldn't stay an extra minute at the Monroe's house. I wasn't long for survival there, or anywhere. No one understood me or where I came from. And that meant somewhere out there were people not understanding my brother and sisters. And I was the only one to save us.

Legs shuddering, I bent over the side of the bed and eased myself onto the floor. Unable to carry my own weight, I pulled my body in front of the dying flame. I saw scarlet specks on my nightdress and looked at the ring of bruises around my wrists, the blooming purple ovals from his fingers. I touched each part of me where he left a mark and remembered the cruelty. His presence still filled the room, no less than before he left. I picked up the fire iron, and on all fours, slid back towards the bed and hoisted myself up on the dirty mattress. I lay sleepless the rest of the night, the fire iron on the pillow beside me.

#

The wind blew like it had a bone to pick. Although I never fell asleep, my mind drifted to some far-off place where Ma, Randolph, and Miss Atkinson didn't exist. Through my window, I watched the auburn sun rise, reflecting off the frosted grass, and the robins flit from branch to branch. I felt like I was outside of my body, watching all these things, I'd seen time and again, happen, but now none of them seemed real. It was as if all the world was play-acting for me, and I was supposed to figure out how to get myself out of this godforsaken story.

Rage flooded my blood, pumping deep inside my chest, my heart, my eyes. I didn't think I could hold it in. But I had no choice. I couldn't go getting myself into trouble if I was going to bring my family back home.

People searched for reasons to turn us Wilsons away, and I wouldn't make it easy for them. When Mama was around, she'd walk us three miles up Shaker Street towards the center of town to see the doctors for a hacking cough that wouldn't quit, or a gash from the rusted wheelbarrow that festered and oozed.

The doctor's voice always sounded deep and angry, like we were in trouble just for showing up at his place. "The likes of you are prone to such conditions," he said each time, patting Mama on the small of her back and sending us trudging back down the dirt roads to home, with not so much as a salve.

Mama didn't read well, and one time when she scribbled my name on the wrong place on the form, the doctor told her not to come back. So we didn't.

I swung my feet over the edge of the bed, dangling them above the rug. I scooted forward until my trembling toes rested in the soft grooves. I tested them, putting little weight on them at first. They shook. Squeezing the quilt in my fists, balling it up as tight as I could, I tried to bring myself back into the room, like I used to do after Papa grew angry and started swinging his fists. A thin ray of sunshine cast through my window and shined onto the slats of the floor. I shifted so the ray warmed my back and so that I didn't have to see it lighting up my dark room.

I pounded my head with my hands, trying to knock some sense into me. If John were here, he'd figure out some escape hatch to have me sneaking out of the Monroe's house in no time. Or Helen; she'd take care of Randolph for sure, because everyone knew if you got in Helen's way, she'd see to it you weren't standing for long. And Alice; Alice would charm herself out of here. Everyone loved Alice. I wasn't good at anything but keeping us together, and turns out, I wasn't so good at that.

I got myself into a clean pair of knickers, a long, blue, serge skirt, and a heavy, brown sweater that matched my hair. I looked at myself in the mirror but turned away at the stranger staring back. I had only been gone two weeks, but already I could tell that when I did make it back to Shaker Street, I wouldn't be the same girl who left.

I swallowed hard and moved towards the door, knowing I was beginning an after. Mama used to say that life turned on an axle so smoothly that sometimes you missed it. Just like when Mama left. I didn't know until about a month after she didn't come back that we had started living an after. But this one, this turn nearly snapped my neck. I knew I'd never be that old Anna again, and I missed her already.

Chapter Six

A week after Randolph laid himself on me, I still felt him all over my skin, like he was some kind of spiderweb I'd walked through. I couldn't seem to shake him.

I walked out of my room and stood in the dark hall, daydreaming, as my fingertips ran across the crinkled wallpaper, still thinking about how I was going to get us out of this pickle. It wasn't just myself I was saving, but Helen, Alice and John, too.

On my life, I couldn't understand why I didn't tell on Randolph. Why I didn't march up to Ma and Pa that very next morning and explain what their no-good son had done to me. But there was a nagging feeling in the pit of my belly that worked its way up to my chest each time I thought about it. For some reason, telling on Randolph seemed like a confession. And it made me afraid.

"Anna, what's your business?" Ma said, as she poked her head out of the kitchen.

"What's that?" I asked.

"Get in here."

I slid my hand down the wall and trudged towards her like I had bricks on my feet. When I stepped onto the tiled floor, I looked up to meet her narrowed eyes. The wood-burning stove pumped out a dry, suffocating heat, drumming up a coughing fit in me.

"Cut that out," Ma said. "You have work to do. Just standing around like you don't have any other business to tend to." She held her hand over the stovetop then pulled it away and rubbed it on her yellow apron. She picked up the percolator from the counter and placed it over the plate.

I had half a mind to tell her right there about what Randolph had been up to, no matter how bad it made me feel, but instead I let the words sit on my tongue and grow bigger and bigger, like a blister I couldn't pop.

"Don't tell me you still can't follow that list."

My excuses for not reading the list were running thin. I thought early on to tell Ma I don't read well. I even opened my mouth one time to show her, so she'd stop harping on me about not doing things in the right order. But I went mum. I thought back to the doctor who wouldn't see us since Mama put our names in the wrong places on that stupid form and figured Ma was no better than a doctor, even if he was a country one.

"I'll get to work on it," I said, eyeing the chicken scratch on crumpled paper. I looked through the doorway to see if I could spot Pa anywhere, it being Saturday and all. Having him home always made my stomach untangle a bit. It even ran through my mind that I might tell him about Randolph, given he always had kind words for me. When I didn't see him, I asked, "Is Pa home?"

I heard the thump of the door opening, and then it slammed. My heart leapt for a moment, then sunk as

Randolph turned the corner into the kitchen, his muddy boots leaving a trail of soil behind him that I knew I'd have to clean up. He took a few long steps to close in on me. His hot breath beat on the back of my neck. I wished my hair hadn't been wrapped in a bun.

"What's she doing standing here?" he asked.

And the confession grew so large, I started choking on it.

After swallowing bitter bile, I snatched the list, sliding it into my apron pocket, and said, "I'm about to do my chores."

The percolator began to hiss and pop. The smell of coffee filled the room.

"Let me see that list," Randolph said, reaching in the pocket of my apron.

Ma shifted the percolator and turned off the stove.

"My list. I don't have to show you," I said.

"Do too."

"Do not."

"Bet you can't even read it."

Ma shouted, "You two stop that fighting right now. Anna, Pa's working. Would do you two good to follow Pa's lead. He's a hard worker. Took an extra shift selling paper today, so we can save up to take the Greyhound Line to New York this spring."

"Anna, too?" Randolph reached out and touched my shoulder.

I smacked his hand away.

"Heavens, no. Remember when we tried to take that last girl some place nice? Their kind aren't made for nice things," she said, without so much as glancing at me.

My blood boiled. I clenched my hands into fists that I pounded on the table without thinking first. The bang bounced off the walls.

Ma shot a look at me, then Randolph, then back at me. As she stomped her foot, she shouted, "What are you doing, child?"

I pushed myself away from the table, landing in the center of the kitchen between Ma and Randolph. I had nothing left to hold those words back. "Randolph done lay on me."

Their eyes went glossy like they didn't hear me.

"He forced himself on me. He done that." My voice didn't sound like my own. Some other girl stood there, braver than me, accusing Randolph of horrible things. But I was going to be the one to pay the price.

Randolph's mouth dropped open. He pointed at me, but nothing came out of his stupid mouth, so I took the chance to say it again.

"He did. He's no good." I watched Ma's face turn red and thought about taking it back. I thought about how much she might blame me for this, but then I thought about my kin and how I hoped that if anyone was touching on them, that they'd stand up for one another. So here I was, standing up for myself.

Her bright face turned to Randolph. "This true?"

"No way, Ma. Ain't true." But his face said it all. He couldn't look at her. He stared right past her but never looked her in the eyes.

I straightened my back to appear taller and said, "Is so."

Ma shook her head and sighed a heavy breath. "You never learn, do you?"

I thought, at first, she was talking to me, then I realized her eyes were squeezing in on Randolph. He dropped his head and kicked at a crust of bread on the floor.

"I didn't do nothing. You're believing a dumb appleknocker?" His words slurred together.

I heard a sound out front and moved towards the window behind the table to see if it were Pa coming home, but it was just the wind rattling the front door. "I'm not lying," I screamed, turning back to look at them. My voice scratched. I hadn't shouted like that in a long time, and part of me felt a little bubble of happiness at the sound of my own hollering.

"Randolph, you stay away from Anna when I'm not here. And no fishing for the week. Do you hear?"

I searched her face for some kindness towards me, a smile or even a glance in my direction. Finally, she huffed at Randolph then shifted towards me. "Anna, you tell me if he tries any more nonsense. And you keep to yourself, too, do you hear?"

"Yes, ma'am." Ma would tan my hide for stalling, even if it was because of Randolph, so I thought it best to get on with things. "I'll get my chores finished right quick."

Although I wasn't keen on telling Ma what Randolph did, I was glad I lost control and blurted it out. It bought me time. If I could stay at the Monroe's long enough to learn to read and know how to find my siblings, I might get them back by end of spring. I figured Randolph would leave me alone for now. Just in case, I took to sleeping with the fire iron on the pillow beside me.

No one had noticed the percolator whistling on the stove. Ma grabbed a dish towel, swung it over her shoulder, and poured us cups of coffee. We each set ours on the table, but no one sat.

Ma sipped hers, and the cup rattled as she set it onto its saucer. "No dawdling. It's already late morning, and it's laundry day. That'll take you right to suppertime."

Randolph gulped his coffee, then choked. He opened his mouth to speak but said nothing. I could feel his stare from across the room, like it was a branding iron.

"I have a pot of water set to boil on the stove. You get yourself set up, and Randolph will bring it once it's ready."

Randolph grunted and scratched his head.

I collected the dirty laundry in a wicker basket and brought it to the porch. The sun lit up the back, screened porch where I set out two galvanized tubs, a rubboard, and the Persil. A clothesline ran along the back of the porch for drying laundry in the winter. I imagined it wouldn't be much longer until we moved it outside.

"Here," Randolph said, walking towards me with a sloshing pot of boiling water. He poured it into one tub.

"Can you fill this with cold?" I asked, pointing to the empty one.

He took the tub without answering and returned a few minutes later with it filled.

I poured a cup of the laundry powder into the boiling water and reached my arm in up to my elbow and stirred. I leaned over to inhale the clean, sharp scent of the soap. It gave me a jolt of energy and opened my eyes wide. I scrubbed the dirty clothes in the boiling water against the rubboard and got most of the soil out of the knickers and dresses. Cleaning those clothes made me feel like I was cleaning myself, too. As I watched the filth rinse into the water and clothes return to their colors, I imagined the same thing happening to myself when I spoke up. I rinsed the clothes in the cold-water tub, rung them, then hung them along the line with the wooden clothespins. Water trickled down the cinderblock wall of the porch, forming a river that winded towards the center of the room.

I thought again to Helen, Alice, and John, and although I wasn't the praying type, I asked Jesus to protect them, wherever they were. And added, if he had anything at all left, maybe he could spare a little for me.

#

Before turning in, I replaced my sheets with fresh ones that I'd cleaned earlier in the day. Then I placed the iron poker

61

on the pillow of the bed, next to where I planned to lay my head. Once set, I lit a fire and took *Peter and Wendy* from my apron in the closet and returned to my reading spot.

I had been reading almost every night since I stole the book, and I was getting better. In my mind, I imagined stuffing my pillowcase with my book, the letter, the doll, and one day's change of clothes. I'd slide open the window by my bed and sneak out on a moonless light, when I could travel in the cover of dark. I'd go through the backyard, hopping the picket fence, to avoid being seen on the street by the likes of Mrs. Rossor. I'd get to the nearest storefront and pretend I was looking for my mother. I'd ask them for directions to wherever it is my siblings were and make it there by the next night. I could do it. I had to.

I opened the book, and the collected lists of chores dropped to the floor. I had been storing each day's list pressed between the pages. Those words, too, would unlock the secret sounds. I set them into the crevice of the binding and stared at the first page. Words leaped and jumped together. I still couldn't make much sense of them. I remembered Mama teaching me how to peel wallpaper off the living room wall. That paper had been there for years, she said, but the leaks from the room made it bubble and mold. I tried pulling off a big strip, but the sucker wouldn't give.

"Patience," she had said. "If you try to pull off too much at once, you won't get any of it."

So I tried one little piece at a time, and in no time, we had that wall as bare as if we'd shaved it. That's how I'd learn to read. One small word at a time. Before I'd know it, I'd be reading a whole book—and that precious letter.

Chapter Seven

Over the past month, Ma changed her tune about not bringing me places. She'd taken me to the corner grocer a few times for the produce and even sent me to the pharmacy one day to pick up Zemo, when Pa had a rash that wouldn't quit. I learned if I put a comb through my hair and scrubbed my face with Ivory, I wouldn't get too many stares from folks.

She had no plans to buy me a ticket for the Greyhound, so when she told me she was taking me to church services with the rest of the family and that I should wear the dress hanging in my closet, I raced to find it. I wasn't sure when she slipped it in there, but the blue ruffled thing hung limp on the wooden hanger. I slipped it on and fingered a few moth holes towards the bottom hem that hung down to my shins.

We four walked in our best clothes down five blocks to the Protestant church jutting tall from a triangle patch of land near the center of the main street, like it was looking down on the rest of us.

Mama and Papa never took us to church, and we weren't God-fearing people, in the sense that we thought if we'd do wrong, we'd burn in hell. Papa used to say nothing good about church people. Ain't nobody going to tell him what to do. Let them try to survive off his land and see if they don't get the devil in their heart and blasphemy on their tongue. Papa never had spoken much, but when he did, his words meant something.

As we walked the stone pathway towards the wide steps, I gazed up at the pointed steeples piercing the sky. Large cast-iron blocks propped open the thick, wooden doors, and deep, low organ music flowed out into the world outside the church. My stomach twisted as we took the steps and walked in towards the back wall.

"We'll stand," Ma said, shuffling us against tall, arching windows with dark, wooden grids so large that there was hardly room for glass.

Thick, white pillars stood like soldiers throughout the room. They blocked my view of the front, which was where sad music sprung from the voices of sad men. The rhythm alone made me fight back tears.

'We shall meet our loved ones gone,

Some sweet day, by and by.'

I slumped under the weight of such heavy thoughts. I missed my family. I wondered, for all my planning and wishing, if I'd ever have them back. Where were they right now? As much as I wanted them to miss me, to want me back as badly as I wanted them, part of me wished that they were some place, feeling so much love, with bellies so full of roast chicken and mashed potatoes, that they didn't have the emptiness in their hearts that I felt.

For the second time since I'd been at the Monroes, I prayed. I asked Jesus to get me the hell out of here and back home. But I was worried my Papa was right. Too much struggling in life put the fire in me, and I doubted I could fool God into believing I had the spirit. A girl like me had too much anger and brimstone to have the Jesus, too.

"Stand straight. No slouching." Ma reached around Randolph, who stood between us, and swatted my belly.

Randolph snickered and shifted his weight towards me. I could feel him, even though he was a half a foot away, as if he were pressed against me. I shook.

Pa, on my other side, reached for my hand and cradled it, tapping it to the music. I inched closer to him, and my stomach settled.

I didn't pay any mind to the pastor or the responses called out by the congregation. It seemed as if everyone knew what words to say and when to say them, so I stayed quiet and imagined how I might follow this route when leaving the Monroes. When the church went silent, and we were supposed to be meditating, I heard the rumbling of trucks not far away. There must be a major road near to here.

After service, the pastor corralled us towards a small door at the side of the church, which led to the basement. The room housed just as many of us as the church, but it was far smaller and windowless. It reminded me of the school room I went to before I stopped going. I was never any good at school, and this place made me feel just as small as that school room. Tiny chairs, that I doubted could hold Ma's weight, sat in rows, and there was a clearing in the front where the children assembled.

"Oh, this must be your newest charge?" Mrs. Rossor asked, pointing at me.

"This is Anna. She comes to us from an old farm out on Shaker Street. An orphan, she is," Ma said.

"I'm no orphan. I have family," I said, eyeing Ma.

"Well, a child without parents is an orphan, Anna." Ma pursed her lips and shook her head towards the woman in a fancy dress that looked like a doily.

Mrs. Rossor said, "You must be so grateful to the Monroes for taking you in. Such kind people they are." Mrs. Rossor looked at Ma, then scanned the room. She did not want to look at me. Facing Ma, she said, "Especially after what happened with the last girl. You really are one of the good ones."

The last girl. Where was she? I crossed my fingers behind my back and hoped she had found an escape like I would.

Ma placed her hand on my back. "You and Randolph go get up front. Make sure you get a seat in front of the pastor."

Randolph moved from behind me. I followed him to the floor and looked back to see Ma pair off with Mrs. Rossor and Pa standing alone by the coffee urn.

From the front of the room came the sound of a man clearing his throat. Everyone shuffled to take a seat. The man wore a black robe with gold crosses on the wide sleeves. He had neatly trimmed hair and thick, black glasses that perched on the tip of his nose.

When he raised his hands in the air, he bellowed, "Welcome, welcome."

The congregation fell silent.

"How are you on this beautiful day that must only be a gift from God?" he asked, as he leaned over to pat the heads of some children sitting on the floor in front of him.

A few elder men shuffled towards the front to shake his hand, then returned to sit with their wives.

"Thank you all for coming to hear from the great Dr. Bisch. I know you have eagerly awaited today's post-service talk, and the women of the Child Conservation League have put forth much effort in procuring the brilliant doctor, a renowned psychiatrist committed to the betterment of society. Let us welcome him."

The grown-ups roared with applause in the back. Their cheers bounced off the walls and echoed even after I no longer saw hands clapping. I looked around at the other children for a sign of excitement, but no one seemed to know what our business here was.

The robed man reached to shake the hand of a balding, mustachioed man as he walked towards the front.

"Welcome. Welcome. Marriage is one under considerable discussion of late, particularly as it applies to the insane and feeble-minded. Several States of the Union have passed laws against such unions, as they lead to the propagation of inferior offspring that will no doubt become a blight to society. We must question marriage selection in the interest of mankind. While some might say that this places the emphasis on race betterment, in fact it promotes family happiness. Much better to be a bachelor or a spinster than to propagate misfits that undoubtedly lead to discord, misery, and disappointment."

I didn't quite catch what he was saying. I tried to see what the others were thinking, but some children stared off towards the giant painting of Jesus sitting on the dirt ground, surrounded by smiling children. Another girl was plaiting her hair.

His mouth grew wide with each word. "The practice of eugenics is not antagonistic to established customs. There is no reason that newer scientific findings should not join with long-held traditions in the cause of race betterment. The waywards, the inebriates, the poor, the orphaned—they must be contained, locked away from the population, or else they shall sink our great nation."

My mouth dropped open. Mama thought I was an orphan. What else did she think of me? My sisters and brother? What would happen if I didn't save us fast? I looked back in the crowd to see Ma, but she didn't see me. She stared at Dr. Bisch like he was God himself.

Chapter Eight

That night, I dreamed I was under a horse cart, fixing the axle when it snapped. Godforsaken thing pinned me to the dirt tracks, crushing my chest. My pulse beat clear in my ears, as the heavy weight crushed my ribs into my lungs. My breath stopped clean, jolting me awake.

In the shuddering light of the fire, Randolph's eyes shined inches from mine. His body lay on me, his hands at either side of my head.

I screamed some ungodly sound that shot through the room so hard that I swear it rattled the knobs on my chest of drawers. But he just smiled. Then I remembered. I groped the pillow beside me for the cold of the fire iron, but I felt only the softness of the pillow. He had me. He took my chin, held it tight and pressed his warm mouth into mine.

"No sense screaming. They're gone to visit Gramps early, Anna."

I hated the sound of my name on his lips. He nodded his head towards the center of the room, and my eyes followed. The poker lay there like a damn fool. Worthless.

My heart kicked in my chest, and my legs fought for something to boot, but my fate was sealed. There were no stars in that sky. Believe me. I searched for them the entire time he lay on me. Not a single one.

#

Family takes more than it gives. It'll bleed you bone-dry if you let it. So I wasn't sure why my heart broke into so many pieces when Miss Atkinson came to our farm that day. I suppose you don't mind bleeding yourself dry for someone you love. But there were limits. Mama had reached hers, which left her not good for anybody.

I remember Mama's sunken cheeks and bug eyes as she looked up from the slop bucket in the yard. She rubbed her face with her apron but didn't bother to wipe the streaks of vomit out of her hair. She hung over it again and heaved more clear broth and stale bread. I stood next to the leaning shed in my work dress, bare feet planted firmly in the hot dirt, and heard my mother say to the bright sky, "Lord, I can't take another young'un." Her voice was a cross between a sob and prayer.

I never saw her so desperate, like she already knew the Lord wouldn't answer her plea. She stood and took two steps towards me, dropping to her knees in soil so dry it formed a dust cloud. I stepped back, not sure what I was afraid of. I had that tingling I'd get when Papa's words swirled, and I couldn't guess what he'd do next.

"Mama," I cried, holding my hands out towards her but stepping away.

She dropped her hands to the ground and started crawling and wailing like a cat in heat. "What have you all done to me?"

A warm trickle streamed down the side of my leg, soaking the soles of my feet, forming a yellow puddle in the dry ground. I hadn't pissed myself in years, and I knew Mama'd be sore, so I squeezed my legs together.

She didn't say a word, just pushed herself up off the ground and puckered her face, as if pissing myself was a good idea. She yanked me by the arm and pulled me straight into the house through the back kitchen door. That sharp scent of piss followed us in.

"They're all yours, Anna Wilson. I've got nothing left in me," she said, nodding to Helen and Alice, who were little ones then.

"Scram," I told them, shooing them out the swinging screen door of the kitchen.

Mama disappeared into the washroom and came out with a wire hanger. I followed her to her bedroom and stood quietly outside while I watched her. For all her crying and jabbing, she left that room with her head hung low, sobbing, saying she can't do with another mouth to feed. Three seasons later, John was born, as the fields thawed from winter.

When my stomach started getting the whirlies in the mornings, a few weeks after Randolph lay on me, all I thought about was how I'd have a piece of him baring my eyes and his nose, meshing us into one. I did not have the stomach for it, or the heart. While retching my breakfast behind the shed when I was supposed to be stacking stones for a new pathway, I thought back to that story of Mama and realized, for the first time, how alone she must have felt. Even with three kids nipping her heels all day, a new life blooming inside her, her loneliness must have felt like chains.

I went around the back of the house, crept in through the back porch door, careful not to slam it shut, and slipped into my room. If Ma looked for me, she'd figure I was still behind the shed, stacking stones. I'd make up an excuse for why they weren't laid right, later. For now, there was business to tend to. As I closed my bedroom door behind me, a rush of heat sprung up my throat, choking me. Darting from my bed to the corner of my room, I spued hot bile into the wicker wastebasket, the bubbling, liquid thick on my tongue, burning my mouth. I knew, after watching Mama, that this meant another chain that would never let me be free, and if I wasn't careful, they'd lock me away and I'd never find my kin.

I was watching myself, some stranger moving about a world that was not her own, as I took the wire hanger from the closet, slunk to the bed, sat on the edge, and stared at the sharp tip. Pressing my finger to its rusted point, I flinched. After gripping the hook, I pulled it as straight as it would go, so that it looked like a needle. Then I stretched out the triangle part to make it as long as I could. In my mind, I imagined what would happen next, how it'd pierce me, and blood would run thick, setting me free.

Once I slipped off my boots, my knickers, and hiked up my skirt, I scooted back onto the bed and opened my knees wide. I reached over my head to grab a pillow and pulled it towards me, shoving the corner into my mouth. I forced the cold wire into me, and the tip pierced my flesh, but I could tell it wasn't deep enough. Opening my legs wider, I forced my bottom down towards the wire and bit down harder on the pillow, just as I imagined Mama doing. My teeth clenched in pain, and a muted scream escaped. I thrusted my bottom down again, this time feeling a sharp jab. I repeated it again and again. Every few times, I'd pull the hanger out to check for some sign of blood, but nothing. I kept trying, each time my heart racing faster and faster until I thought it'd explode.

Still nothing. I threw that thing across the room, smashing it into the mirror above my chest of drawers. An animal wail tore through me. Felt like my entire body was sobbing.

I held my hands over my face as if I could stop the tears from pouring. Footsteps pounded down the hallway, and I knew what that meant, but I didn't move a lick. The door slammed open, and Ma's face turned red as she looked at me, dress yanked up, knickerless. She done lost it.

"You are a sin. There is nothing I can do to fix you," she shouted.

I said nothing.

"You're not fit for this world. I should have learned my lesson before."

She slammed the door behind her. The sound of her feet moving further away was drowned out by my cries.

Chapter Nine

I knew there was no time for fixing holes in my plan. If I was going to run, it'd have to be soon and fast.

The smell of the metal hanger filled my room, as I pulled up my knickers and pushed down my dress, and the whole time I was wishing it was the metal scent of blood. I couldn't bear the thought of Randolph's baby growing inside me.

I searched my closet for my pillowcase that I had brought with me. I took my apron off the hook and slid the book out of the pocket. Then I went to my drawer and slipped out the letter, placed it between the pages of *Peter and Wendy*, and placed them both in the case. I rolled it up as best I could and hid it under my bed.

In the living room, Pa sat reading a newspaper, his reading glasses falling off the tip of his nose. I hadn't realized he was home and wondered if he heard my screams and Ma's shouting.

"Hi, Pa," I said in a low voice. I searched his face for a smile, and my heart slowed when I saw one.

"Anna, my dear. How has your day been?"

Pa still felt like a warm quilt to me, so I wasn't sure what I knew. "Fine, Pa. It's been fine." I could hear Ma fiddling in the kitchen, pans clanging on the stove. I stole a last look at Pa before going to Ma.

Randolph sat at the table reading funnies, and Ma was setting her purse straight, counting her bills. "We're going to the grocer," she said.

At first, I wasn't sure if she meant she and Randolph, or me and her, but I realized she was looking right at me. "I can stay here and finish stacking the stones."

She huffed. "I'm not letting you out of my sight. Randolph will come with us."

He snorted as he stood up, pushed his paper towards the center of the table, then walked towards me, grabbing my arm. He squeezed so tight that his fingers dug moons into my flesh.

"Ouch," I said, yanking my arm away.

"We're not letting you out of our sight." He laughed and let me go.

Ma swung her purse over her shoulder, and we three set down the four blocks towards the corner store.

I wondered if they were on to me, all this keeping a close eye on me. Why not let me run? If I had someone in my house causing trouble, I'd look the other way as they ran. Good riddance. But I got the sense there wasn't going to be any cheeks turning.

I had been to the grocer a few times before. The colors in the market grew brighter and brighter as spring took hold. A few older women in fine dresses held wicker baskets and wore ribboned bonnets wrapped around their heads.

Long stands stretched the length of the storefront under a green awning. Baskets overflowed with dark carrots topped with drooping leaves, crisp green celery, and all kinds of fruit, some of which I couldn't name, but they looked sweet as candy. The tomatoes, bright red and overripe, drew me towards them. I had to touch them, feel their spongy flesh. It wasn't their season. At home we ate the crops we grew or that our neighbors grew. We ate nothing not sprouted on Shaker Street.

Each step I took, Randolph was never far behind. Backing away from him, I moved towards the alley, but he stuck to me like honey, so we both got a good whiff of rotten potatoes from the dumpster.

Afraid to be out of sight with Randolph, I walked back to the front of the shop and spied Mr. Roberts, the grocer, in his doorway.

He tipped his green hat. "Good day, Mrs. Monroe. How are you today?" He turned to the pair of older women and greeted them the same, but I didn't catch their names.

Ma raised her basket in greeting but said nothing. She went about filling it with wilting spinach, some red and green peppers, and a long loaf of crusty bread from a barrel.

A delivery driver parked a faded green truck, loaded with more goods for the grocer, on the corner by a fire hydrant. Randolph walked over and touched the light on the front then patted the tire. The smell of the exhaust filled the air and mixed with that of rotting potatoes. I held my hand over my mouth to keep the stench from gagging me.

While Randolph ran his hand on the knobs of the truck, I moved about a row of vegetables, finding myself again by the tomatoes. I wanted to bite into one, see if it tasted like Shaker Street tomatoes.

I touched another one towards the bottom, shifting the pile, which caused them to tumble onto the sidewalk. I rushed to catch them in my apron, but a few splatted on the ground into red mush. The sight of the mashed fruit and the heavy scent of rot and fumes got my stomach swirling again, so I raced to the alley, slipping on a tomato.

"Anna, you imbecile!" Ma shouted.

The grocer returned to the door to watch the scene.

I hopped on all fours and started crawling away from the older ladies who had moved towards me to help. I vomited there on their patent leather shoes.

Both jumped back, gasping.

Ma's face scrunched up. "Now look what you've done. You awful girl. You made a mess of things."

The old ladies backed away, watching us with wide eyes.

"You must apologize this instant," Ma said.

I retched again, but nothing came up except some syrupy bile that clung to my chin. I wiped it and said, "I am sorry, ma'ams. So sorry."

"There is nothing that can be done with you," she said. She leaned down to pick up a fallen tomato but changed her mind. "Clean this up," she shouted, shoving me towards the tomato mash.

Mr. Roberts said, "No, no. No reason to get upset." He pulled off his cap and wiped sweat from his forehead with the back of his hand. "I can have a boy clean this up in no time." He turned in the doorway to shout towards the back of the store. "Henry! Henry! We need your help here."

"No. She will clean it up." Ma leaned down and pushed me again, knocking my hand into a squashed tomato.

"It's not my fault. It slipped," I said, holding the tomato remnants in my hand. "It was an accident." My belly grew topsy-turvy, as my anger started bubbling up through my chest. I squeezed the flesh in my hand then hurled it at Ma, splattering her floral dress.

The old ladies shrieked, and Randolph laughed from beside the truck.

"Please, please, Henry will take care of this."

A freckled boy in dark overalls appeared from behind the grocer, poking his head out to see the commotion.

I stayed on all fours, not sure to stand up or clean up. Figuring I had already gotten myself into a heap of trouble, I began taking the no-good tomatoes and tossing them in a metal pail under the vegetable stand. When I finished, I wiped my hands on my dress, streaking it red, and stood up.

"You girls have no idea how kind I've been. There's no helping you." She snatched my shoulder and pulled me away from the storefront.

"Told you they're no good, Ma," Randolph said, biting into a pear. "No good."

She handed Randolph a bill and nodded towards the grocer. Randolph took the money. Ma and I set out towards home, both of us filthy.

Chapter Ten

I spent the night sounding out letters in my book, by the little light shining from the full moon. It grew too warm for a fire, so building one would raise a fuss. I couldn't take the risk of Ma finding one more thing about me that she didn't like.

I thought about running that night. I did. I even peeked my head out the bedroom door. When I didn't hear even the pattering feet of mice, I crept down the hall to see if everyone was sleeping. But Ma sat like a grinning fairy doll on the chair and yelled for me to get back to bed. She knew I was up to no good, but I couldn't figure out why she didn't just let me run like the dickens out of that house. I apologized for leaving my room so late and pretended like I had to use the water closet.

I didn't sleep that night; just lay in bed thinking about how I was going to get the devil out of me and me out of the devil's house. My mind spooled thread after thread of worry over how I'd raise Randolph's child. I looked up at those stars that night and cursed them for punishing me for the rest of my life for Randolph's sin. I couldn't imagine ever looking in that newborn's face, knowing he had

Monroe blood coursing through him, not even if he had my smile.

When the sun stretched out over the horizon, I sat up as a rumbling came over my tummy, that made me know I had no time to waste. In my nightdress, I raced out of my room, turned down the hall toward the back patio, and swung open the screen door in the nick of time. I threw up my boots over the edge of the railing into the forsythia about to bloom.

Once I cleaned myself up and dressed for the day, Ma ordered me to start laundry. On the back porch, I set out the buckets like I always did and worked on a load of darks from the wicker basket.

The harsh scent of the Persil scorched the back of my throat and brought on the urge to vomit again. I swallowed bile and held my breath as best I could. The whole time I scrubbed, thoughts raced through my mind about how I was going to get out of here. Ma was angry, too angry to let me go, and I thought back to the girl before me. Where was she now? I figured if Ma had anything to do with it, that girl did not just up and walk out. I hated to think of what happened to her. And what would happen to me if I couldn't escape.

Once I finished washing the first load, I hauled it to the backyard where the clothesline stretched between two rusted metal poles outside the open kitchen window. The weather turning meant hanging clothes outside, and I was grateful for that bit of freedom. The Monroe's house felt like a hog pen.

I set the laundry basket on the ground and reached for clothespins in the small tin pail hanging from one of the poles. Even on my tiptoes, I couldn't reach. I grabbed a nearby bucket that was full of dead leaves and dirty rainwater and tipped it over, the muck running over the toes of my shoes. I tried moving out of the way, but it was too late. My socks got soaked clean through. I stepped on the bucket then picked out a handful of clothespins.

I moved the bucket down the line as I hung garment after garment, watching them drip onto the muddy ground below. A voice came from inside, and I looked to see Mrs. Rossor sitting at the kitchen table with Ma. I stepped down from my bucket and moved it a few inches closer to the window.

"Thank you for making the call. I can't go through this again," Ma said, her voice sharp.

The air outside was so still I heard Mrs. Rossor's teacup rattle as she set it on its saucer. "I never mind calling in a favor, Lucille. We can't delay something like this. There is nothing else to do with these kinds of people."

The two kept chatting, but their words blended into mush. My head got so swirly that I lost my balance and slipped off the bucket.

A chair screeched across the floor, and Ma raced to the window. "What are you doing, child? You must be more careful."

"Sorry, Ma," I said, looking up at her scowling face in the window. But I wasn't sorry. I hated Ma more than Miss

Atkinson, and I would not let another old meanie take me further from my family.

I had to run now.

#

I left the soaked laundry still to be hung and darted into the house, through the back porch door. I shut the door behind me, careful not to make a sound, then tiptoed through the porch and peeked down the hall. Empty. I scurried to my room.

In the center of my room, I took slow, heavy breaths, but I couldn't seem to get enough air in my stupid lungs. I wanted to leave so bad that it buckled my knees. Turning towards the mirror, I glimpsed my reflection, and for the first time in a long time, I recognized myself. I was ready for a fight.

I dug under the bed to find the pillowcase I had packed. I found it and took hold. The front door slammed shut, and Randolph's muffled voice echoed down the hall, reaching my room. I couldn't make out what he was saying, but his voice was loud and excited, and it didn't sound good for me.

No time for checking halls and sneaking around now. If I didn't pull out everything I had, I'd never taste freedom again.

I took off out of my room and tore through the back of the house, through the back door.

"Ma! She's running!" Randolph screamed.

Speeding up, my strides grew longer and longer to reach that old fence in the backyard. I swung the pillowcase over my shoulder and ran faster than I ever thought I could.

Ma screamed from somewhere near the house, "Stop her!"

Randolph tore after me like a rabid dog. When I got to the fence, I grabbed the top of the pickets and hoisted myself up, then swung one leg over. From the corner of my eye, I saw Randolph closing in.

As I was about to make it over, Randolph yanked a clump of my hair and pulled me back. My leg snagged on the wood and ripped open, but I'd fight 'til I had nothing left. With all my might, I swung my loose arm at his face and caught him in the cheek. He pulled my shoulders towards him and threw me to the ground, my one leg still dangling on the edge of the fence. He swatted it off and fisted my hair again. I punched his calf, the only thing I could reach. He smirked and kneeled down to pin my shoulders to the dirt with his dirty hands.

"You're gone," he whispered. "Like you never were."

Ma screamed, and I leaned my head up to see a black car pull beside the house. Randolph's panting grew loud. I couldn't make out what Ma was saying to the man, but I watched him as he stepped out of the car, wearing all blue, and opened the back passenger door.

Ma bounced up and down, pointing towards me. I dropped my head to the hard ground, not wanting to see anymore.

Randolph eased off me and took my arm to pull me up. I struggled to gain my footing. He clenched a clump of my hair by my scalp and held tight, leading me toward the car and the man. I walked bent-legged all the way through the yard, past the soppy laundry I had never finished hanging. I still had my pillowcase in my hand and did my best to hold it tight to my side, so that no one would think to take it.

As we grew close to the man, Randolph let me loose a minute too soon. I kicked and swung my arm, but I wasn't doing anything but making a scene. Finally, I took one last chance and clawed that man's rough cheek, knowing full well that Randolph would yank me to the ground by my hair. And he did.

Another man came out of the car and said, chuckling, "I thought you said this was a one-man job."

They left me there, on the ground, my arms punching my own belly with every scrap I had left. "No, no, no!" I shouted. If I was going to leave those Monroes, I would not bring a piece of them with me.

By the time they wrestled me into the car, I had no more fight. I slumped in the back seat against the door, my cheek pressing against the window. Neither man said a word about where we were headed, and I gathered I had no say either way.

The engine roared then hummed, as we pulled away.

I looked through the window, back at the Monroe's house, and saw Pa standing on the front porch, his hands dangling by his side like he done given up—no better than the rest of them.

During the long, weaving drive through county streets, not a word was said. The quiet vibrated in my ears like an echo. My mind set itself to thinking about how this hole kept getting deeper and deeper. No matter how much I tried to set things right, nothing I did seemed to matter. No one listened a lick to what I had to say or cared a smidge about what I wanted. I knew that wherever I was headed would be worse.

When we pulled into a paved drive, I thought I heard a baby's cry pierce the silence. I placed my hand on my belly to quiet the child growing inside, but the wailing grew louder. Suddenly, as I looked up at a stone tower with iron bars across the windows, I realized the screams were coming from me.

Chapter Eleven

The sun hung high overhead as we weaved through a winding, curved road that swerved like a garden snake.

The buildings. I'd never seen so many on one patch of land. Brick, stone, wood. They sprouted like wildflowers without any sense of order. A farm, peppered with mismatched stables and sheds, stretched across the background. Hunched bodies dotted the fields, all laboring away in dresses as gray as the stormy sky overhead.

Tears soaked my face as we approached the biggest structure. My heart beat like a punching fist. I looked up to see a three-storied tower dotted with rectangular windows, every one of them barred. On the third floor, I could just make out the silhouette of a girl pressing herself against the glass. Through the black iron bars, I saw she was naked, her mouth a wide gash across her face.

I was still howling when the man in the passenger side whipped around, rearing a nightstick over his head. He reached his free hand into the back seat to grip my shoulder, so I bit him. I hung on like a rabid dog protecting her litter. When he yanked his hand away, the iron in his blood spread out over my tongue.

"Don't make me use this," he said in a sharp voice, waving the nightstick.

I leaned forward and dropped my head between my knees, sobbing until the stick came down hard between my shoulder blades. I collapsed on the floor at the same time that the car jolted to a stop.

I watched the driver step out and walk to the back of the car to take out a white coat. He opened my door and said, "For your own protection."

I wasn't the smartest, I knew, but I was wise enough to know none of this was to protect me. It was as if the whole world conspired to destroy me. I couldn't understand why. I hadn't hurt anyone.

He forced one arm into a sleeve and then the other; my pillowcase dropped to the floor. From behind, the passenger door creaked open, then the other man appeared. He took thin straps from each sleeve, crossed my arms around my chest, tying them at the back. He tugged at the ties to check they would hold, before they returned to their seats. We continued the short way up a circular drive towards the front of the towering building. I pressed my head against the car window, watching the naked girl stare into nothingness.

#

A tall, thin woman with short, black hair opened the wide door. She looked like a ghost in murky white from head to toe. Even her hat, with its sharp angles and folded edges, was the color of old cotton. When she reached the car, the driver stepped out and handed her some papers. She pulled a fountain pen from her apron, signed, then returned them.

They talked a few minutes. All the while I lay with the side of my face pressed against the window, too tired to sit up. I couldn't hear their conversation, but I didn't try. I couldn't even feel my heart beating no more. I was no good to myself. To anyone. As I was slipping further and further away from my home, all I kept thinking about was how I had let everyone who loved me down.

I heard a door slam, then looked up to see another woman—shorter than the first, with curly hair escaping from her cap—spring out the same door, holding a rug and flat iron beater, then she lay the rug across the railing and began pounding it. A dust cloud as thick as wool formed around her, but she did not let up. I watched her. Our eyes met, even though she was some distance away and covered in soot. A trace of a smiled crossed her lips. I wondered how anyone could find a reason to smile at this place.

The car door swung open, and I tumbled out, unable to catch myself with my hands wrapped around my chest. The tall nurse grabbed me by the scruff of my hair and pulled me up as if I were a mangy hound. I swallowed the thick air, as I prepared to enter the dog pound reserved for women. I avoided her eyes and instead kept mine on the lady beating the carpet, because she still held a smile I couldn't understand.

"Thank you, Mr. Hughes. I will take it from here," the nurse said. She turned towards the one with the carpet. "Millie. Millie, come get her."

The shorter nurse placed the beater upright against the railing. She raced over. "Yes, Nurse Gladys." She set her hand on my back and guided me towards the door.

Ten stone steps led the way to the building. I counted as we took each one, careful not to trip, with my shaking knees and trussed arms. As we reached the top, before entering the door, I turned to watch a herd of women walking along the path. They were silent, each one staring down at her own feet, disinterested in anything around them, unaware of my arrival. My eyes followed them as they seemed to disappear into the fields.

We stepped through the old door, the tall nurse in front of me, the shorter one next to me squeezing my shoulder gently. I thought back to Pa and his wink the first night at dinner. Then I remembered his hands dangling by his side as the car took me away. Some people wanted very much to be kind but never had the courage for it.

"You are Anna Wilson," the short one said, but it sounded more like a question.

I didn't answer.

"I am Miss Millie. This here is Nurse Gladys." She pointed to the spindly nurse who was shuffling papers on a large wooden desk. "You are at the Farview Training School, formerly the Village for Feebleminded Women." The tall ceiling set with dark beams echoed her words.

I said nothing.

Miss Millie, wrapping her arm around me, leaned towards me and said, "If you remain calm, I can remove your restraints. Can you remain calm?"

I never answered.

She turned me so my back faced her and worked the ties until they loosened. Shaking the fabric, she adjusted the jacket so that my hands hung loose, then she turned me around again and shimmied it off. "Now, isn't that better?"

I said nothing.

"What are you doing, Millie? We've got work to do," scolded Nurse Gladys, as she stacked a neat pile of yellow papers on a desk then pulled out a metal drawer in a tall filing cabinet that looked like it might tip forward.

"Yes, Nurse Gladys. I'll see to it that Anna is acquainted with the grounds and return right away." Miss Millie darted towards a side room with the jacket and came back empty-handed. She stood inches from my face. Her dark-brown eyes stared into mine, as she brushed a tangle of hair from my face. Her breath smelled of peppermint.

"Stop fussing over the inmates, if you see yourself long for this job." Nurse Gladys slammed the file drawer shut, shaking the cabinet. "People much smarter than you or I will have our heads if we don't get the work done around here." She picked up the neat stack of papers and disappeared into the room beside the desk.

Miss Millie shuffled towards the table; she looked to be searching for something.

I walked towards a long wall lined with the most gorgeous windows I'd ever seen. They were taller than me, with pine arches at the top, each curve having a tiny point like a star at the center. Outside, the view expanded for acres and acres. There were fields of crops, a brood of hens, and a stone well placed in the center of it all. My mouth hung open. To the east, I watched a group of inmates dressed in the matching gray dresses and white aprons, digging trenches, their bodies hunched like weak flower stems unable to bear the weight of their petals. One woman could hardly hoist the dirt over her shoulder, so she kept dumping soil onto her own head. She shook it off each time and went back to her digging. On the opposite side of the grounds, lay long rows of crops that looked like collards—spinach maybe. Women pushed wheelbarrows through the rows, squatting every few feet to harvest a patch.

"Anna Wilson. Anna Wilson."

I jumped at the sound of my name and turned towards the voice.

Miss Millie raced towards me, her eyes wide. "You startled me. You mustn't walk away like that." She glanced out the window, shaking her head, then placed her hand on my shoulder again. "Do you like the grounds? Our inmates keep the farm in working order. There's a lot of work to be done." She tried shuffling me away from the view, but I planted my feet. "You'll eat most of what we grow here. We sell some to cover costs. There are many jobs here." She watched me still looking out at the fields. "What's your favorite?"

I pointed to the hutch and the penned hens.

"Oh. You like the henhouse? Have you worked with hens before? Have you been on a farm?"

I stayed mum but shook my head a bit, my throat too dry for talking. Thoughts of who I was, before they tore me from my farm, spun. *Yes, I raised hens. No one could raise them better. Before Miss Atkinson, Randolph, Ma, I was proud of my work on my farm. They took it all away from me, blow by blow.* Anger boiled in my blood as I wiped my sweating brow.

"Quiet, aren't you?"

I turned to face her and watched her face flinch. I was sure that mine was pinched in rage. She dug in her apron pocket for a handkerchief and dotted the corner of my eye. It felt raw, and I realized I must have a bruise from one of the hits I'd taken trying to escape the Monroe's.

"You poor child. Why are you here?" She leaned her ear close to my lips, but all I could muster was a sigh.

She was one of them. I could never trust her.

Chapter Twelve

"This way," Miss Millie said, pointing towards a gated doorway on the opposite side of the large room.

I walked slowly behind her, aware of the pattering of my boots echoing off the high ceiling. The thick bars of the gate curled and wound into beautiful flowers with long arching stems. Miss Millie drew a long iron key from her apron pocket, unlocked it, then pushed it open with a creak. After we walked through, she slammed the gate shut behind us and locked it. The click of the key rang throughout the hall we entered.

I had never seen so many doors next to one another. The pale, daffodil walls were lined with skinny wood shelves on one side, each holding a small, shaded lamp. On the other side, the closed wooden doors were spaced evenly down the row. The narrow hall and high ceiling inhaled me, pulling me deeper and deeper into the place, further and further from where I wanted to be. My stomach grew queasy, and I remembered they were locking me away with this baby. Randolph would forever be a part of me. At the thought, my head spun and dropped me to my knees, unable to catch my breath.

Miss Millie propped me up and kept us walking, passing a narrow alcove between two of the doors that had round pegs holding pulleys and leather straps with buckles. They reminded me of equipment we had had for the horses when we had a few. I paused at the nook until a waft of body odor and ammonia hit me. Miss Millie pulled my elbow to move me along, but I couldn't walk. I dropped my hands to my knees, leaned my head over and struggled to slow my quickening breath. Miss Millie placed her hand on the small of my back and rubbed soft circles. I flinched at first, but then the touch felt so good that I wanted her to do it forever.

Once I calmed myself, we continued. When we reached the end of the hall, we turned to find an open door. I stood behind Miss Millie. Blooming spots of mildew covered the white ceiling. Paint chipped away at the corner wall, leaving brown flecks on the floor. Despite the tall windows, high ceilings, and fancy wooden chairs, the room was bleak. A few inmates clustered around some round tables lining the sides of the room, leaving a wide aisle in the center. On each table sat a jigsaw puzzle and a deck of playing cards, although no one was playing with them. They all seemed to stare off into nothingness, or at least something I couldn't see. Not yet.

Miss Millie walked towards the front of the room, so I followed her. "Anna, this here is an orderly. His name is Paul."

The man, not much older than me and with a thin mustache you'd miss if the sun wasn't breaking through the window, grunted and nodded.

"Orderlies keep everyone safe and make sure everyone is where they should be," Miss Millie said. She turned her head towards a crash on the other side of the room.

One of the women fell on the floor, her chair toppled over on her.

"Damn it, Wilma. You son of a bitch," shouted a silver-haired woman in a loose dress. She stood over the woman on the floor and pressed the chair down onto her back. The woman shielded her head with her hands but said nothing.

"Let's move on, Anna," said Miss Millie, as the orderly walked around us towards the fighting ladies.

We left the room too quickly to see what happened to the woman under the chair.

"That was the game room," Miss Millie said, as we walked down the hall. "When you have some free time, it might be fun to—" Her voice trailed off.

Miss Millie shuffled a little further down the hall as I trailed her. She passed a door on her right, stopped, then turned back. I followed her in.

"This here is a laboratory."

A wretched scent hit my nose. I gagged with no warning, vomiting onto the floor in front of four rows of long tables. I wiped my mouth with the back of my hand before Miss Millie could stop me.

"No, Anna. Use this." She handed me a towel from a shelf in the front of the room. "It's the formaldehyde. It can do a number on your stomach."

I waited for her to mention the pregnancy. Morning sickness. But I got the sense she didn't know about that. Ma didn't tell. There were plenty of other reasons to send me here, so Ma kept that secret. I wondered how long it'd be before they found out. I placed my hand over my belly and wondered if I could get out of this before they were on to me.

Despite the sickening scent of pickles, I stood in the room, looking at the glass jars filled with brains and I wasn't sure what else, while Miss Mille scrubbed the floor, leaving no trace of my being sick. I wished she could wash me away too, leaving no trace that I was here.

As we were leaving, she said, "This room is for experiments. Most of the time, you won't participate."

I was filled with such emptiness that I couldn't even find it in my heart to be glad for that.

She placed her hand on the small of my back. "Let's get you out of here. The smell does not agree with you."

We returned to the hall and kept walking. A low din hummed throughout the place, then a sudden shriek. It was as if the walls were screaming. The low lighting and no windows made it hard for me to breathe. My eyes welled up and I sniffled, unable to hold it all in. Miss Millie must have noticed, because she reached for my hand, but I jerked it away and wiped my dumb tears.

Every step we took felt like I was moving further and further away from my sisters and brother, further from my farm. I wanted to turn back, run back to the other side of the gate, but I knew it wouldn't help. I was already erased from the world outside. I thought back to Randolph's words: 'Like you never were.'

Further down, we stopped in front of a sewing room lined with small tables, each staffed by a girl in a gray dress, working at an iron sewing machine. I'd never seen one before, but I knew what they were. I'd always wanted one. I used to hand sew dresses for Alice out of flour sacks, and a sewing machine would have made it lighter work.

The fabric the girls used was mostly gray, that matched their own smocks, but a few worked with lemon-yellow pieces that lit up the room like fireflies.

"Hey," a voice said to me, from a sewing machine near the door. A matted-haired, blonde girl about my age was fashioning a daffodil top with small, flower buttons. "Pretty, isn't it?" Even with a wide gap between her front teeth, her smile filled the whole room and made the edges of my lips curl a bit, too.

"It's beautiful." The sound of my own voice surprised me. They were the first words I'd spoken since I'd been there.

She set the blouse against her chest and shimmied. "Wouldn't I be the bee's knees in this?" She giggled, and I giggled back.

"Let's press on, Anna," Miss Millie said. "I'll show you to your cottage and dormitory."

We walked a few steps then turned towards a large door that led outside. She took a key from her apron again and unlocked it. "You must be careful about who you fraternize with. Some people look for trouble, and they will bring you right along with them."

I seem to find trouble just fine on my own, thank you.

We walked outside down the same path we drove in on. I shielded my eyes from the bright sun and tried my best to memorize the patterns of stones and patches of flowers, so that I could find my way back again later. We entered a building that had a sign out front. The word started with an A, but I couldn't read it. I remembered then my pillowcase, my book, the letter. They were left in the motorcar. A sinking feeling struck me, as we turned into the first doorway of the cottage to see an enormous room filled wall to wall with small cots, each having a thin, white sheet, a flat pillow, and a metal trunk at the foot. I gasped. How many of us were there?

Chapter Thirteen

After I changed into the gray dress and white apron everyone else here was wearing, Miss Millie led me back to the main building and into a narrow office near the desk. Scratching the whole way there, on account of the papery fabric, I had several raw spots on my arms by the time I reached the office. I pulled my baggy sleeves over my hands to hide them. The windowless room, lit by a wide, shaded desk lamp, smelled of ammonia, burning my nose with each inhale. I tried breathing through my mouth, but the thick scent coated my tongue. I was afraid it'd make me throw up again.

Across from Miss Millie, who was seated in a tall, soft chair behind the desk, I slumped in a wooden chair. She leaned over the desk and spoke in a soft voice. "Would you like some water before we get started? Soda crackers?"

I shook my head.

"Let's begin then," she said, her voice bouncing off the cracking walls. "You are at the Farview Training School. Here at Farview, we train the residents to contribute to our work. We have farms, sewing rooms, even a cannery. If we all work together, we can fully support ourselves." Her voice rose like the nice gray-haired teacher lady who used to drive Helen, Alice, and John home from school when the rain fell in buckets.

"Get on with it," Nurse Gladys shouted from outside the door.

"OK, then," she continued. "I have a few questions for you. Do you think you could answer a few questions?"

I thought, for a minute, if this might be my chance to tell Miss Mille there had been a mistake. I was no orphan. I had a family. A place to live. I opened my mouth to speak, but nothing came out.

"Do you have any questions for me before we begin?" She flipped through some papers on the desk and adjusted herself in her chair. She pushed her curly hair from her eyes. When I didn't answer, she went on. "Do you have any parents we can contact?"

I thought of Mama. Maybe even Papa. But it wasn't worth the words. I didn't have a way of reaching them.

"We do have a few Wilsons here. Do you have family at Farview that you are aware of?"

I didn't answer. My stomach got all knotted up at the thought of Mama being here. But I couldn't get my hopes up. And if she were, what use would she be to me? The further I got from my home, the more her leaving got stuck in my craw. If anything was to blame for us ending up where we were, it was Mama's leaving.

She continued asking a few questions about schooling—mine, Mama's and Papa's—of which there wasn't much to say. Staying mum on that one wasn't hard. She asked about some history, like if we were inebriates or bastards. Again, if I knew what was best for me, I'd keep my family business hush-hush, just like Papa used to say.

Miss Millie just stared at me like I didn't have a brain for answering questions. Then she went to the office door and closed it. When she returned to her chair, she reached under her seat, shuffling around for something. When she placed my pillowcase in the center of the desk, my mouth dropped wide open, and my blood grew so hot that I bet Miss Millie could feel the heat rising out of me.

"Medication time," Gladys called, from the other side of the door.

I jumped as if she had caught me in a trap. I moved closer to the desk, hoping Miss Millie might slide the pillowcase towards me. I could take it and be on my way. But she just let it sit there between us.

"We found this in the motorcar. Is it yours?" She tapped her hand on my pillowcase.

I nodded so hard that I thought my head might roll off and fall right there on the floor.

"Are you reading this book?" she asked, taking *Peter and Wendy* out of the sack. I spied the tip of the letter poking out from between the pages.

I stayed mum.

She asked again. "Is this yours?" She looked around me, as if trying to see if the door was still closed. Then Miss Millie said, "I'm sorry, Anna, but there are no personal belongings here at Farview."

A loud roar shot through me. I didn't realize I had been holding it back, but I must have, by the way it blasted out of me. And I didn't stop. I reached across the desk and nabbed the pillowcase, opened the door, and flew past Nurse Gladys, knocking over a tin tray with tiny cups of pills that scattered to the floor like thick snowflakes. I never looked back.

"Stop her!" Nurse Gladys screamed.

Suddenly two orderlies appeared, and one tackled me to the floor before I ever reached the front door. I held the pillowcase like my siblings' lives depended on it. Because they did.

Miss Millie rushed to my side and put her arms around me. She whispered in my ear, "Let me help you. You must talk to me if you need me to help." Then she forced the pillowcase out of my hand. "I can't let you take this, though."

I didn't need the likes of Miss Millie helping me. I learned now that people outside of Shaker Street were bad news. No one was looking to help the Wilsons or anyone else who didn't fit in with their kind.

The orderlies stood over me, their eyes burning my skin.

Nurse Gladys barreled through them. "Enough. This girl is unfit for intake. Remove her."

"But Nurse Gladys. I'm trying to speak with her." Miss Millie's voice sounded like cotton, even though she must have been cross with me for stealing. But they were my things. And I deserved to have them.

"Put her in solitary until she calms down," Nurse Gladys said, as she pulled at the neck of her white uniform.

Miss Millie adjusted her small hat that toppled to the side to reveal a fit of wild curls. "I believe she's calm. Right, Anna?" She looked down at me and nodded just enough to let me know I should listen. "I'll show her to supper."

Nurse Gladys stepped aside, giving us enough room to stand up. "You spoil the inmates, Millie. You are not long for this place. There is no saving them." With that, she went about setting the tin cups back onto the tray, slamming each one so hard that it sounded like hail pinging a window.

Together, we returned to the metal gate, and Miss Millie unlocked it again. As the gate screeched open, she leaned down and whispered to me, "This is a dreadful place. You must let me help you."

The gate snapped shut, and the click of the key echoed through the long hall. I said nothing.

#

Miss Millie directed me towards the dining hall in a building a short walk down the path from the main one and bid me farewell. I walked outside, surprised by how the fresh air and being alone made my skin squirm and prickle with life. It felt strange to be on my own. For a moment, I was Anna Wilson again. I squatted by a patch of wildflowers, blue and yellow, poking their sleepy heads through cracks in the pavement, and rubbed their silky petals between my fingers. The sun beat down on me, so I looked up to the sky to warm my face. I plucked a few of the flowers, tucking them into the pocket of my apron so that I'd have the scent of wildflowers following me around. If Alice were here, I'd give them to her. I was grateful she was not. As much as I missed my kin, I hoped they were someplace much better than the Farview Training School. I held my breath and closed my eyes, as I wished they'd never know a place like this existed. I didn't think they'd have the stomach for it.

Four tarred steps led to the building with the dining hall. I took them one at a time, not two, which I used to do at home. The noise from inside—screaming, calling, wailing—all meshed together into one sour note. I entered with my head low, watching my feet as I stepped through the mass of people in gray, to reach the serving area. The long room held four of the longest tables I'd ever seen, each with white tablecloths. The ceiling was lower than the main buildings, so low that I felt like it might crush me. There were ceiling lights hanging above each table; if the tables weren't there, you'd whack your head. I had never seen anything like it.

I took a tray and stood in line, but a little woman with strong arms knocked me back, so I waited a little further away from her. Once I filled my tray with soup, string beans, and pale-looking bread, I scanned the room for a place to sit.

"Over here." A girl's voice cut through the racket.

I looked up to see the blonde girl from the sewing room, her blue eyes staring right at me. She slid the spindled chair next to hers, and I sat down. Something leaped from her head, so I jumped.

"Ain't nothing you can do about that," she said, pushing her hair from her face. "I'm Abigail. Who are you?"

"Anna. Anna Wilson."

"Well, welcome to hell, Anna Wilson." She shoveled a spoonful of string beans into her mouth.

My stomach churned. I hadn't realized how hungry I was. I sipped my soup. It was bland, tasting like lukewarm carrot and celery water. "I'm not staying."

Abigail broke off a hunk of her bread and popped it into her mouth. While chewing, she said, "How'd you get here?"

It felt so good to speak to someone like me. I hadn't realized how lonely I'd been until the words started pouring from my mouth. "My mama took off. Somehow the authorities found out and took us. I ended up with some family I don't want much to talk about. Then they sent me here." I paused to sip my soup, then said, "I don't know what happened to the rest of them."

"Who's the rest of them?" Abigail asked. She dunked the hard bread in her soup and swirled it around.

My stomach sank at the thought of my family. "My sisters, Helen and Alice, and my brother John. We were living fine on our farm, but someone must have told that we didn't have parents at home."

I didn't think she heard what I said. She stared at a boy across the dining hall, dressed in all white. An orderly.

He smiled over at us, and I saw her cheeks redden. She turned to me. "You know who that is?" She pointed at the boy with her dripping spoon.

I looked at him, then at her, then back at him. He moved closer to the door and stood talking to another boy his age, dressed the same. They both had slicked-back hair that shined. "No. Who is he?"

"He's how I'm getting out of here. Isn't he a sheik?" She slurped her soup and giggled. In that hall, with the shrieks and cries echoing off the ceilings, her giggle sounded like a lily in a cornfield.

I said, "But how? How do they let you out?"

"Don't most people get out. But I have a plan." She set down her spoon then wiggled her fingers at the boy. He shrugged and wiggled his fingers in return, but he kept his hand by his side. I noticed his eyes were wide-set, and his nose curved like the fish hook we used when the minnows and carp filled the creek that ran behind Shaker Street.

I pressed. "What's your plan? I need a plan. I'm in trouble here." I wondered if it was right to tell this strange girl my story, how desperate I was. But I had nothing to lose. And I didn't think her word counted for much around here, so if she turned on me, no one would listen. I was sure of that.

Huffing, she said, "Everyone's in trouble here. You don't end up here unless there's trouble."

I didn't feel hungry anymore. I placed my hand over my belly and pressed hard, as if Randolph himself might feel an ache in his head from all my pushing. Screams roared from across the room, and I wished I could plug my ears.

She went on, "There's a test you take if they think you're fit to be out. But it's a hard one. And that stupid committee don't like nobody. Don't know anyone who passed."

My eyes narrowed in on Abigail. "Who's the committee?"

"No one knows who they are. Doctors? Folks with money who pay for this place? I heard once there was an old lady on it. Fainted at the sight of the wards."

"When'd that happen?"

"Before I was here."

She looked around at the women. They seemed to be acting like they weren't sitting elbow-to-elbow with strange ladies. Maybe they stopped noticing after a time? I didn't want to get to that point. I needed to be out before.

Abigail went on, "People aren't exactly conversating around here much. All I know is that they ask a bunch of questions and make you do some school stuff. Reading. Math." She took a bite of bread, and as she chewed, said, "Then they tell you that you can't leave."

I gasped, "No one passes?"

She smiled and nodded her head, then leaned in close and whispered, "But there's another way."

"How?"

"You have to find someone to take you. Bobby," she said, nodding towards the boy. "He's my ticket."

I scanned the room, looking at the women eating. Their heads hung over their food as if they were going to slop up their dinner like swine. One woman, gray-haired with a patch of black hair in the back, had the curving spine and sharp nose of my mother. I realized how she wouldn't be such a misfit here. "Who can be my ticket?" I asked.

"You got any family?"

I thought to mention Mama and Papa but realized they were why I was here. "Just my sisters and brother. They're too young. It has to be me who takes them in." The bitterness of those words stung my tongue.

"What about your ma or pa?"

The boy, Bobby, walked towards us. He was hiding something in his hand. Without saying a word, he plopped a piece of cornbread onto Abigail's plate. I looked around to see if anyone was watching, but they weren't.

"See?" she said, looking at me. "Told you he was my ticket."

Her happiness warmed my heart. She broke the bread in half and slid me a piece.

I took a bite and smiled. Then my smile vanished. "My mama and papa took off. I don't think they're coming back," I said. And I knew they weren't. I looked over at the woman again. She sure looked like Mama.

The spring before Mama left, we had a mama cat who used to come by our house every day to lap at water dripping from the pump. Each day, after collecting eggs from the henhouse, I'd sit stroking her fur. That peach never bothered those hens a bit. Back then we had a dairy cow, and I used to put a little milk into a tin cup as a treat for her sometimes. I figured if she knew I had milk, she'd come back and visit. And she did. Even started letting me rub her belly.

Her belly started growing, though, so I knew she had a litter on the way. I begged Mama to let me keep her as a pet and take care of her babies.

"We ain't got two wooden nickels. No business taking in more mouths to feed."

It seemed like no time, and I found the mama cat laying in a small ditch surrounded by five black and white kittens that looked just like her, aside from the gray mixed in their tails. She'd gone from plump to skin and bones in what seemed like a minute. She looked like she was trying to bury herself in that dirt hole. I ran to the cow stall to get a little milk to get those kittens off her teats, but they only wanted their mama's milk. No matter how hard I tried, those buggers wouldn't get off her.

Mama came up from behind me. "What are you doing? You've got to shoo those chickens out and get to cleaning the henhouse."

"But Mama, they're killing her." I pointed to the limp cat and her hungry kittens.

She shook her head. "Those damn young'uns are sucking her teats dry. Nothing you can do about it. They'll shrivel up, one by one, and die themselves. Taking so much, they'll be dead in a week."

Mama was right. In less than a week, they were all dead, no matter how much milk I stole for them. I dug a proper grave behind the coop and set them there, covered with plenty of dirt to keep the hounds from digging them up. I plucked the heads off a few dandelions and placed them as a marker.

No, Mama was never coming back for us. I looked over at the woman again and thought, *Maybe?*

Abigail's voice shocked me. "So if you don't have anyone to take you, you'll have to answer all those riddles." She looked up towards where Bobby was, but he was gone. "Did you meet the great doctor yet?"

I didn't answer her. I couldn't take my eyes off the woman with the dark patch of hair. Once she stood up to set her tray on the counter, I knew. "I have to go," I said, jumping up.

"Your tray. You don't put your tray away, they'll come after you."

I started moving towards the door. I looked back at Abigail. "Please can you take care of it?" I followed the woman as she walked out of the building and onto the path draped in the orange of the setting sun.

Chapter Fourteen

I stood on the stoop of the dining hall and leaned against the railing, as I watched her shuffle towards the cottages further down the lane. The sun faded from orange to a beige that cast everything in shadows. I wondered if her eyes were my mother's, gray ovals set wide above her narrow nose. She was thinner than my mother, but short like her, and the dark patch made me wonder if there wasn't a chance.

I raced off the stoop and paced her, mimicking even the slumping shoulders and bowing head. As she neared a cottage, I moved faster, closing in on her. When she turned towards the steps to the brick and stone building, I was sure.

"Mama!" I shouted, racing towards her, taking her by the shoulder.

She jumped and shooed me away. "Hands off me! Don't touch me."

"It's me, Mama. It's Anna."

She turned towards me, her sunken cheeks made darker by the shade, but the eyes were hers. "Anna?"

"Why are you here?" I asked. It was all I could think to say. My heart slowed, as if it stopped beating altogether.

She shook her head. "Why are you here?" she asked. At first, I thought she was copying me, but then I realized she didn't hear me.

"Because you left. There was no one to take care of us." Her forehead didn't crinkle in thought. It was as if she didn't understand what I was saying. I asked her again, "Why are you here?"

Her face flinched. "Why am I here? Why are you here?" she said, flinging her arms wild.

I took a step back and raised my voice. "I told you, Mama. They wouldn't let us stay on the farm without you. Or Papa."

She snapped at me. "You were supposed to take care of them. I couldn't do it."

I stepped towards her and grabbed her wrist. My breath quickened until I panted each word. "Me? Why me? What about you? You are our mother."

She shook her head as if offended. "You can do better than me. You always did." I looked into her eyes and saw a glare of resentment.

"That's not true. And so what if it is? You are our mother." I yanked her wrist, and the waif of my mother flung towards me. I gripped harder. "This is your fault. All of it." I watched myself from above as if this weren't me and my lost mother here, at an asylum, arguing over facts. It was as if we were on stage, play-acting. I became aware of my fingers pressing deep into her thin skin, the bones of her wrist protruding. I let go. "How did you get here?" I wasn't going to let her wriggle out of this.

Her shoulders slumped even further towards the ground. I thought she might collapse, and I suddenly felt guilty for being rough with her. I put my arm out to steady her, but she shook me off.

"I left. I didn't know where I was going, but I knew I couldn't stay."

I heard the anger in my own voice echo as if trapped in a soap bubble, the words muted and fuzzy. "You are our mother. How could you leave?"

"It had been a long time coming, Anna. You knew that. I couldn't do it anymore. You could."

I stomped my foot and turned to walk away from her, unwilling to hear. I swung back towards her. "How dare you?"

"You were better off without me. You all were. I couldn't care for you no more."

I shivered at the weak sound of her voice. She had no fight left in her. "How did you get here?"

"I walked down towards the butcher, then out to the fruit stand by Cuthbert."

"Where were you going? What was your plan?" I grew tired from talking. I hated her for abandoning us. I no longer cared what she had planned, only that she had left.

She huffed. "I didn't have no plan. Only that you'd take care of the kids."

My voice pitched. "Why didn't you tell me?"

"You would have tried to stop me."

"Of course, I would have. We needed our mama."

"You needed a mama. I was fighting to keep my mind out there on the farm, with you four hungry all the time, always calling for me. It got to be that I couldn't fight it no more."

I took a deep breath, realizing I wasn't going to be satisfied by anything she said. "Then how'd you end up here?"

"At the fruit stand. It got late, and I realized I didn't have a place to sleep. That old bench that's missing a few slats? I lay on that. By morning, the police came and took me in."

"Why didn't they bring you home?"

"I told them I didn't remember who I was. If I told them the truth, they'd know you were out there alone. I couldn't let them take you in. So I told them I didn't know my own name. I came here as number 83."

I looked her in the eye. "If you told them your name, they may have brought you home. I could have taken care of all of us."

"I couldn't stand going back there. I couldn't breathe there anymore. When I did finally say my name, it wasn't on purpose, but they asked, and I forgot about not telling."

"That's how they found us, and they split us up now. I've been through terrible things because of you."

Her lips pursed, and her voice grew louder than I'd ever heard it. "It's not my fault you got caught!"

My mouth opened to shout at her, but I smacked it shut. The anger held too much power over me, and I knew now that it wouldn't help me get home. I turned away, but my feet wouldn't move. My mama's words sounded in my head like pelting rain. We both stood there, the smell of wisteria filling the air.

I knew Mama wasn't cut out for family. But I didn't expect this. Part of me had always hoped that she had planned to come back, that she had tried desperately to return to us, but something stopped her. But now? Now I couldn't lie to myself. She abandoned us. Anger burrowed in my chest and made my insides burn.

I heard her sigh and felt the air shift as she turned to walk away.

"Stop!" I shouted. I didn't realize I was going to say it until it popped out. "I'm having a baby." I said it to hurt her. I wanted her to know how dreadful life had been since she left. I waited for her face to fall in grief, in guilt, for her to drop to her knees, apologizing for how selfish she'd been.

But her expression went blank. "You will never get out of here. You'll be lonesome forever."

"But my child." I wanted so much for her to wrap her arms around me, to hold me, but that wasn't my mother. Not then. Not now.

"They'll take him from you. You'll be better off." She wrung her hands together then dropped them by her sides. "You need to get back to your sisters and brother."

I quickly realized that telling her had been a mistake. "I'm trying to get back. But I'm only getting further away."

"From where?" she asked.

"From home."

"Well, where are the young'uns?"

"I don't know. They dropped me first, and I don't know where they took them." I thought of mentioning the letter, but I knew she wouldn't understand what I meant. She already seemed lost to this place.

Mama shook her head again and started to turn away. "Looks like neither one of us is cut out for much," she said, waving her hand as if showing me this terrible place for the first time. "Once you're here, there isn't much left for you to do. They don't give you those kinds of choices." With that, she stepped away from me and went up the steps towards the door. She never looked back.

#

I was grateful that nighttime came fast. I craved time alone to think of how to fight myself out of this mess. I wished, though, there was quiet. There was never quiet at Farview, I was learning. Noise bounced off the walls, no matter where I went. Screams, cries and wails cut through the air like a steady wind, but there were so few words. Despite the constant chatter, no one said anything.

Barred windows lined my row of beds, about one window for every other cot. I set my head on the pillow and could smell the chicken feathers it was stuffed with. I wiped my nose then looked out into the sky, searching for stars. When I saw them, one bright one twinkling like it had something to say, I tried listening real close to see if I could hear over the screaming. But they said nothing. Those stars must have figured there ain't no use trying to talk to me anymore.

As I lay in my bed, my baby stirring away in my belly, I thought about how sickly Mama looked, like she'd given up on living. If you don't pay attention, life keeps moving on without you realizing it, dragging you along the whole way, either kicking and screaming or completely ignorant of the whole thing. You must pay attention if you want to be the one in charge of where life goes. I felt sad for her. As much as I knew I couldn't win, I'd never give up. There was no way I could let my family stay apart any longer than they had to. I'd bring us together, even if it was the last thing I did. But Mama? Mama gave up fighting a long time ago. She always did say I had too much fight in me, but it was going to take every bit of fight I had to get us all home.

Abigail's familiar voice broke through my thoughts. "Get up, you fool," she said, swatting at the feet of my neighbor. She had a pillow in her hands, and she picked up the pillow of the woman next to me and tossed it onto the empty bed. The woman, dressed in the same nightdress everyone wore but with a wide slash in the skirt, scurried to the other bed and climbed in without saying a word. Abigail plopped down, driving the legs of the metal bedframe to squeak and crack. "Where'd you run off to?"

I sat up on my bed, facing her. The windows behind us cast a slight light that stretched across the narrow space on the wood floor between us. "My mama."

"What about her?"

"I saw her. She's here."

"Not surprised. Once your family's in, they're in. That makes it harder for you, you know?" She lay back down and started picking at her fingernails.

"What do you mean?"

She turned onto her side. "If your family's no good, you're no good. They'll figure it out." She flipped her hair over her shoulder then scratched a matted part on her head. "That's why I can't get out."

A screech of an old woman, her voice garbled by age, echoed from the hall.

I raised my voice so that Abigail could still hear me. "Why not? How'd you get here?"

"My daddy."

"Your mama didn't stop him?" I asked.

She sighed. "My mama died years back. My daddy found me running around with some neighborhood boys. Wasn't nothing."

"So, what happened?"

She laughed. "He brought me here. No daughter of his was going to be gallivanting. But no matter. I've got Bobby now." She paused, then said, "But I cried my eyes out after he dropped me here. I swear he was just looking for an excuse to get rid of me."

"I'm sorry," I said. I took a deep breath. "I asked my mama how she got here, and she said they picked her up while she was sleeping on a bench. But she doesn't seem all that broken up about being here."

"Son of a gun. Why do you think that? I can't imagine anyone would want to stay in this place." She lay back down and stared up at the ceiling. "Why on earth would anyone be okay being here?"

I wondered that since she told me. I thought back to the kittens, to the night with the hanger, to the day she packed her few things and the screen door slamming behind her. "I guess she couldn't take much more of not getting by, is all." I didn't think enough about what I was going to say next. It shot out, pulling the conversation a safe distance from my mama. "I'm having a baby."

She popped up in bed. A scream came from the other side of the room. We scooted to the edges of our beds, facing each other, our socked feet touching in the narrow space between us, and we kept our voices loud enough to hear each other over the cries.

"You're lying." Her clipped voice made her sound jealous, and I wished I could take my confession back, but the secret had been chewing away at me. I never was good at secret-keeping, and this one felt so big, I couldn't carry it by myself.

"Nope. I'm not." Since I said it out loud to Mama, it felt real. I wanted to keep saying it, no matter how much trouble it got me in.

Shaking her head, she whispered, "Whose is it?"

Here's where I fell apart a bit. I wasn't expecting the question, but looking back, I couldn't understand why I didn't. "I don't know," I said.

"Can you guess? Can't you guess?"

"No idea." I decided then and there, without actually deciding, that this baby was never going to know how he came to be. I might never find it in my heart to love him, being he'd be Randolph's blood, but I'd never tell him his story.

"They won't let you keep him."

I flinched, and my eyes widened.

"Did you think they'd let you keep him?" She hunched over and swatted my knee. "If there's no daddy, they'll send him to the almshouse the minute he's born. He won't be yours. He won't be nobody's."

I put my hand to my belly to protect him. As much as I didn't want him, he deserved better than being nobody's. "They can't do that."

"They can. And they'll see to it you can't have any more."

"Any more what?" I asked.

Abigail laughed. "Babies, silly. They operate. Make it so our kind can't have any more."

Gasping, I said, "That's not fair."

"Nothing about this place is fair." She wrung her hands in her lap. "You aren't anybody's here. You have a baby; he isn't anybody's either. That's why I got Bobby."

"What do you mean?" I asked.

She lowered her voice to a whisper. "When Bobby marries me. I'm his. He can take me away from here. We can go live out on the county road, in a trailer by the river."

Her plan made me realize that mine was never going to work. I couldn't read myself out of this kind of trouble. "Take me with you."

"Why on earth should we do that?"

I thought for a moment. What did I have to offer? I had nothing. Nothing but more mouths to feed once I got out and got my family back. Then I realized that if they got me my freedom, I might be able to get them something in return. "I've got a farm out on Shaker Street. I know how to run it. If I get out, I can get it back to good, and there's enough land for all of us."

"Where's Shaker Street?"

"What difference does that make? It's a farm. Got horses, milking cows—" I lied.

She shook her head. "You're fibbing."

"Well, the horses and cows ain't there no more. Been a bad year, and there's no one to watch the farm now. But I could wrestle up some chickens, no problem, and we can start with them."

"What are we going to do with them?"

"Eggs, of course. Get some broilers, too. And we can clear the fields. Work those three seasons a year. John will be getting bigger. Alice and Helen will be, too. We'll all pitch in."

She sat cross-legged on her bed, leaning towards me. "Who are they?"

"My family. If I get out. If you get me out. I can collect them. They'll pull their weight, and we'll have that farm the best in the county."

"So, if Bobby and I take you on, as our ward, you'll get us that farm." Her voice rose. "We can live like sisters."

"Sisters," I said, reaching out my pinky.

She wrapped hers around mine, and we both whispered, "Pinky swear," while the wails of the other women drowned out our voices.

Chapter Fifteen

That night, I dreamed of freedom. As I sprinted through rows of corn in winter, cold nipped my ears and bit my cheeks. The faster I ran, the colder the wind turned, but I never slowed. As I neared the edge of the last row, the field opened to an early summer prairie filled with bright yellow goldenrod and deep purple irises. The irises' plum scent drifted through the soft breeze as it turned warm. Suddenly, the dryness of an unforgiving summer drought covered the place; those beautiful flowers withered. The fiery sun burnt my skin and dried my throat like a prune.

Just as quickly as things turned cold to hot, they turned cold again, and the withered flowers froze into icicles. Out of nowhere, something knocked me down and pinned me. I flipped over and swung my arms. Randolph. He pressed his chest against mine. I had no breath in me. I stared into his black eyes and lost myself. As if all that breath I lost rushed back at once, I inhaled so sharp that I felt my chest explode. I woke, my breath catching, to see the weaselly eyes of a mangey rat staring at me. I screamed and jutted up, tossing the rodent across the floor. He darted down the row of cots and disappeared into a crack in the plastered wall at the far end of the room.

The light broke through the clouds and cast a dim glare into the room. I realized that this was the signal for the women, myself included, to step out of their beds and retrieve the day's clothes from their trunks. We lined up along the foots of our beds like gray, paper dolls. When I opened my trunk, my eyes must have outshined the sun, because there was my pillowcase. I rummaged through it to check, and sure enough, my apron, the doll, the book, with the letter pressed between its pages, were there. I vowed that as soon as my day allowed, I'd escape to my room to read my book in hiding. Hope swept over me like a mist, and I knew I'd wrap my arms around my loved ones again. It felt so real, I could taste the sweetness of their cheeks on my lips.

I rushed to breakfast with Abigail, as if starting my day might bring me home faster. Miss Millie found me nibbling on a piece of dry toast from a loaf that was about to turn, based on the sour scent. I dropped it onto my plate when I saw her. She smiled and slipped me a fresh piece of cornbread just like the one Bobby got Abigail the day before. I devoured it.

Then she said, "I have your assignment. You'll be out in the fields. I will see you there now."

I tried to catch her eye to thank her for sneaking me my belongings, but she turned from me too quickly. Thinking it best to keep the secret, I stayed mum. After tossing my breakfast into the bin, I followed her, my hands pressed against my belly to quell my morning nausea.

As the sun cut through the clouds, shadows cast across the fields. Skinny stalks of hay and wild grass darkened long stretches of land. If you looked too quickly, when the wind blew, you'd think ghosts floated over this place.

Miss Millie told me to wait beside the old well near a chicken coop for Mr. Lucas. I didn't ask who he was. I stepped close to the stone well, placed my hands on the lip, and looked down.

"Gone dry," a man's voice said from behind me.

I jumped. "What's that?"

A man in soiled overalls towered over me, his eyes dented with dark circles. "Dried up years ago. We keep hoping we'll see some life in her again, but like everything else in this place, it's been nothing but disappointment." He took his hat off and wiped his brow. After replacing his hat, he said, "You the new inmate? You're stepping in for Shirley. She's gone now, and these hens are about to worry themselves into a tizzy."

Although I wondered what happened to Shirley, I didn't ask, for fear the answer would make my knees rattle. I followed him through a narrow gate into the coop. The long, sloping roof fit me fine, but Mr. Lucas hunched so that his head wouldn't bump the ceiling. There were dozens of hens, far more than we'd ever had on my farm. Nesting boxes were stacked three high, each row having at least five or six lining the two long sides of the walls. By the doors, hung rakes, baskets, everything else I'd need, and some things I wasn't quite sure what they were. I used to tend our chickens every day at home, even when I had other chores piling up. The chickens felt like home to me, and gathering their eggs was like finding a present every morning. For the first time since leaving Shaker Street, my heart beat steady, as if it recognized this place.

"Wow, I never seen so many hens," I said.

Mr. Lucas swatted one off a top box and dug his hand in the hay. "See. Nothing." He walked towards the center of the hut and kicked a bow rake to the side. "These chickens need to lay enough eggs for all of Farview and some to sell. In this place, you eat what you sow. They don't start laying again, you don't eat."

At home, we followed the same rules. I smiled, knowing that if anyone could get these hens laying, it was me. A bubble of pride ran up my spine.

He grabbed a strand of hay from the floor, dusted it off, and placed it between his teeth. "You'll see to it," he said, walking out of the coop and booting a bent piece of chicken wire as he left the run.

I noticed a hen who looked to have been attacked something awful, from the gash torn by her eye. I bent down to pull some loose feathers from her wing. "That's the problem, isn't it? You're too busy fighting for yourself—ain't got time to lay no eggs," I said to her. Hearing my voice out loud made me jump, but it felt nice to have someone to talk to out there, even if it was an old hen who couldn't win a fight.

I mended the fence first thing, to keep any critters from trolling the henhouse at night. Fear knocks the laying right out of a hen, so I figured that would be my first step to fixing the problem. Next, I took that rusted rake and scattered the hay about the floor. I realized it was a concrete pad, not dirt like mine at home. I stepped out of the coop and walked over to a pile of hay sitting next to a wheelbarrow. I took a mess and scattered it along the floor of the coop to keep the chickens from getting too cold at night. I added a little more to a few of the nesting boxes.

I stepped over a few clucking hens to reach a wire basket. To be safe, I went through each box in search of eggs. Mr. Lucas was right—nothing. I hung the empty basket up and walked into the chicken run. The sun began to peep from behind the clouds. I rested my hands on my hips and looked around at the enormous farm. It was larger than mine, or any of the farms on Shaker. I noticed, for the first time, about five feet from the well lay a thatched roof that someone must have taken and tossed out of the way. It still had a broken chain, but there was no bucket.

Along the wall of a nearby shed, inmates lined up, waiting for water from a tin pail. Each woman sipped the murky water from a ladle passed down the line. The well, I imagined, once meant plenty of clean water for everyone. Looked like that was a long time passed.

The crops nearest me looked like broccoli, but their stalks drooped under the weight of the small heads, and the leaves were a dull blue, not the bright green of healthy harvests. I thought back to my promise with Abigail and imagined the two of us, and our jigsaw family, having a welcome-home picnic. I touched my belly, as my stomach churned with the fear of what would happen if Abigail and Bobby didn't take me with them. I shook the thought from my mind. It wasn't any use worrying about things like that. I returned to the work of the coop to distract me.

After a few hours passed, and it was nearly lunchtime, I hopped when I heard my name called at the door of the coop. I looked up to see Miss Millie standing in the enclosure.

"Dr. Fender would like to see you, Anna."

If Alice were there, she'd have said I was trying to catch flies with my mouth dropped open so wide. "Who's that?"

"He evaluates all the inmates. Gather yourself, and we'll head to see him."

I held a trowel in my arm and raised it. "What if I don't want to?"

"It's not a choice." Her voice was all grit and sandpaper.

"Why not?" I asked, planting my feet firmly on the hay-covered ground.

She shook her head and looked at me with sad eyes. "You don't always get a choice. Come now."

I walked towards her, my shoulders slumped like Mr. Lucas' and tossed the trowel into an empty metal bucket. The ding echoed in the coop as I followed her out.

Chapter Sixteen

Doctors made me feel like I had creepy crawlies all over my skin, ever since that day Mama bungled those forms. All I wanted was to go home, and if Abigail was the only way to get there, I'd take it. Sweat dripped down my back and pooled along the waistline of my dress, just thinking about how much I didn't want to mess this up. If I did, there'd be no getting my sisters and brother back. I wondered, for a moment, if I couldn't convince Mama to change her mind, if only for appearances. I'd do the housework and tend the farm, just like I did before. But better this time, so no one could take it away. She wouldn't have to care for us. Just sign some papers, is all, or whatever she needed to do to get us out of this mess she had caused. I crossed my fingers behind my back and swore that as soon as I was done meeting with whoever this doctor was, I'd find Mama and beg her. One way or the other, I was getting myself out of this place and back home before this baby let out his first cry.

After we walked through the main building doors, the same doors I walked through that first day, Miss Millie leaned down and whispered in my ear, "You do good now.

You do just what he says." She placed her hand on my shoulder, but I shrugged it away.

I realized the big door behind the desk was his. We stood there waiting for a few minutes, me shifting away from Miss Millie, her shifting closer to me, when it finally creaked open.

I blinked then rubbed my eyes, unable to believe what I was seeing. Her gray hair was sticking out wild like she never saw a comb, dark bags puffing out from her eyes. I had to squint to be sure. "Mama!" I shouted. "What are you doing with the doctor?"

She rubbed her eyes too, as if she couldn't believe it was me standing there in a matching dress and apron. "He's a good man. He'll help—" Her voice trailed off, and she slunk away from me, looking like she was sleepwalking, not even a look back.

I peered up at Miss Millie. "That's my mama."

"Oh, Anna," she said. And I don't think Miss Millie believed me.

"What's wrong with her?" I asked. "She looks like a ghost."

Miss Millie glanced up at the door then back at me. She whispered, "She's taking medication. Sometimes it makes people sleepy."

"Why? What's she taking it for?" I asked.

A voice boomed from inside the room. "You may come in."

She gave me a little shove towards the open door. "Go on. I will wait here for when you finish."

The dim room had no windows and was lit by one heavy shaded table lamp with pretty glass panes in reds, blues, and greens. It smelled of sweet tobacco and peppermint. On the yellow walls hung rows of what I imagined were framed degrees and certificates. Each one had a shiny round seal and curly writing. I wondered how I'd convince this man of anything.

I inhaled sharply but couldn't seem to fill my lungs. I breathed faster, which made the room spin around me. I placed my hands on my knees and leaned forward, gasping as if there was no air in the room. Behind the desk, the doctor sat upright in a suit, his elbows resting on a desk calendar which had '1928' printed in large numbers. He spun a pencil between his fingers then scratched his dark mustache with the point. Round, wire-framed glasses rested on the tip of his nose. He pushed them up before he spoke to me.

"Wilson. Have a seat," he said, pointing to the chair across from him.

To the left there was another spindled chair, and I wished I could sit there to keep more distance between us. I caught my breath then crept towards his desk, which must have been as long as I was tall. I sat in the small, wooden chair that was too low for someone my size. I could hardly see over his desk.

As he leafed through papers, I fidgeted in my seat, straightening my apron, pulling at the hem of my dress.

He cleared his throat. "I'm Doctor Fender. I'm the resident doctor here at Farview."

I bit a nail too short, flinched, then wrapped my hands together in my lap. "Hello, sir. Umm… Doctor."

"You are acclimating to Farview?" His voice didn't raise at the end, so I wasn't sure if he was asking me or telling me, so I nodded. "And the meals? I'm sure you are finding them an improvement from where you've come."

I wanted to say that while we were hungry on the farm, we enjoyed what little food we had. But he was already on to his next thought.

"Are you sleeping, Miss Wilson?" He drew out my name, as if his tongue got stuck on the letter 'l'.

I cringed at the sound of my name on his lips. I hated when people who wished me evil spoke my name. It was the only thing that was really mine. They had no right to use it.

I considered not speaking, to force him to whittle down a diagnosis of me from what little he had. But then I remembered the warmth of Miss Millie's hand on my back and the promise between Abigail and me, and bravery boiled up inside me. If I wanted my freedom back, I'd have to figure out a way to do it by their rules. It was time to start helping myself.

I said, "Yes, Doctor. I'm sleeping fine."

After I finished speaking, I looked up at him. He was reading a paper and made a mark with his pencil. Then he said, "I had your mother in my office a few minutes ago. Did you know that?"

His question felt like a trap. "Yes." I breathed slowly, trying to calm my racing heart.

"She told me all about your family situation. Your history."

I closed my eyes and hoped she hadn't said too much, but then my heart sank as he continued.

"I'm aware you are carrying a child? An illegitimate child?" He pushed his glasses back to the edge of his nose and waited for my response.

How could she? I thought of lying. I wondered if, possibly, I could escape with Abigail before anyone knew I was having a baby. But then I placed my hand on my stomach, and I could feel the bulge of my belly. They'd know soon enough, no matter what I said. "Yes."

"The Monroes sent you here, is that right? They are good people, the Monroes." He nodded his head as if I had no choice but to agree with him.

I bit my tongue.

"And you were destitute before that? No father to speak of. Your mother, living here."

I knew it best to agree, but instead I said, "Not destitute. We were getting by just fine."

"No parents? No schooling? Now a bastard child? Around here, we don't call that fine." His voice sounded sharp enough to cut glass.

I looked down at my hands clenched in my lap. "Nothing I can't handle, Doctor."

"We'll see about that. We'll have to run some tests. Quite possibly we may move to put you before the committee, if we think there's a chance you're fit, capable." He ran his eyes over me. "There's always hope."

He paused then went on. "I'll be traveling this summer. The islands are lovely this time of year. You're not far along?" He stared down at my belly. "When I return, I'll make a determination. If we see to it, there are almshouses for bastard children. In the meantime, you keep yourself out of trouble. You should not take advantage of our charity."

Blood rushed to my head, making me hotter than a red coal. Finally, he excused me.

Miss Millie was waiting outside the door for me. She placed her hand on my shoulder and said, "I'll walk you out. It's lunchtime."

I couldn't keep in the tears after her kindness and Dr Fender's threats. They streamed down my face, and I gasped for air. "I... I..." I wasn't sure what I planned to say, but I didn't have a clear thought.

"Anna, what's wrong?" We stepped onto the front steps. She took my hand and stooped to look me in the eyes.

I gripped her hands tightly. "They're going to take my baby. They won't let me keep him." I huffed to catch my breath. As much as I didn't want this baby, I couldn't see him turned out into the world like I was.

"Anna? Are you with child?"

I nodded my head.

"Let me help you. You don't have much time. I can help you," she said.

I moved away from her, trying to race down the stairs, but she grabbed my hand and pulled me back.

"You can do this, Anna. You are enough."
But I didn't believe her.

Chapter Seventeen

Early September saw my belly blossom with life, yet that old Dr. Fender still hadn't returned from his voyage. I did as he said, stayed out of trouble as best I could. But would it be enough to get my freedom back? Every day I read by the light of the setting sun. As summer faded and the edges of the leaves turned from bright green to the color of rust, the hours of daylight seemed in short supply. There was never enough time to get myself set with my book before those stars poked their heads out, taunting me every night. *You're no longer invisible.*

Their words struck me each time, and one night, those words gave me the chills so bad that I thought I struck a fever. I started off unseen, and no one paid any mind to what we Wilsons did. I never realized how dangerous it was for my kind to be seen. How it'd destroy everything I knew. What I wouldn't do to go back to being invisible!

Mama and I hadn't crossed paths much over the summer. She worked in the laundry, and in the heat of the summer it'd get so hot in that room, you'd damn near boil yourself right there with the whites. My anger at her never wavered. I wasn't sure I'd ever forgive her. I wished I could go back to being a fool, believing that she thought we'd be better with her gone, but I wouldn't lie to myself anymore.

Abigail and I figured that if we stuck together and I minded my Ps and Qs, Dr. Fender would have no choice but to let me go with them, even if I was carrying a bastard. The henhouse, too, would make Dr. Fender see I was all the worker any other person was, free or locked away. Those hens laid more eggs that summer than they ever had, according to Miss Millie. She even gave me a special pineapple upside-down cake with bright-red maraschino cherries, that she had made especially for me with some of the money they earned from selling all those eggs at market. The day she gave it to me, Abigail and I ducked out of our afternoon chores and snuck behind the henhouse to eat the delicious cake with our hands. My belly near busted from all that sweetness, but I never had something so delicious. Abigail neither.

I had begun to grow on Nurse Gladys, and I hoped she'd give Dr. Fender a nudge when Abigail asked to bring me along. She had to.

All summer I'd been egging Abigail to move things along with Bobby. She and Bobby would sneak away almost every day back into the dormitory, but for all his talk, he hadn't yet set a date for leaving.

On a late summer day, when I knew it'd be the last of the warm weather, I heard the voice of Dr. Fender ringing in my ears. Time had moved so quickly, yet I stayed in the same place. If I didn't act now, I'd be in this place forever.

Abigail and I sat together at lunch like we always did.

"Have you talked to Bobby?" I asked Abigail, as we ate our beef stew with a nub of bread.

Abigail dropped her crust. "You keep asking. These things take time."

I scooped a mound of peas into my mouth. While chewing, I said, "Time is something I don't have. If you don't figure out when you're leaving, before Dr. Fender gets back, how am I getting out of here? I don't think I can pass no test. My reading isn't much better than when I started."

I realized that on my own, my reading only could get so good. I wished on a star that Alice was here to teach me. But then that'd mean she were here, and I cursed myself for even thinking such a thought.

She smirked and stopped chewing. "Guess what?"

"What?" I said, my belly starting to jump. "What is it?"

She bit off a hunk of bread. "I'm having a baby, too."

I dropped my fork. It clanged on the tin plate. "What!"

"I'm having Bobby's baby." I looked up and saw Bobby across the room, standing by the doorway like usual. He smiled at me, and I looked away.

I moved in closer to her and grabbed her hands. Whispering, I said, "You're going to get in trouble, Abby. They won't let you."

"Silly. He's going to marry me now. He won't be able to wait any longer. Don't you see? This is a perfect plan."

My heart raced. "But what if they find out? What if the doctor finds out?"

"We'll be gone before that. We'll get married at the courthouse and be living on your farm by the time my belly pops." She put her hand on mine and giggled. "We'll be raising babies together. Like sisters."

I picked my fork back up and took a small bit of stew potatoes. "So you told Bobby?" My voice rose at the end with hope.

"Not yet. Soon. I promise. And we'll be out of here and bringing you along and living on your farm and setting up house and being so happy, our eyes will pop out." She grabbed my hands, leaned towards me, giggling for a few minutes while I tried to figure out how all this might work. "And look what he gave me," she said, slipping a shiny, carved circle from her pocket.

"What is it?" I asked.

"Silly. It's a compact." She clicked open the clasp to reveal a small, shiny mirror. "So I can get myself pretty for him."

I'd never seen one before. "Can I hold it?" She passed it to me gently, and I cupped it in the palm of my hand. It felt cold against my warm skin. I closed it then tapped it open again. I looked at my face in its tiny reflection and saw how much thinner I'd grown, the whites of my eyes overtaking my irises. Even my nose seemed slimmer, pointer than it was. I handed it back to her and said, "You better not get caught with that."

"I'm no dummy. I'll keep it tucked at the bottom of my trunk in a pair of knickers, until I tell Bobby about the baby. Then we'll be hightailing it out of here."

Her promise wasn't enough for me. Abigail didn't understand what was at risk. "You need to do it soon. I can't wait any longer. My baby will be born soon after the new year, and I can't have him here."

"Well, I can't rush it. You know how boys are. If I start rushing it, he'll get cold feet." She spooned the last of her stew into her mouth and chewed slowly. "These things take time. You just get yourself ready."

"I have to talk to Mama. See if she'll give me use of the farm. Papa's on the papers and don't know where he is. But the taxes are done paid up. So they couldn't have taken it from us yet."

"Talk to her. Because we'll be there lickety-split." She looked me square in the eye, her blue eyes looking like water, and said, "Promise you'll talk to your mama, and I'll talk to Bobby. Old Dr. Fender won't know what hit him when the two us pack up and walk right out the door."

#

Abigail acted as if her plan held water like a tin pail, but I wasn't so sure. I thought about how I might need to start thinking for myself again. After lunch, I asked an orderly if I could return to my quarters to change my soiled knickers. He did not ask questions, so I took the steps in a rush, ran into the empty room, and darted to my trunk. I pried open the heavy wooden lid and dug under my scratchy uniforms and underclothes to find the pillowcase hidden underneath. I slipped the book out and slid it into the pocket of my apron.

When I arrived at the coop, I looked to see if any orderlies were milling around to catch me up to no good, but all I saw were some inmates, dressed like me, who moseyed around the fields with buckets of grain or handfuls of hay like they were lost.

Before stealing away to the back of the henhouse, I noticed an older orderly with a patchy beard and a stooped body caving under a sunken cap coming my way. He wasn't no match for me. I walked between the rows of nesting boxes to check on my chickens. After picking up a wire basket, I reached under each hen in its hay to fish for fresh eggs. The ones who I knew had a mind not to lay, I left a nest egg to keep them feeling like they could do it. Sometimes you just needed a little reminder to make you believe in yourself.

I thought about that as I finished collecting the eggs and tucked myself into the back under a row of rakes. I read the title, *Peter and Wendy*, a few times to remind myself I wasn't just memorizing now. I was reading, sounding out real letters and making them into words. My head rested alongside the clucking chicken on the side of the enclosure, as I cracked open the stiff book that I hadn't found time to read in a few days. I needed to get moving fast. Only a few weeks stood between me and my sisters and brother all getting to go home. Dr. Fender would return any day now, and I was going to be ready for him.

I tried not to think about the baby that'd be coming with me when I finally did make my way out of here. I touched my belly; it was growing bigger each day. I still wasn't sure how I'd come to love this child who was brought to me from the worst moment in my life, but I vowed that I'd be out of here by the time he breathed his first breath.

I thought for a moment about Randolph and all the evilness he had spread on me. And the part Ma played on getting me here as well. And I swore I'd keep those secrets and never tell a soul how he touched me. My baby would never know how he got here. No one would. I couldn't bear to tell anyone. The fear of Randolph still gripped me every day, even though I knew he couldn't reach me here, and talking about it would only make my nightmares feel more real.

I wiped a tear from my eye as I returned to my book. The letters leaped from the page and at first did not translate to words; my mind couldn't make sense of it. Then I concentrated on how those letters paired with sounds, the way Alice used to practice her reading, and things started coming together.

My eyes darted around the page in search of words I knew: all, one, up, that, will. I whispered them as my heart beat heavy in my chest. The henhouse, the clucking chickens and the scent of hay all seemed to disappear like a smoke cloud when I started reading. A lightness came over me, as if I wasn't at Farview anymore.

A shuffle through the door spooked me, so I scooted lower in the corner, inhaling the scent of dirt and feathers. A chicken hopped and clucked, but that was all, so I went back to my book. From outside, a tin bucket rattled and clanged, then a woman screamed for water, and my mind lost all sense of letters again.

After reading the same words over and over, I was done tuckered out. I had learned so much, but I still had too far to go. I couldn't do it on my own. There was no way I could impress Dr. Fender with my smarts and get him to let me out to live on my own. Wiping a tear from my eye, I realized Abigail and Mama were my only hope. I needed Abigail to convince Bobby to marry her now and take me with them, even if it meant sharing my farm forever. And I had to convince Mama to let me live on that farm with everyone together, for we had no place else to go. There were no other choices. If I wanted to save my baby, myself, and my kin, the only way was Abigail and Mama. I could never do it myself.

#

The next day, I snuck out of the henhouse and searched for Mama. She wasn't hard to find. In the basement of the Garment building, I found her stirring a pot of boiling laundry, her eyes glossed over from the heat—or the sadness. I didn't know which.

"Mama!" I shouted over the din of chatter. "I need to talk to you."

Her eyes grew wide, and I wondered if she remembered I was here at Farview. I waved the acrid-scented steam away from my nose. I had prepared to ask her if I could stay on the farm, but the image of her walking out of Dr. Fender's office stuck in my mind. She had no stake in that farm. It was mine, and I deserved it.

"I'm going to find a way out of here—" I paused. My eyes filled with tears until she was so blurry that she looked like a reflection in a pond. "And when I do, I'll stay at the farm."

"Dr. Fender said you could leave?"

"Not yet. But if I have to stay, they'll take my baby. And who will care for the others?"

"What did Dr. Fender say?" She kept stirring the bubbling laundry.

The steam moistened my face. I thought for a moment she was crying, but I figured the moisture was from the boiling water. She had no tears for me.

I snatched my breath, feeling like I couldn't get enough air. "The doctor said they'll take my baby. He'll end up in an almshouse. Then they'll make it so I can't have any more children."

She set down the large wooden spoon she was using to stir the laundry and hoisted up her dress. Above her bloomers was a silver scar that ran the length to her waist. "You should listen to the doctor."

The tears started falling. "Did he do that to you?" I couldn't believe what I was seeing.

"I can't have more babies. The doctor says it's for the best."

"But Mama, why'd you let him do that?"

She looked surprised that I'd asked. "He's a doctor, Anna. He'll do what's best for you."

"No. I'm not letting him. I'll make those choices for myself. I'm getting out of here with my baby." I swung my arms to keep the heat of the laundry away from me. "And I'm taking the farm." I ran my fingers through my matted hair. "I'll have to have a place to go if they're going to release me. He's returning any day now. If I don't have a plan—"

"You should listen to the doctor," she repeated, then looked back at the laundry that was hissing in the pot. It was about to boil over. "I need to get back to work."

"But Mama—"

She picked up her spoon and turned back towards the pot. "I need to get back to work."

Chapter Eighteen

That night I lay in bed, Mama's words simmering in my mind. I couldn't believe she placed her faith in this place, that man, just because he was a doctor. He didn't seem to have any interest in protecting her, or any of us.

Abigail reached over and smacked my arm. "Psst. Anna."

"What?" I asked. "Abigail, it's the middle of the night."

A woman's wail cut through the room, then it quickly fell silent.

"I can't sleep."

The pattering of racing paws broke the quiet. We watched a wiry-haired rat dart between the rows of beds and disappear into a crack in the wall.

The full moon shone through the barred windows, reflecting on the metal bed frames lining the room. In each bed lay a person, someone who had had a life before they were brought here, and I couldn't help but think about all the lives that wouldn't be lived. Just suffered through. It wasn't fair. A woman cried out, and I realized she'd been crying all night. I had become so used to it that I didn't notice it anymore.

"I can't sleep either. Keep thinking about what Mama said." I placed my hand on the roundness of my belly.

Abigail huffed. "It doesn't take much to convince the sheep to side with the wolf."

My voice cracked. "But how could she?"

"Some people don't think very much of themselves, is all. Got their worst enemy living inside their head." She popped up on her bed and faced me. "You know what you need?"

"What?" I asked, sitting up to face her.

"Some fun."

"And how are we supposed to have fun in this place?"

Abigail smiled wider than I'd ever seen. "I have an idea."

It had been so long since I had a friend. I missed dancing to my own humming in the fields and skipping rope on the grass. Leaning towards her, I said, "What's your idea?"

"Wait here," she said, holding up a finger to her lips. She rolled over, swung her feet off the bed, then tiptoed to the wide door of the dormitory. A low creaking sound filled the room as she cracked the door open a foot wider. She peeked her head out and looked down to the right and left. Leaving the door open, she ran back to me and whispered, "Let's go."

My mind raced with worry. "Where? Where are we going?"

"We're going to have a little fun." She pulled my arm to nudge me off the bed. "Bobby says the orderlies like to smoke Luckies outside all night when the weather's right. They prop open the door at the far end of the dormitory in the stairwell, so they don't get locked out."

"What does that mean for us?" I asked. I didn't want no trouble. But I needed Abigail on my side. I couldn't risk losing her now.

She pulled my arm. "Come on. We can go out. Just get some fresh air. No one will notice."

I swung my legs over the bed and pulled my nightdress down. The thought of fresh air, freedom, even if it was for a short time, tugged at me. "How do we get back in?"

"The way we got out."

I pushed my hair away from my face. I imagined it looked like a lion's mane. It had been so long since I had washed it, with only getting every other week to tend to the task. There were so many rules here to see that they made every decision for us.

"What if we get locked out?" I turned to look out the window at the full moon and a sky full of bright stars. "We'll get into trouble, Abby."

"Oh, what could go wrong?" She squatted by the side of my bed and scanned the room. "Do you think someone is going to tell on us?" She waved her hand at the bodies in the bed. Some screaming, some chattering, none of them making a lick of sense. She laughed so hard that she toppled over.

I looked around the room at the lifeless women, all suffering in their own world but sharing this one. It didn't seem fair. Had they given up, like my mother? I thought of my sisters, my brother, my baby on the way, and knew I'd never give up. I was going to stay Anna Wilson, if it was the last thing I did. And when they set me free, they'd know my name and that I wasn't the worthless person they thought I was.

"OK, Abby. Let's go."

#

We crept down the long hall, away from the door we usually went in and out of. They bolted that each night, and I bet no one would take the risk of keeping that propped. Then we passed by two orderlies in a small office, arguing over a game of cards. The older one slammed a card face-up on the table and cheered. They never looked up at us. I glanced into the other rooms, similar to ours, beds laid end to end filled with sleeping or screaming bodies. As we neared the edge of the hallway, I could smell the thick scent of hay and dust and feel the cool air drifting in. I pulled my nightdress tighter around my neck.

When we reached the stairwell, I pressed my body to the iron railing in the dark, careful not to trip. My heart raced. At the bottom of the stairwell stood a tall five-paneled door with a small, square, wired window at the top, too high for me to see out. As Abigail had promised, the door was wedged open a bit, with a large rock. I could smell the faint cigarette smoke, but the scent wasn't strong enough for someone to be still smoking. I pressed my eye to the open slit, but the door wasn't propped open wide enough for me to see out.

"We need to look out before we go. Make sure no one's out there where they can see us," I said, pressing Abigail down towards the ground and pushing her hair to the side. I found a bit of flatness on her back, braced my hands on the door careful not to push it, and hauled myself up to the window. She wiggled under my weight. "Don't move," I said.

"You're stepping on me. How do you expect me not to move?"

I stretched a little higher and finally got a clear view through the wire-trap window. Through the window, the fields looked endless, but I saw no one. "It's all clear," I whispered to her. I stepped off her back and reached my hand to help her up.

Wiping her hands on her nightshirt, she said, "Perfect. Let's go."

We opened the door only enough to squeeze through and then carefully rested the door onto the stone. I stood for a moment taking in how beautiful the farm, the fields, the henhouse and the well looked when you didn't know why they all existed. At night, clear of any inmates or orderlies, it looked peaceful. For the first time, I smelled the tartness of raspberries in the light breeze.

The moon hung like a lantern in the dark sky, its reflection turning the black night a deep blue. Stars twinkled and shined, as if they were competing for brightness. Even the crops glimmered under the shine of the moon and waved with each gust of wind. Our bare feet stood in the dry, cool soil, sinking into the earth. It felt like home and made me miss my farm more than I had in a long time. I had forgotten how free I felt on my own land.

Abigail snatched my hand, and we ducked down. "Come on."

We ran, backs hunched, hand-in-hand, through the rows of corn. Finally, we reached a patch of ripe raspberries next to the well that, from their soft, dark flesh, looked like they should have been harvested a few days ago. Abigail plucked one and popped it into her mouth.

"We shouldn't eat them, Abby. They're not ours," I said, then wiped a red smudge from the corner of her lips.

"They're so sweet. Like candy. Here," she said, plopping an overripe raspberry into my mouth.

It was mushy and delicious. She started plucking as many as she could and stuffing them into a basket she made out of the front of her dress. I followed her, folding the front of my nightdress to cradle the bright red berries, revealing my gray knickers and bare legs.

"We're taking them with us? Where will we hide?" I popped one into my mouth then looked around the shadowy grounds.

The well seemed to reflect the starlight, casting a faint glow that drew me towards it. As if in a trance, I wrapped the berries tightly and walked to the well.

I leaned forward to gaze down the shaft, careful not to smush the berries against the rugged stone. "Come here,"

I called to Abigail in a hushed voice. "How deep do you think it is?"

Abigail wrapped her nightdress basket tighter and scurried over to me. The cool breeze howled around us, rustling the cornstalks and carrying the crisp scent of soil and grass. I watched her with wide eyes as she placed one hand on the lip of the well and hoisted herself up, managing not to lose a single berry.

"Up with you," she said, motioning for me to join her.

Careful not to lose my pickings, I did the same, placing my feet squarely on the ledge of the well. The breeze felt stronger from up there, as if it was waiting for me to take the perch so it could knock me down. "How deep do you think it is?"

She kicked at a piece of chipped stone and leaned down to pick it up. When she wiggled a bit, I reached out to steady her. "Careful, Abigail. You're going to suffer a fall," I said.

She didn't answer me, just held her free arm out straight in front of her over the dark hole, the stone clutched in her hand. The other hand still held the berries, and as the wind picked up, she swayed like a ghost. My breath caught in my throat. I wanted to scream, but her face, the stillness in her eyes and her shoulders, not shrugged up to her ears like mine but resting low, like she didn't have a care in the world, made screaming seem silly somehow.

She turned to me and said, "Ready?"

"For what?" I asked. I looked down and suddenly caught a scent of the stale, moist earth at the bottom.

Her eyes caught the light reflecting from the well, or the moon, or the stars. I watched them glow as her hand opened as slow as an opossum who doesn't want to give up an apple core.

She started counting, "One, one thousand; two, one thousand; three, one thousand; four, one thousand; five, one thousand; six, one thousand." She got to twelve, one thousand by the time the stone crashed into the rocky bottom of the dry well, its echo sending a smooth vibration that blended with the night's breeze.

"What's the counting for?" I asked.

"Every second means three feet. My momma taught me. We had an old well in the backyard."

"Wow," I said. "So deep."

She leaned forward, her bare toes teetering, folding along the ridge of the stone. "Do you know what happened here?"

"Here? Farview?"

"No. The well, silly."

She switched holding her dress basket to her other hand, so that her hand closest to me was free. I did the same. We clasped hands. I could feel the stickiness of the berries, gluing our palms together.

"Before I got here, a girl went missing. They say she suffered bad dreams, screaming fits every night, like so many around here. One night, she wouldn't let up. Got so bad that the orderlies didn't stop her when she moseyed right out the door into a thunderstorm."

I stared down the well and felt the unease of my balance. "What happened?"

Abigail sighed. "They say she never even stopped. Just walked right up to the well, placed her hands on the ledge, and dove in headfirst, like it was a swimming pool."

I gasped. "She fell down."

"They never even bothered to get her body out. Just left her there for the worms to feed on. Even the buzzards knew she was down there. They'd circle the well when I got here. Never did see one swoop down there, though. I guess even they knew they'd never make it."

"That's horrible."

"Sure is. They could have at least tried to scoop her out. Bury her in the graveyard." She looked over to our right, away from the cottages and towards the picket fence behind the fields. It was tucked so far back on the land that I hadn't noticed it before. "That there is where they bury the lonesome."

Dizziness overtook me, and I placed my hand on her shoulder. I couldn't imagine being left here to die alone. I thought about all the women there, rotting under the soil, and no one noticing they were here one day, gone the next. And no one caring. I hated to think of Mama here, dying alone then buried with not so much as a song to send her off. I vowed then, that even if Mama stayed like she wanted, I would see to it that I'd bring her home after it was too late for her to stop me. She'd be laid to rest on our farm, and I'd never let anyone forget about her, no matter how much she made my blood hot.

I held my berries tight and scooted myself off the ledge. I didn't want to see anymore. But then I couldn't stop my brain from thinking. "Why do they bury them here?"

She laughed. "If you're here, you're forgotten. Do you think anyone wants to come claim you after you're dead? No way. They dump you in a hole back there," she said, nodding towards the overgrown land dotted with stones, "and put up a marker. No name or anything. Just a rock, so they know not to bother digging another hole there. The women themselves dig the graves, you know. Ever see them out digging?"

I had, but I didn't answer. My mouth felt dry, and I lost my taste for raspberries. But Abigail tap-danced right into her old self. Before I knew it, she hopped backwards off the well and landed on the ground with a thump, a cloud of dust puffing around her. She was laughing so hard that she dropped half her berries.

I couldn't help but laugh with her, grateful for a taste of freedom for the first time in so long, even if we were stealing it.

Suddenly a bang came from a building, but I couldn't tell where. We both jumped and turned towards the noise. I scanned the field, the cottages, the path leading up to it all, but nothing. Then it sounded again, and we took off like the dickens.

Chapter Nineteen

"Let's go," she said, taking my free hand and leading me towards the back of the fields, where an old stable sat abandoned.

We raced, the wind in our hair and moistness of berries soaking through our nightdresses. We didn't stop laughing until we came to a hidden clearing. We were so close to the graveyard now, that I could smell the fresh dirt someone had dug.

We lay down on the soft grass, our heads pressed next to one another, our knees bent towards the sky, and gazed up at the stars. I saw it, Orion's Belt, glimmering like diamonds I hadn't ever seen in real life. I touched my swollen belly and thought back to all I'd been through these past months, all the heartbreak I'd known, and wondered what happened when your heart done broke so many times that you couldn't put it back together again. What becomes of a person who ain't got the will in them to fight anymore? I figured that must have been what happened to Mama. Once you lose so much, you stop trying to find a way to get people to see you and start wishing you'd disappear. Ain't no better place than

Farview to disappear. I glanced again at the lines of stone markers scattered behind the old fence.

Abigail broke my thoughts. "You want to know a secret?"

"Um hm," I said, shoving a fistful of raspberries into my mouth.

"I wanted this baby. Bobby was all about biding time and nonsense. If I didn't get this baby in me soon, he'd never get me out."

She took a handful of berries, raised her hand straight towards the sky, then one by one dropped them into her mouth, missing it most of the time but not caring in the least. She giggled then reached her hand over to drop one into my mouth. I caught it and choked a little. The little sucker came down fast.

She sat up and pulled me up too. "Holy cow. We're going to be mamas!" She hugged me, forgetting all about the raspberries tucked in our dresses.

I felt the smush of the soft flesh against my round belly. She stood up and let the remaining berries drop to the ground. She looked like she had just butchered a rabbit.

Heat ran up my spine and burrowed at the top of my head. Bobby wasn't as in on the plan as I had thought. What if he didn't want me to come with them? What if he didn't want Abigail at all?

"Did you tell him yet? No sense waiting now."

"I'll get to that, silly. For now, I just want to enjoy being grown-ups." She touched her stomach and then mine, then twirled around, fanning her nightdress as it caught the wind. "Can you believe we're going to have babies? We're all grown up."

I stood up next to her and let my berries fall. They smattered my feet red. "I don't know, Abigail. I think I turned grown-up a long time ago."

"How you figure? You just, bam, grow up one day?" she asked, then squatted down to run her fingers through the grass in search of berries. She found a whole one and popped it into her mouth.

"Nah. Ain't' like that." I paused a minute to look up at the stars, then stared at my red-streaked feet as I went on. "You grow up without realizing it. It sneaks up on you like a critter in the night, when you so done from working all day that you can't feel their little feet tickle your leg, or their whiskers prick the heel of your foot." A sigh got caught in my throat. "Once all the ones who done grown up long before you show they got more flaws than you'll ever have, and you love them anyway—that's when you know you're grown up."

"What if you don't have any grown-ups to love?" She stood tall and held her arms out wide like butterfly wings, as if she thought the wind might sweep her away.

"I guess you never grow up then."

She held her belly. "Well, my baby sure as rain going to be a grown-up someday. She's going to have me and Bobby to love. But we ain't ever doing her wrong. She'll never end up in a place like this. And we're going to be so perfect, she won't ever wish for other parents. I promise."

"When will you tell him?" I asked.

161

"Soon. I need the right time for this," she said, scooting berries around the grass with her toe.

I huffed. The air between us felt thick. "I don't have time. I done told you the doctor will be back any day. I need to have my plan set."

She snapped back. "You didn't even get the farm from your Mama yet. Why am I the one who has to rush?"

"I'll take care of that. I deserve that farm. But it'd be easier if I knew I was leaving. She wants me to listen to the doctor, so she won't talk about it unless he's saying I can go."

"Uh. Fine."

"Fine meaning you'll tell him? Soon?"

She shook her head. "Soon as I see him. The sooner we get out of here, the better our babies will be." She paused. "Plus, he's going to go bananas for a little one."

We stood for a moment, quiet in the still air. Even the wind felt calm. I heard them then, the stars, in their faint voice that shook like an echo. *You won't be invisible for long.* I stomped at them, and their horrible wish for me, and felt the berries squish under the soles of my feet. Just then, I noticed the soft light break from across the edge of the graveyard. I looked up, and the stars were disappearing in the rays of the rising sun. We were too late.

"Run!" I shouted, pulling Abigail with me towards the cottages.

We tore through the long fields, scratching our feet on stiff strands of hay and prickly gravel. The scent of early morning, the soil mixed with dew, struck me.

"Hurry!" I raced as fast as my skinny legs would carry me.

When I reached the well, I paused a moment to look behind me for my friend. I leaned my hands on my knees and caught my breath, then sprinted again when I noticed the sky lit like a candle.

"Please, please don't let those mean nurses be waiting for me," I said. All the world blurred through my tear-soaked eyes. But then I saw it. The stone, tossed off to the side of the closed door. "We're too late, we're too late!" I screamed loud now, unafraid of anyone hearing.

My mind spun with excuses for being locked out, as we pressed against the door that we had slipped through hours earlier. I pressed my fingers into the jamb, trying to pry it open.

"Out of the way," Abigail said, pushing me off to the side. She tried the same, but still no luck.

"They'll never let me out! They'll never let me out!" I started screaming, pulling at my hair. "They'll never let me out." I collapsed to my knees and began banging on the door in the hopes that Bobby, or someone kinder, would find us and let us in.

"That ain't going to work. You've lost your mind. It won't work!" Abigail shouted, then she smacked me, and I fell back towards the wall and slid down to the dirt. I crawled back towards the door but couldn't stand up. My body had done given out on me. I sat there, my head in my hands, crying like I didn't have no more reason to go on.

Suddenly, Abigail froze like a scared mouse when you shine the lantern on him. Her eyes grew wide, and her bottom lip dropped. She took a step back. That's when I heard it. The click of the door, then I saw the turning of the knob. The door opened to a red-faced Nurse Gladys, looking like a mutt ready to scrap with a runt over old stew bones.

Chapter Twenty

I scrambled behind the door, so she didn't see me at first, but I knew she locked eyes with Abigail based on Abigail's scrunched-up face and raised fists. Abigail stood there, in her firecracker-red-stained shirt, ready for a fight, like that's what she came to do. Not me. I curled up behind that door, and for the second time in my life, prayed to Jesus. If he couldn't make me invisible no more, I prayed he'd at least make me fast.

I pushed myself up to run, but she must have spotted my bare feet from under the door, because just as I went to stand up, she slammed that door into me so hard that my head cracked, and I flew back into the wall. I tried to make the bleeding stop by holding it tight with my dress, but red poured all over, and I wasn't sure if it was raspberries or blood, but that red nearly covered me.

Oh, how I wished Miss Millie would have been the one to find us.

Her knocking me with the door must have sent Abigail into a rage, because she swung, hauling her scrawny fist right at that baddie's cheek, but Nurse Gladys was faster than she looked. She snatched a clump of

Abigail's hair and twisted it good, until Abigail dropped to her knees and begged her to stop.

"Come with me," Nurse Gladys said.

I knew we'd lost. I expected my chest to heat up with anger and my fists to clench so tight that my nails would dig crescents into my palm, but instead I felt like a tire that someone had let the air out of. I reached under Abigail's shoulder and pulled her up to her feet. Shaking, we both followed Nurse Gladys towards the main building, our heads hanging low and my belly grumbling all the way, as the dawn sunlight poured down on us.

When we reached a side door I had never seen before, she took out a mess of keys and flipped them until she found one to fit the lock. After she opened the door, my head grew woozy, but I wasn't sure if it was from the bleeding or if I was too scared to see straight.

She pointed for us to go through the door and then up the steps, and being that we already had ourselves in more trouble than I cared to think about, I did exactly as I was told. Her rubber soles squeaked on the wooden steps the whole way up four flights. I had never been up four flights before and wondered what it must look like from up so high, like I was a robin in a tree, but I didn't get much time to think about that, because before I knew it, we were standing in a narrow hall that had just one tiny light and three gray, metal doors, each with one small window covered with chicken wire, and wide mail slot.

The only sound in that place was Nurse Gladys' squeaking shoes. I wondered if we were the only ones on the floor. Since I'd been to Farview, I'd never heard such silence, but for the moment, between the squeaks of her shoes, I realized how much I missed it.

Nurse Gladys stopped between two doors and fumbled her jangling keys out of her pocket again. She thumbed through them until she found the largest of the bunch. Abigail stood on one side of her, I on the other. I stared at my red-streaked bare feet, afraid to so much as glance at Abigail or else I might find myself in more hot water. The floor was unfinished, a raw cement that scraped my soles and reminded me of the cellar floor where Miss Atkinson first found me cowering.

I could never have imagined the storm of trouble that followed.

For a moment, I had a bubbling up of blood in my head and a tingling behind my temples that I figured must have been courage. I thought of running, racing out the door and tearing off in search of my family. I imagined myself running through miles of dirt road, coming across a home on the side of an empty road and spying John in the window, waiting for me. I ran in, grabbed them each by the hand and pulled them out to the lawn. We spent just enough time to hug each other tight, like we used to when the thunder rolled out across the farm. Then we raced down a winding path towards home, shouting, 'I'm going to beat you,' at one another. We were running and laughing, our bare feet kicking up a dust cloud behind us. John began, and we all joined in, 'A tisket, a tasket, a green and yellow basket. I wrote a letter to a friend and on the way, I dropped it. I dropped it, I dropped it, and on the way, I dropped it. The little boy, he picked it up, and put it in his pocket.'

The click of the lock snapped me back to the empty hall. Abigail stepped in first through the door in front of her, while Nurse Gladys unlocked the one next to it for me. I watched Abigail's knickers drop to the floor. She untied her waistbelt and then grabbed the hem of her dress, pulled everything over her head, and let it fall by her feet. With her foot, she formed a little ball with the clothes, then kicked it right out the door. She'd done this before. I thought back to Miss Millie's warning: 'Be careful with whom you fraternize,' and realized I was too late for thinking. I glanced up at Abigail's naked body, a softened belly with a baby no one could see a sign of yet, then looked away, embarrassed for her and for myself. I knew what was coming for me.

I didn't want to go. But Nurse Gladys glared at me and pointed to the next room that wasn't much wider than the door itself. My eyes glued to the floor, I stepped in, then looked up and saw a tall window barred from top to bottom and realized this was the room where I saw the naked girl screaming when I pulled up my first day.

"Off with your clothes," Nurse Gladys said.

I took a slow breath before I undid the button on the back of my gown and untied my belt. I yanked it over my head, dropped it, then used my hands to cover my breasts. My belly, wide with life now, felt heavy. I tasted my stomach in my mouth and gagged.

"All of it," she said.

So I dropped my drawers to the floor and kicked all my clothes towards her in the hall, like I saw Abigail do. I shivered like I did back home on nights when howling wind whipped through cracks in plaster, but the room I was currently in felt like the inside of a firebox. I opened my mouth to speak, unsure of what to say. I wanted to ask how long I'd be here. Would she tell Dr. Fender? Would she hold a grudge when it came time to discuss my leaving? But the door slammed shut before I had a chance to utter a word.

As I pushed my hair from my eyes, I listened for the squeaking of Nurse Gladys' shoes to see if she walked away, but the door, the cement walls, were so thick that I didn't think I'd have heard myself scream. Abigail being right next to me made no difference, because I doubted that we could talk through the solid walls. These cells were made for keeping noises and misbehaviors inside. I imagined that even if there was a fire, no one would be the wiser that we were here, unless I hung in that window like that girl my first day. But then, who would care anyway?

I avoided the window because of the image of that poor girl crying for help. Instead, I took four steps in the tiny space, not much bigger than a toilet room, and reached a bare mattress lying on the hard floor, some black mouse droppings scattered next to it. In the corner was a rusted tin pail that I figured I'd have to use as a slop bucket. The stench of urine already filled the room and would overtake me within a day, unless someone came to empty it. I figured it best to plan on things only getting worse from there.

I shivered again, the heat of the room refusing to warm my blood, but I saw no means of covering up—no quilt, no sheet, not even an apron.

When I realized how alone I was, it felt like pinpricks dotted my skin. I paced the room, counting the steps of the border, like I used to do in order to figure out how much chicken wire we'd need to fence a coop big enough for six hens and a rooster. Twenty-two feet, it was. Might be big enough for a patch of tomatoes, if you spaced them out right.

Soon my body grew so tired that I couldn't move to count no more. The rest of the day I spent curled in a ball on the mattress, staring at a blooming patch of mildew in the corner of the ceiling, while repeating Helen, Alice, and John's names, as if they were a song. I thought if I said them enough, maybe they'd hear me, at least in their dreams, and know I was thinking of them. I hadn't forgotten they were in the world with me. And I was going to get them back.

The only light in that place was from the window, so once the sun set, I had only a half-moon and a few meager stars to see by. After dark, I stood in the window, certain at this hour that no one could see me back. I didn't want no one to bear witness to me locked up like this, tucked in an attic room, hungry, naked, and forgotten. Then I heard the stars speak again, their voices as soft as the cotton we used to shove in our ears to keep from hearing Papa's hollering after too much whiskey. *You're no longer invisible.*

And I done had enough of that. I banged on that window with my fists, and this time I screamed back, "I don't want no one seeing me! It ain't got me nothing but trouble!"

The tears sprung like someone done turned the knob of a spigot. My nose snotted up, and I had nothing to wipe it with but the back of my hand. I wiped that on the side of the bare mattress, then fell face-first onto it, the springs poking into my face and belly. I only wept harder then, and I thought that if Alice had been there, she'd be trying for a laugh to get me to stop this nonsense. All this crying was only making my mind too cloudy to think.

After a while, hunger gnawed at me. I knew I shouldn't be so long without food—couldn't be good for the little one. This baby knew nothing but heartache and sin. The pain ate me from the inside, like my stomach needed food so badly it was going to get right to eating itself. I screamed out, unable to take it, but that was the last thing I remembered until the sun stretched into the window and lit up the room.

Just then I heard a loud screech at the door and jumped up to see who was coming in, thinking that this must be my punishment done. I had learned my lesson. But then I saw the mail slot shift and realized it was for food. A tin tray with a few crusts, a small cup of water with a tin lid, and a tiny bowl of clear broth. I'd never seen a bowl so

171

tiny and wondered if it weren't a measuring cup of some sort.

I paid no mind and gobbled it up so fast that I didn't care about the green mold on the bread. Once I had finished, I realized I had eaten too fast, because I hurled it right back up. I was thankful for the small favors I got, and so I was glad to have made it into the slop bucket, though I wished it were empty. I wasn't so great at being grateful.

After I finished yucking up my breakfast, I felt the pangs of hunger start again. I smelled the crisp scent of rain, fresh and clean, mixed with the sour scent of urine and bile, then I heard pelting on my window. Storm clouds covered the sun, and my bright room went dark again. I stood by the window, not caring a lick now who saw me, and watched a roaring storm move in across the land. The rain across the way was so thick that it looked like a sheet of water moving towards us. For a moment, it sounded like pecking at the window, like a woodpecker searching for a mite, but then the sheet hit the building, and the room roared with the pounding. The sting of the mildew hit my nose, and I could tell that the patch must have been growing, because I struggled to catch my breath.

I curled on the bed in the dark, listening to thwacks of thunder and watching the room light up with each spark of lightning.

Back home, we'd hide in the cellar in a heap, waiting for storms like this one to pass. We'd count one, one thousand, two, one thousand, between each flash and rumble, so we knew as soon as the storm was moving out.

Mama taught us that. Said we'd be safe when the counting between the two grew longer. She said, back then, that we needed to keep ourselves safe. I thought, for a moment, how she could ever think I'd be safer here than on our farm, how my kin would be safer when we didn't know where in this wide world they were. I wasn't so sure, anymore, how I could trust anything Mama ever said to me. But one thing I did know—I couldn't go on without my kin to hold onto. And the little one, I thought as I rubbed my belly, deserved to know his mama, even if she was me. I was still his mama. And then I knew that Dr. Fender would have to come to see things my way, or I might as well stay locked up in this room forever, because there'd be nothing else for me outside of these four walls if I didn't have my family to care for.

Chapter Twenty-One

After two days in solitary, with no fresh air in the hot room, my skin cracked like a dried corn husk. I was picking away at my flaking skin, flicking flecks onto the bare mattress, when I heard the metal of a key in the lock. The click echoed in the room. At first, I thought I imagined it. I believed Nurse Gladys was going to lock me away forever. The emptiness made hope drip, as if through a sieve in my heart. I had nothing left by the time the door opened, and an orderly I'd never seen before tossed in a heap of rags. My clothes.

I squinted and rubbed my eyes, blinded by the faint light in the hall. I looked around for something to cover myself before standing, not wanting this man to see me bare, but I remembered there was nothing in this place to hide me. For a moment, I imagined rolling from the bed to the floor and tucking myself under the mattress where no one could see me. I wondered what he thought of me and his job. He probably thought me nothing more than a drifter with no one to care for. I imagined he felt right in his duties, and at night, before he drifted to sleep in a warm bed, surrounded by soft things, he told himself that he had helped another helpless girl that day, showed her how to act civilized and tame, rather than rabid and feral.

I forced myself to stand up and pick up the mangled clothes. I backed towards the window, far from the door where the orderly stood, and dressed there. The dry-rotted dress scratched my skin as I slid it over my bare body. I pulled up the knickers, but the elastic had worn so loose that they wouldn't stay up, or I had lost so much weight that they no longer fit me. I rolled them then wrapped around the apron, tying it tight to keep my drawers from falling down.

As much as I wanted out of that room, I walked a snail's pace to the door. The orderly didn't budge, so I sidled beside him, our bodies almost pressing against each other in the musky hall.

Abigail's door was open, and when I looked inside, I saw her face smacked raw on the side, a purple bruise framing one blue eye. I shot my eyes down to the floor, staring at the spider cracks in the cement, trying to hold back tears. I watched the tiny specks of water drop to the cement, turning its pale-gray color to almost black, and figured I wasn't doing such a good job at fighting those buggers after all. Nurse Gladys didn't have to be so cruel to us for our indiscretion. She didn't have to beat Abigail like that.

Abigail darted out and wrapped her arms around me, hugging me so tight that I thought I might wretch. Her force made the gash in my head ache, and I touched the cut to feel the crusted scab.

"You're OK," she said, in a voice so chipper that I lifted my head to look around, thinking someone else might be talking.

I pushed her away just as the orderly shouted, "No touching."

Truth was, I didn't want her touching me, anyway. No hug would undo the trouble she got me in. I wanted to shout at her, lay the blame where it belonged, but I knew there was no sense shooting a dying cow when she's still got a drop of milk in her. I needed Abigail more now than before. The only way out of this place, I saw now, was for her and Bobby to walk me right out that door. I figured the old doctor couldn't stop me if they two were married and took me in. But there was no way she'd take me if I didn't get my farm for them. I was making a deal with the devil, but it was that or risk staying in hell for the rest of my life.

#

I scarfed down my breakfast so fast that I didn't taste the toast and porridge, which I figured made me lucky for the first time in quite a while. They assigned me to scrub the floor of the dormitory, on account of the rain soaking clean through the coop and there being not much to do until it dried out some. I spied Abigail walking on a path opposite me, while moving from breakfast to the cottage, but I stared up at the clouds in the sky so that I didn't have to pretend like I wasn't still hot about the trouble she got me into. Those papery clouds caught my eye so long that I tripped, but I stopped myself before I done hit the ground. Part of me wondered what might happen if I smacked clean into the pavement, bumping my belly around, and if that would be enough to make me no longer be carrying a baby. Blood would drip down the insides of my thighs, a thin, winding trail to freedom from Randolph, and I'd follow it wherever it led.

I kept thinking I never was going to be able to care for my kin, because I didn't have the wits or the sense. Spending just a few years in school and not paying a lick of attention then wasn't helping me. And my sense, as Papa would say, didn't add up to a hill of beans, so I might as well just give up on fighting my own way out this.

When I got to the broom closet, I pulled the chain for the light. I figured a pail, some ammonia, and a good scrub brush would do the trick. I tore up some old aprons lying in a stack, because I didn't find any brushes. Tearing into them, ripping them shred by shred, white streamers like papier-mâché, made me feel powerful and strong, if only for a few minutes. After pumping water into the bucket in the toilet room, I sloshed my way down the hall towards the dormitory.

Beds lined the room so tight that I'd have to lie on my belly, scrubbing that floor. I couldn't see another way to do it. I poured ammonia into the bucket, bringing a rainbow shine to the murky water. It looked like the casing of a bubble and reminded me of when I blew bubbles in the yard with Alice, Helen, and John. The sharp scent made my dry nostrils bleed. My cracked hands burnt from the sting of it, so I blew on them to cool them down. Then I got to work, trying real hard to block out the screaming coming from a few rooms away. I thought, by now, I'd get used to it, and sometimes I did—didn't even notice cries so loud that they blocked out my own thoughts—but today I couldn't help but hear those women hollering a sad cry that made my temples tingle and my head fuzzy.

I was so busy scrubbing the floor, tucked underneath the row of beds by the windows, that I didn't hear her come in, until she stood there in the middle of the floor where I had just mopped.

"Miss Millie," I whispered, peeking my head out from under a bed frame. "What you doing here?"

"Anna," she said in a low voice. She squatted down to look me in the eye. "I was worried about you."

Worried about me. I done laughed at that one—been so long since anyone cared a mind about me. "Why?" I asked.

She shook her head then leaned over to grab my wrist, careful not to touch the wet rag in my hand. She pulled me out from under the bed. I squatted on the floor beside her.

"You got yourself into some trouble, I hear."

"Sure did," I said. And I decided I was going to keep my voice nice and even, so she didn't know how sad I was about the matter.

She slipped something from her pocket, wrapped in paper, and handed it to me.

I unwrapped it. A blueberry muffin. "Thank you," I said, before I ate it down in three bites. My stomach had been so empty that I had stopped noticing the hunger pains a long time ago.

"I know it must be so hard for you here," she said, and I knew she wasn't fibbing, by the tears welling up in her eyes. "But getting yourself into trouble like that will not help you get back home."

She said that like I didn't know already. I huffed a little, just enough to let her know she wasn't telling me something I didn't figure out for myself.

"And your baby? How are you feeling?" She reached to touch my belly, but I shifted away.

"I appreciate the kindness, Miss Millie, but ain't none of it your business."

"You need help, Anna."

"Again. I appreciate your kindness, but I got myself a plan. And once I find my kin, we'll be right as rain."

"Do you know where they are?"

Her question hit me like a gut punch. The room swirled around me, and I nearly toppled over as I dropped my rag, splashing onto the both of us. All this time, and I still didn't find my Helen, Alice, and John. I was only getting further away. For all my plotting and planning, I hadn't made a lick of progress. I might as well have been filling a hole-riddled bucket all this time. Who was Anna Wilson to think she had the smarts to find anyone? I stubbed my foot on the hard floor, so that I could feel the ache of my toes. I deserved much worse than that. I had failed my family.

179

Doubts skittered in my head, as I realized I could never get my kin back on my own. Then I remembered Miss Millie here was the one who got my belongings, and her voice always wrapped me up like a quilt when she talked to me, so she had no reason to bristle now. Her kindness looked as real as the crack in my tooth. And if anyone found out how she had snuck me my things, she'd be in as much hot water as I. But I had to be sure.

"Miss Millie," I said, picking my rag up and scrubbing like I had a will to get the job done right then. The ammonia scent made my eyes burn, but I didn't pay it no mind.

"Yes, Anna." She placed her hand over mine to stop me from working. Her eyes met mine in a way that made my heart slow.

"Was it you who put my sack in the trunk by my bed?"

"It was. I knew if it made it this far, it must be important to you."

My lips cracked a smile, and this strange feeling swept me, like I wasn't me anymore, like something hauled me up in some other person's body. "There's a letter."

Her back straightened. "What letter?"

I stood up and sleepwalked over to my trunk. The hinges creaked as I opened it, and I dug underneath the few aprons and dresses until I found it. As I slid out the letter, my neck grew hot, and my heart sped up. There was no going back once I shared this secret. I sat on the bed near Miss Millie and handed it to her while my palms grew tacky with sweat.

"Can you read it to me?" I asked.

A scream cut through the halls, shuddering my spine. I looked up towards the door, but no one was coming. We were alone.

"Please," I asked.

She slipped the letter from the white envelope. I could tell by the way she took care unfolding it that she understood this letter meant more to me than the moon on a pitch-black night.

Her eyes swept back and forth over the words, but she didn't read out loud.

I couldn't take it no more and grabbed her wrist. "I want to know what it's got to say."

She began:

#

'Miss Anna Lee Wilson,

The Children's Aid Society of Pennsylvania has determined you without guardianship. As required by law, you will be taken into custody by the Children's Aid Society and placed in foster care until the matter of custody is resolved, or until you reach the age of majority; if, by such, you are deemed fit for society and no longer indigent.'

She paused and looked at me.

I shook my head. "I don't know what any of that means."

"Anna, when is your birthday?"

I had to think on it a minute. Birthdays weren't much with Mama. 'We ain't got two sticks, so we ain't got birthdays,' she used to say. "September," I said. "The twenty-third, I think." I tasted my stomach and swallowed hard. "What's that matter?"

"Well, according to this…" She spoke slowly, her words skipping like stones, so gently that I thought I might pee my pants from so much fret. "Once you reach eighteen, you could possibly be on your own again."

My heart lifted. I hugged her, for the first time in a long time, wrapping my arms so hard that I thought I couldn't breathe. "It won't be long. I'll be out and get my siblings back." Stepping back, I noticed a strange tingling on my face. I was smiling. I thought back to that day with Pa in the shed, when a little kindness felt like a gift.

But Miss Millie's face fell, and suddenly, I didn't want her reading no more.

"Give it back," I said, snatching it from her hand. "I don't want you reading my letter no more." I collapsed onto a bed and started crying. The tears wouldn't stop coming.

She sat beside me and rubbed my back, just like Alice used to do when I couldn't make enough mush to fill our four bowls. She whispered, "It's not quite what you're thinking, Anna. It's not so easy now that you're…" She paused a moment, then went on, "… here. And having a child."

"Why is that the problem? I'll be that age in no time. I can sign myself right out."

She slipped the letter from my trembling fingers. "Things are different once you're placed in an asylum. They've got reason to think you're not fit to take care of yourself. Let alone a child."

"What reason they got?" My words shot out like pellets from a gun, but it wasn't Miss Millie I was angry with. I wasn't sure who to be angry with. I felt it all boiling up and had no place else to put it. If I kept it inside, I thought I might blow.

I pushed her right off the bed, and she toppled to the floor onto her bottom. Watching her eyes fill with tears and her pretty lips shake, I scooted off the bed and onto the floor next to her. Miss Millie didn't deserve that no more than I deserved what they were giving me. It seemed like life gave you all sorts of grief, even when you didn't ask for it.

She placed her arm around me and squeezed my shoulder, and I knew she wasn't mad at me. She was softer than my kind. "Let me finish reading."

'As such, Helen Marie Wilson, Alice Joan Wilson, and John Joseph Wilson are deemed without guardianship, and consequently, under the care of authorities until such a guardian surfaces. Placement of each minor will be determined by the state. Barring no guardian lays claim to said individuals, each shall remain in the care of the state until the circumstances outlined above.

Any questions regarding this decree shall be addressed to the Children's Aid Society of Pennsylvania.

Sincerely,

The Board of the Children's Aid Society of Pennsylvania.'

"So what's that all mean?" I asked, still nestled in the crook of Miss Millie's arm.

She set the letter down and took the breath you know means bad news. "It means that in order to be released from here, in order for you to lay claim to your sisters and brother, you'll need to prove to Dr. Fender that you are fit to do so. It might not be easy, Anna. But you can do it."

I shook my head so hard that I thought it might roll off. "Oh no, I can't, Miss Millie. I won't pass none of the doctor's tests. We ain't the same kind. I won't do it."

"You have to. It's the only way."

"What about my birthday? Ain't that a way to do it?"

"You'll be eighteen. So it may help. But it's not enough. You'll need to prove yourself. I don't see how you'll get around that."

I shifted away from her. "I have a way. I might not be enough to pass Dr. Fender's old test, but I got another way."

"How?" She didn't believe me, but then she didn't know about Abigail's plan, even if it was shaky. She didn't know how Abigail could trick them all into letting us both go.

Just thinking about that plan made the smile on my face creep back. "No matter. But I need to talk with my mama. I've got to square something with her."

"I will see to it. For now," she said, handing me back the letter, "you keep this in your trunk where no one can find it. And know that I will help you."

I took the letter back and felt my heart slow a bit. "Oh, it's OK, Miss Millie. I don't think I'll need any help. I've got a plan."

My heart sunk when I said it, knowing Abigail wasn't to be trusted. But I couldn't risk depending on my own wits to get me out of this. Abigail was trickier than I was smart. If anyone could spin a web to get us free, it was Abigail.

Chapter Twenty-Two

My foul with Abigail saw to it I had more chores than I had time. I'd have stomached it if I thought multiple tasks would make things even, but I knew that it was just the start of my punishment. Thoughts of how I'd get out of this jam spun in my mind and tangled into a mess of a knot, so much so that I couldn't figure out what to do. I listened to orders, grateful for not having to think.

My blood still boiled about the trouble she got me in, but I thought back to my spat with Ma, my kicking that old Miss Atkinson, and none of that set me right. This time, I was going to speak like I had sense about me and wasn't all thunder and lightning, even though thunder and lightning was what I felt in my heart. A voice in my head said I was lying by trying to make nice with Abigail, but then I told it to hush, because without her, I'd have no chance to get my family back. If a lie gets you where you need to go, then there ain't no harm in telling it.

I had not caught sight of her shock of blonde hair all week, so when I showed up to sort silver in the kitchen and saw they assigned her to the same duty, I smelled a rat. No way Nurse Gladys didn't think she was setting a trap for me, but she didn't know our plan, and that gave me the leg up.

The kitchen lights swung from the ceiling, like stars toppling from the sky. They shone on the crusted bits of hardened flour caked in the corners of the walls and tiny mouse droppings peppering the floor. I walked over to stand next to Abigail, and I could feel her lift like someone filled her with air.

She dropped her silver and hugged me. "Finally. I thought they'd never let us be together again." The quiet room made it feel like we were someplace else, someplace far from Farview. I felt like I was watching myself, as I began working at the knot of thoughts tied in my mind.

Someone was laying a trap, but I had little choice or time, so trap or not, this might be my only chance. I grabbed a handful of knives, spoons, forks, and a stack of stiff napkins, and lay them in front of me. I kept my eyes forward. "Shh. Someone might be listening."

"Oh, they ain't no bother. We just two dumb inmates. No one cares about us."

I swallowed a deep breath. "We can't be stupid now. We have to get our plan going, or else we'll be too late."

"I have it all set. Don't be such a handwringer." She scooped up a mound of spoons and sprinkled them onto the metal counter, sending a clanking sound through the kitchen.

"Shh." I looked around to see if anyone was listening. "Did you tell him yet?"

She huffed. "I will. I tell you, once he knows, he's going to scoop us out of here so fast that we won't remember Nurse what's-her-name's name."

"Just do it. All right. I can't wait no longer."

She stopped sorting and looked at me. "What about you? You ain't even sure the farm's yours to have."

"I thought about that," I said. "All I've been thinking about for the past week. That and you marrying Bobby."

"Well, what's your plan?"

My words stumbled out of my mouth. "It's mine. She can't keep it from me. I lived on that farm after she left, and I will promise her I'll get my sisters and brother back and show her I don't belong here."

"How you going to do that?"

"She trusts the doctor, right? Well, if the doctor lets you and Bobby have care for me, then why wouldn't he think we should have the farm? It's perfect. How could she argue that?"

Abigail slid a pile of sorted silver off to the side and started with a new pile. "Anna Wilson, you are brilliant. Even if you did get us into a mess of trouble."

My head grew so hot that I felt like I might burst into flames right there in the kitchen. "You're the one who got us into trouble. It was all your idea." I should have held my tongue, but that's something I wasn't very good at.

"You kept us out too late. You should have known the time. You know I'm not good with that stuff. It's your fault for all that thinking you do." Each of Abigail's words was tightly clipped.

"This is not my fault. I would have never done that if you hadn't thought of it. You and your bright idea got me into so much trouble. You owe me." My voice rose too high. Before I knew it, I was shouting. "It's all your fault!" I looked down at the table and saw my blurry reflection in the metal and flinched at the stranger.

"How do I owe you?"

"I never found trouble in here until you. Now, if you don't get me out of here with you and Bobby, they'll never let me go."

"It was not my fault." She slammed a pile of spoons onto the metal table, and they clanged throughout the kitchen.

I needed to mind myself. If she didn't think we were a team, she could leave without me. "Let's not fight. Just tell him, OK?"

"You think that was my fault? You don't have a lick of sense."

My voice scratched. "I'm just mad. Neither of us deserved what we got. Now we just need to work together, to find our way out of here."

"You're right. No sense fighting about that now. I will tell him."

"Tomorrow."

"Tomorrow? These things take time. I need him in the right mind when I do it." She placed her hand on her belly.

Her eyes glowed when she touched her baby growing inside her, and I was pretty sure mine glazed over like hot cross buns. I couldn't even bear to touch my belly, which now bulged out so far that my apron had to be tied above the bump.

"I don't get why it has to be so soon."

I pointed to my wide waistline with a butter knife. "I'm out of time. If I have this baby in here, they'll take him away. They'll send him to the almshouse." I took a few butter knives from the pile and separated them into rows. No matter how much I didn't want this child, I couldn't see sending him to a wretched place like that. I'd carry that guilt forever.

"Fine," she said, grumbling. "You talk to your mama then, so that we got our ducks in a row." Giggles ran through her so hard that she braced herself on the countertop. "Can you believe we'll be mommies? What a hoot!"

But I couldn't figure out what she found so funny. The thought of this child being an orphan, of me being locked in this godforsaken place for the rest of my life, not laying claim to Helen, Alice, and John ever again, made my head so dizzy that I could hardly stand straight.

"I need to be set before Dr. Fender gets back any day. You're my only hope."

Laughter shot through her again. "Well, that stinks. I'd hate to have me as my only hope."

I thought back to the trap and wondered if I had just stepped foot into it—again.

#

After sorting the silver, I snuck outside while Abigail was still laughing. The scent of hay filled the late September breeze. I was glad to be out of that kitchen. I couldn't stand to hear her laugh anymore, the cackling of someone slipping into madness. I didn't want to let go of hope just yet, so I rushed to the main building to find Miss Millie. When I entered, Nurse Gladys shot me a look that made me drop my head and slump my shoulders.

"What are you doing here? Don't you have work to do?" she said.

I coughed, my throat dry with fear. "Miss Millie, ma'am. She told me I could find her here."

She pointed to the corner where I saw Miss Millie picking the nits from an old lady's gray hair. I could smell the scent of her unwashed body from across the room and gagged. The smell reminded me of my first day there, when my morning sickness peaked, and every strange scent had me choking back bile.

She stopped when she saw me and handed the comb to the woman whose body caved into itself like a shell. "Agnes, you keep combing. I will be right back."

Miss Millie walked towards me, her white shoes tapping in the quiet hall. "I have her waiting," she said, and led me towards the gated doorway.

She unlocked it, and it creaked open as we both stepped through. I didn't mention my duty with Abigail or my heart racing in my chest. I wiped my sweaty palms on my apron and tried to appear calm. Really, I wanted to run. The closer I got to figuring out how to get myself out of this mess, the more afraid I got. Suddenly, the thought that none of it would work plowed into me like a rogue horse, and it knocked the wind out of me. I gripped the wall to steady myself.

She led me into the game room where there were a few other inmates arguing over a game of cards. They scattered the torn cards along the tabletops, and one woman's deep voice boomed about how her opponent cheated. I ignored them and went to sit next to my mother.

"I'll be back in ten minutes," Miss Millie said.

I wasn't sure why, but I was hoping she'd stay. *This is my mama,* I told myself. But she didn't feel like my mama. Didn't even sound like her. And I wondered if this was the same Mama as back home, but I never saw it then. Maybe I'd been too worried about pretending things were fine, to see that my own mama had been slipping away from the world. Or maybe it was this place that changed her. I couldn't tell, and the thoughts made my throat close, so I pushed them away. If I didn't keep it together, I'd never get to telling her I was getting myself out of here, and that I was taking the farm once I did.

"Hi, Mama," I said.

Her head hung low and swung like it was tethered by a shoestring. It bounced a bit, but she didn't look up. I had heard about the medicine they were giving people, the ones Nurse Gladys had set out on my first day here, and I wondered if Mama got that. She seemed like sleep was all she wanted, and a talk with me wasn't something she was up for. But I had no choice.

"Hi, Mama," I repeated, this time placing my hand over hers.

"I do hope you've been listening to the good doctor," she squeaked out in a voice so low that I leaned my head towards her cracked lips. "He's a good man."

The lady boomed again, her voice rattling lights dangling from thin chains.

"I need to tell you something. I need you to listen good." Mama seemed to be good at taking direction here. She did whatever the doctor told her. If only she'd listen to me the same.

She didn't say a word but looked at me, her eyes dry and yellow.

"I think I have a way out of here, but I need to know about the farm. You and Papa still own it, right? And I paid the taxes last time they were up, so we can't be too far gone on it, right?"

"Oh, Anna, that farm has been in our family for years. Papa's granddad started that farm a long time ago. He was a brilliant man." She smiled at the memory. "Ain't no one taking that farm from the Wilsons."

"Then, when I'm out of here, I can run it. Just like I did before." I put my hands on my hips and stomped my foot.

Her faced scrunched, as she looked down at my cracking boot. "You can't run that farm from in here."

"I'll find a way out."

"But the doctor? He'll have a plan for you."

"No doctor is going to tell me I can't have my own life. I'm going to get out of here."

Mama sighed. "It's best you listen to the good doctor. He has seen a lot of our kind and knows what's best."

My voice rose over the inmates squabbling. "How can you say that? He knows nothing about our kind. I bet he can't even harvest a crop of tomatoes before they turn. He doesn't know what it takes to be us. Our kind, you say? Our kind wakes at dawn, to dust out the fireplace ash from the night before so we can start another before the little ones freeze to death. Our kind makes stew from scraps we wouldn't feed to the hogs, so that we don't starve when winter goes on a month too long. Our kind huddles in a single bed to keep warm when the wind gusts through the wallboards. He doesn't know a thing about what our kind can do."

Mama shook her head and furrowed her brow.

"You don't get it, do you?" I slowed my words so she could understand the weight of what she was saying. If I stayed here, that'd be the end of all of us. Those people out there, the ones who wanted to do us in, they'd win. "Everyone will forget us. No one will remember us. What about Helen? Alice? John?" I placed her hand on my round belly. "This little one? They all need me. I won't let them disappear, too."

"But he's the doctor. He knows what's best for us. Don't you think if I could have done better, I would have? It's hard out there, Anna. And you've got no one to help you."

I snatched my breath. "I should have you."

"I'm not enough. It's not enough to just want things to get better. You're not a child anymore. Wishing ain't enough."

I huffed. Screaming came from the far side of the game room, followed by the iron scent of blood. I looked over to see a woman cupping her bloody nose. "Wishing ain't enough? Well, then, I'll prove I'm better than some girl who relies on someone to tell her when to take her meals—if that's what it takes."

I wanted to argue with her more. Our ending up torn apart and in this godforsaken place was her fault. I opened my mouth to tell her as much, but I stopped myself. It wouldn't help me to pick a fight with Mama now. So instead, I said, "Well, I'm going to get out. Whether or not they like it."

"I don't know what you're talking about," she said. She started looking towards the door over my shoulder.

Heat rose in my chest, and angry words crouched on the tip of my tongue, but I stopped myself and breathed nice and slow this time. Doubt crept up my spine, and I shivered at the thought I couldn't trust Mama. But I had already said too much. She knew I had one on the way. "They'll take my baby to the almshouse if I stay."

"A nice family will care for him. A family better than you."

"No one can love my child better than me. I won't let them take him." That was lie, I thought. I wasn't sure I

195

could love this child, but I'd be damned if I'd let him disappear into the world with no one.

She put her hand on mine, as if she were offering some wise words I hadn't heard before. "That's not for you to say, dear."

"What if it is?"

"What?"

"What if it is for me to say? What if I have a choice in all this?"

She smiled a kind smile, and I finally felt like she understood what I was saying. "Our kind don't have a choice. The doctor knows all about such things, and he'll see to it your child is taken care of."

My voice rose with the anger I was trying so hard to keep inside. "I'll see to it my child is taken care of."

"What?" Her voice trailed off, and I wasn't sure she was even listening to what I was saying. She didn't have the wits about her to hear my entire plan, so I told her only what she needed to know.

"If I get out of here, I'm taking the farm. I'll be eighteen. Papa is still missing, so no one can raise a stink about it if I keep it up and keep out of trouble."

Her voice hitched somewhere between a laugh and a cough. "If you find the good doctor sets you out, then return to the farm. But it's not the dream you seem to think it is. That kind of life isn't easy."

I jumped up and wrapped my arms around her stiff body. "Mama, I know it's not. But it's my kind of life. The one I choose."

The voice boomed again, and I looked over to see the large woman swipe the cards onto the floor.

"Don't celebrate yet, child. You are still here. And you'll see that once you're out in that world, being invisible isn't such a bad thing for our folks."

I got up to leave then turned around, one more burning question egging at me. "Why'd you really come here?"

Her eyes stared off into something I couldn't see, like she was watching a memory. I thought back to our days on the farm before she left. The kittens. The squabbling between us kids. The horse that run off in the night because I forgot to lock up his pen. What had we done to make her leave? What had I done?

"I couldn't do no more. I done give everything I had to you kids. To your papa. And I had nothing left. If I stayed, I don't think any of us would have lived through that spring."

"But why would you stay here?"

She smiled again, and this time she really looked at me. "Here, you can disappear, dear. Everyone knows that."

Chapter Twenty-Three

Each day felt like a lifetime, and yet, before I realized, the leaves on the trees turned bright orange and red, and the rumors of Dr. Fender having returned spread through Farview. He hadn't called me to report yet, but I knew it'd be soon. I had to be prepared for the day. Once I made sure that Mama wouldn't or couldn't fight me on taking the farm, the only piece missing was Abigail and Bobby.

Abigail and I had been up at nights, dreaming about her wedding, but she still hadn't told him about the baby. Her belly grew enough that he had to notice swelling, but she was sure he hadn't a clue. A kernel of a thought popped into my head. She didn't have faith in Bobby. I pushed away the idea, knowing I couldn't pull off my plan if she was right.

I had taken to slipping my book into my apron pocket and sneaking reading in when I was alone in the henhouse. Those chickens didn't mind my reading, and I knew my way around a coop well enough to get a day's work done in the morning hours, so that left time enough for learning. There were so many inmates, and hardly enough orderlies to mind their own work, let alone ours, so I worried little about being discovered.

One day, when I was walking to the pen, I found the most beautiful stone, gray and black and shinier than a nickel. I knew it was a wishing stone, so I rushed over to that old well and made my wish I'd had since Miss Atkinson showed up on Shaker Street. I blew on it for good luck, rubbed it in my palms, then leaned over to look down the deep well. I doubted it'd bring much luck from the looks of it, but then I wondered how many people here ever had enough hope to bother. After blowing on the stone one last time, I kissed it, then dropped it in. My stomach sunk when I couldn't hear it hit the bottom.

"Good morning," I called to the chickens, as I entered their pen.

Since I'd done mended the fencing and rubbed the insides of chili peppers all over the chicken wire each week, the hens had been laying good, and I hadn't seen any signs of foxes. I picked up the wire basket on the hook and started rooting through the hay in the boxes for fresh eggs. I filled two baskets, leaving a few eggs for the ornerier hens, so they'd remember what they were there to do.

I was setting the last of the eggs into the basket to bring up to the kitchen when a scuffle broke out. There was always one weak hen of the bunch, and that poor soul got a sharp beak to her eye and one to her wing. They knew there was only so much power to go around, so it seemed like every day they were fighting to move up in the pecking order. I felt bad for this one. Queenie, I called her. The only one I named. She didn't have fight in her, and so even the weak ones would gouge her when they felt crotchety. Her light-white feathers were always streaked red, and even her little orange hock sported scars from battles she'd lost. I patted her little feathered head and told her she needed to fight back, or she wouldn't make it much longer. If she wasn't as strong as them, she'd need to fake it.

I shooed those mean old gals out into the pen and picked up Queenie to check on her cuts, then I put her in a high nesting box to rest a bit.

Once she settled, I nestled into the crook in the back of the coop and took my book out. I was getting better at reading, I could tell, because the long string of words was starting to add up to sentences. I didn't know the story yet, but I knew parts. I knew Peter was looking for trouble and that he could fly, and that Wendy was too good for Peter, because he'd bring her nothing but trouble. But I wished I knew the whole story in and out, and why Wendy would be such a fool for Peter.

As I was hunting for words I could make sense of, I heard my name.

"Anna."

My eyes sprung up, and I saw Miss Millie standing there in the center of the coop. "Miss Millie. How'd you find me?"

She laughed. "You're here every day. And that hiding spot isn't as hidden as you think."

My face must have reddened, because I felt as bashful as Queenie. "I've done collected the eggs. I'm a fast harvester. I thought I'd—"

"Oh, I'm not here to punish you. I'd like to help. Do you want help reading?"

I didn't want help. I had done fine by myself, and I didn't need anyone pointing out all I didn't know yet. Then I noticed she had something hidden behind her back.

She pulled out the most beautiful cupcake I'd ever seen. It was vanilla with frosting and a maraschino cherry plum on top. "This is for you. I missed your birthday."

"Thank you," I said, setting down my book and standing up to take the treat. Without saying another word, I ate it in three bites. "It was delicious." I wiped my hands on my apron. "I forgot all about my birthday."

"Read to me," she said, sitting down next to where my book lay.

"Oh, I'm not good. I'm learning, is all."

She smiled. "We all start somewhere. Just pick a line to read."

The sounds came out mixed at first, nervous and as unsure as I was. I mixed up the 'w' and 'r' sounds, and forgot the 'th' was special, but soon I caught on and read a few lines that seemed to make a bit of sense. Miss Millie corrected me a few times and taught me a few new words that I had been struggling with. Then she started reading some of the story to me, and I realized what I'd been missing out on all this time. It felt like Alice was back with me, reading her tales. The story created all sorts of pictures in my head, so much prettier than real life. Suddenly, a giant ache for my home grew so big that it could swallow me.

#

That afternoon, I raced to the dining hall to find Abigail. My stomach, chock-full of worry, had no room for the butter beans and soggy bread set out for lunch, so I took an open seat by the door and sat waiting for that mess of blonde hair. Then I saw it. She turned the corner, bouncing like we were at the dance hall.

"Abigail!" I shouted. "Sit here."

She held up a finger and turned to fill her tray. She plopped next to me and flung her hair from her face as she chomped on a nub of bread. "Today."

"What?" I asked.

I watched Bobby walk through the door, his bright-white uniform a little wrinkled and untucked.

"After lunch. I'll tell him. I have it all planned out." Her voice hitched like she already had good news to tell.

The ache of a smile crossed my lips. "That's great. You're going to do it."

"Of course, I'm going to do it. You don't think I'd fib to you, do you?" she said, rubbing my head.

"I've got good news, too," I said. "I told Mama I'm going back to the farm when I get out of here. It'll be all ours."

"Hot dog." She rubbed my belly, then her own. "These babies going to be like sisters."

"Or brothers."

"Definitely sisters," she corrected. "Mine's a girl."

"How you so sure?"

"I'm so fat it has to be a girl." She blew out her cheeks and pretended to waddle in her seat. "These babies are going to have a home for sure."

I picked up her bread and pulled off a piece, my appetite returning. I popped the crust into my mouth and said, "I can't wait. I owe it all to you."

She laughed. "Yes, you do. Me and this," she said, pointing to her bump. "Bobby's going to be so happy. I can't wait to see his face when I tell him."

The dining tables were packed with hungry women eating slop. I watched their faces fall as they dug into their meals, and I could feel their sadness like a storm cloud hanging over me. This placed shoved so much sadness into it, a woman could hardly breathe.

"How are you going to tell him?" I asked. I slid a little closer to her, on account of all the wailing some ladies were doing in the back corner.

"Well," she said, spooning beans into her mouth, "I'm ahead on my sewing. I sewed two full shifts today, plus an apron. That's a full day for me."

"What's that have to do with it?" I asked.

"Be patient," she said. "Since I'm done, I'm going to sneak off with him to the dormitory. Everyone will be working and won't notice I'm gone." She paused a moment then went on. "Or else I'll do that tomorrow. Maybe tomorrow, if I don't get a chance to call him away today."

I stomped my foot. "Today, Abigail. It must be today. I can't wait any longer. Dr. Fender is back. I know it. He's going to call for me, and we need this plan set for it to work. I have to know what to tell him." I smashed her hand onto the table, and she dropped her fork. "You do it today, or it's off. I won't let you share my farm."

She huffed and pulled her hand away. "Fine. I'll do it today." She started piling everything back onto her tray, even though she wasn't finished eating. "You have no idea how men work. They take time to come around to these things."

I stood up and stared down at her. "Well, I'm telling you, we ain't got time left. Today."

"Fine," she said, pushing out her chair and picking up her tray. She emptied her tray and stacked it on the pile, then came back to me. She leaned down and whispered in my ear, "But if the timing ain't right, I'm blaming you."

I hated to be the one to push her, but time wasn't something we had left. Bobby would have to marry her if he wanted the baby. And if he wanted the farm, that sapsucker would have to take me, too. It was the only way. I knew she'd be thanking me by the next morning. She'd cuddle up in bed with me by tonight, thankful I nudged her.

Chapter Twenty-Four

Abigail still stood by me when a loud bell rang in the hall. My heart jumped. I scanned the room, trying to figure out what to do when a bell rings, and watched every woman pop out of her chair and toss whatever lunch was left into the bins. Eyes poised at their toes, they shuffled their feet into a single line by the door. Everyone except Abigail, who spun quickly without saying a word and ducked under the table, pulling a chair in to hide herself.

I stood like an opossum stuck in the light stream of a lantern, afraid to move. My eyes glanced down to Abigail, trying not to give away her hiding place. For a moment, my mind flashed to Alice ducking into the cupboard when we'd play hide-and-seek, her knobby knees tucked up under her chin.

I whispered, "What's going on? What do I do?"

She held up a finger to her lips. "Just go. They have some detail they want the whole booby-hatch to work on. It ain't nothing. I've got to find Bobby." Her voice slipped from muffled to clear as day. "Those crazy old bats won't miss me."

I did as she said and followed the other women into a long line that stretched down the wide length of the dining hall and wrapped through a row of tables. Not wanting to be the caboose, I snuck behind a wretched old woman with shoulders so slumped I imagined she had spent her life shoveling heavy piles of dirt. Maybe she was one of the grave diggers?

With all of us lined up for the first time since I'd been there, I realized how hopeless a lot we were. Dresses hung ratty and torn, and the arms of the women hung lifeless. I'd have thought that seeing us all together would have made us seem normal, but I realized what outsiders we all were. We didn't fit in with the world. Maybe we never would again. When pushed together, we smelled like a farm gone to rot. I covered my mouth as I gagged. I crossed my fingers behind my back, hoping we'd be herded outside where I could breathe, but then that made me feel like lambs to slaughter, and I started hoping we'd be inside, sweeping up and dusting.

I was far back in the line, so I couldn't see where we were headed. One foot in front of the other, we moved in pace, but the women behind me were shoving and jostling, to get us going faster. One younger girl, about my age, elbowed me between the shoulders so hard that I reeled around to clock her. I raised my fist and looked her square in the eyes. She looked like Helen, those blue eyes staring back at me, making my heart stop for a second. I grew so woolly-headed, I thought I might fall over. I dropped my hand, shaking out my fist that so wanted to spend anger. Then I remembered this place didn't look kindly on fighting or rule-breaking, and I kept my temper to myself.

But that sucker, she stepped on my heels the entire time we held that line.

After we went through the door, we tripped down the brick steps. No one in that line knew how to keep a safe distance so we could see where we were going. Packed so tight, I wondered if these ladies were jamming together out of fear or stupidity. It mattered little, either way, because soon we reached where we were going. A bald man with a thick mustache doled out orders like any of us had sense enough to know what he was saying. He was older than the orderlies and not as neatly dressed as the doctor. I wondered where he came from and how I'd never seen the likes of him until now.

His voice boomed over the nonsense chattering of the inmates. I worried at a raw spot on my hand, flicking bits of dried skin onto the ground, while I listened.

"The Board of the Farview Training School is coming for a visit. We need to get the grounds in tip-top shape for their arrival later this week." He cleared his throat, then pointed to a cluster of women in the front of the line. "You take the front grounds entering Farview. It must be impeccable, with no weeds to speak of." He carefully clipped the end of each word like a carpenter cut wood.

The inmates slumped off, following an orderly who pushed a wobbly wheelbarrow packed with rakes, buckets, and shovels.

He then turned and pointed to what I imagined was my group. I moved a little closer towards the front and away from the girl who looked like Helen, so I could get on with my job. I didn't want to be working near that shover, and I sure couldn't stand to see Helen's eyes no more, unless they were on my Helen herself.

He assigned us to the lawn of the main building, the lawn I looked out on when I was in solitary. I hoped I'd get a chance to look up at that window and spy another soul pressed against the glass, wishing to get out. I don't know why I felt that, but I had this hopeful feeling someone might be in there, suffering like I was. And I wanted to witness it.

Miss Millie appeared with a wheelbarrow with similar tools to those in the first wheelbarrow, and my breath caught at the sight of her. I couldn't believe my luck getting Miss Millie to be doling out orders for my group. Luck never much came my way, but when it did, I made sure to be grateful, so that I'd bring more of it.

When we got to where we were going, she handed us each a tool and pointed to where we should work. Three women bounced towards the shrubs with a pair of trimmers, and I wondered if that was the task they were hoping for, because I'd never seen someone bounce like that around here.

To me, she handed worn yard gloves and a small hoe. "You weed the front bed."

"Yes, ma'am," I said. I waited a minute to see if anyone was joining me.

Finally, a girl about my age, with tight braids and coal-colored eyes, appeared next to me. I recognized her from around, seen her a time or two out in the fields and at meals, but I didn't speak to anyone there except Abigail, Miss Millie, and Mama.

"You may go," Miss Millie said to the two of us.

As we set down our tools and started fighting to get our old gloves on, a gray hawk screeched overhead, and we both looked up. Its wide wings fanned out in the clear sky, as it caught a gust of wind and glided to perch atop the pointed stone roof of the solitary room. No one was in the window. My stomach dropped a little, sad that no teary eyes were looking out.

I hated myself for that, for wishing bad on someone else. For wanting someone to be feeling the loneliness I felt, but I couldn't help it. Suffering was one of those unfair things that made you want others to be alongside you. Not so much you wanted them to suffer, but so that you knew someone out there understood. It made the lonesomeness a little easier to bear.

I worked without saying a word to the girl with the coal eyes. Someone across the yard screamed and hollered. It made me want to shout too, louder than her, to prove I was real, but instead I focused on raking out the winding vine that snaked around a dead rose bush.

From behind me, I heard my name, but it sounded so far away that I thought it was my imagination. Then I heard it again and again. When someone touched my shoulder, I jumped and swung my hoe. Turning, I saw Miss Mille standing over me, blocking the sun and casting her long shadow over the flower patch. I tugged my soiled gloves off, set them on a pile of weeds, then stood up.

"Hello, Miss Millie."

"There's someone I want you to meet," she said, holding her hand out towards the coal-eyed girl. "This is Rebecca."

The tall girl walked towards me and slouched next to Miss Mille so close that their shoulders were touching. "Hi," she said, glancing up just long enough for me to see her eyes looked like midnight, even up close.

"Hi," I said.

Miss Millie took my hand, and I held hers back. She let go, but I didn't. I wanted to hold on forever.

"This is Anna. She stayed with the Monroes, too."

My eyes grew wide at the word Monroes. This was the girl I had heard about. *She's here. With me.* Rebecca's black eyes teared up like a rainy night sky. She blinked, and I watched as they trickled down her pale cheeks. I wanted to speak but didn't know what words could say all that I had in my heart, so I stayed mum.

Rebecca reached down and touched my belly, and I knew I didn't need any words to say what I felt.

"It's Randolph's?" she said, in an angry voice that gave me the shivers.

I didn't mean to, but I snapped. "Of course my baby ain't Randolph's."

She cried harder now, and my stomach tangled in knots. What was Miss Millie getting at, bringing us together like this? I didn't want to think no more of Randolph. I'd worked every day to push him out of my mind, and I didn't need her making me talk about him.

"It's not his," I said.

Miss Millie looked from Rebecca to me, then back to Rebecca. She breathed so loudly that I could hear it over the screams.

Rebecca said, "I had a Randolph baby. That's how I come to get here." She pointed up at the stone building like I didn't know what she meant. "They took him from me the day he was born. I never got a chance to hold him."

"That ain't happening to me," I said. I stared at Miss Millie so hard that I thought she might have felt a punch. "Why she telling me this?"

"They fixed me good after he was born. I can't ever have no babies." Rebecca placed her hand over her belly and winced, as if the pain was still there.

"How come they do that?" I asked.

She hardly waited for me to finish when she answered. "My mommy died, and it was just me left at home with my daddy. He gave me up when he met his new wife. She had three youngsters of her own, and four was too much. My mommy never had schooling, and I never much paid attention to the lessons, so they figured I wouldn't be bright enough to have a family of my own. And there was no place for me to go but here."

I shook my head, not wanting to hear any longer. But I couldn't help but ask, "Where'd your baby go?"

"Almshouse, they say. They never told me. Never asked to take him, either. They didn't see him as mine."

She kicked at a pebble on the ground, and tears kept coming. I watched, as her shoe worked at the pebble and

211

teardrops darkened the soil. If I didn't know better, I'd have thought rain.

I set my hands around my belly. "That ain't going to happen to me." I turned to go back to my gardening, but Miss Millie called my name again. I liked Miss Millie, so I turned back. "What?" I asked in an angry voice.

"I didn't introduce you to her to scare you. I wanted you to know that you're not alone." Her voice sounded soft and made me feel bad for what I was going to say next.

"Don't mean a lick to me. I bet they filled this place with Annas and Rebeccas. We don't mean nothing to nobody."

I thought about that, about how it wasn't quite true. Abigail meant something to me. As much trouble as she made, she was my friend. And I wondered how lonely it'd be with no Abigail. How lonely was Rebecca? Still, I wasn't planning to stay long enough to make more friends.

I went on. "I thank you for meeting us. But I won't be staying long enough for them to take my baby."

Miss Millie sighed. She didn't believe me. "Rebecca doesn't belong here any more than you do."

She put her arm around Rebecca, and I felt hot with jealousy. I thought Miss Millie and I had something special.

"I really hope your plan works, Anna."

And I knew she meant it.

Rebecca went back to gardening, so I had Miss Millie to myself. "You knew?" I asked.

She clenched her lips together real tight and said, "I did. Your paperwork has the name of the home you came from listed on it. I recognized it from Rebecca's paperwork. I've wanted you two to meet since you got here."

"Why?" I asked. "What's she got to do with me?"

"She's been where you've been. Sometimes it's nice to know you're not alone."

I thought about that. How I wanted to see some wild lady hanging in the window in solitary. How come we want other people to have it as bad as we had it? "I wish she'd have gotten to keep her baby. She should get out of this place."

"You're right. I will help her as best I can. But I want to help you, too."

I looked up at her. "How can you help me? You think the doctor won't let me out?"

"I was going to wait to tell you, but he has called for you tomorrow," she said in a low, calm voice.

The hair on the back of my arms stood tall.

"You may ask him then," she continued.

"What do I say?" My heart beat in my ears so loudly that I could hardly hear her reply.

"Ask him what you want to know. He is an honest man, if not somewhat a stickler for the rules of Farview."

"What rules?" I asked.

"Don't you worry about that now. Let's keep practicing your reading. That's a good place to start." She

213

placed her hand on my shoulder. "You can do this, Anna. You've got this little one counting on you."

She rested her hand on my belly, and I flinched at the memory of Randolph and the thought of how so much of life was out of my control. I ached to forge my own path and wondered where I'd be if I could. Would I still be on our old rundown farm without any plan for making it better? I hadn't realized all the choices I had failed to make, like not reading and learning or patching the roof. If I didn't start making choices for the better, how could I get myself out of this hell?

The warmth of her palm spread through my body. I held her hand there, feeling the whirling of life underneath the pulse of our palm, imagining it slipping away from me, imagining my pushing against the tide to bring it back.

Chapter Twenty-Five

That night, as I lay listening to screams, I imagined my meeting with Dr. Fender. In my mind, I walked into his office, with my head high and my shoulders rolled back like I saw the girls at the Monroe's church do. Their eyes seemed to know something I didn't, but I figured I could fake it for the doctor until I figured it out. No sense going in there thinking I had already lost. I was going to see that once Abigail and Bobby had themselves married, I'd be able to leave with them. We'd tell the doctor I was working for them, so I wouldn't be trouble to nobody, and I'd be able to care for my own kin. That and a place to stay had to keep him from forcing me to stay locked away.

Rebecca popped in my mind like a hiccup—hit me so fast that I jumped. I pushed any thought of her out of my mind, because I couldn't stand the idea of me being done like she was. I wouldn't make it. And it wouldn't matter if I made it, anyway, if they took away all the things that I loved. I figured I'd just as well find some way to make myself disappear for real. Being locked away in the asylum wasn't disappeared enough for me.

The night moved on, and I watched, through my window, the moon that only shined half full. Abigail hadn't come to bed yet, and I kept glancing over at the doorway to see if she was going to bounce in and hop on her bed. But she never came. I waited and waited, fighting sleep, because I wanted to see what Bobby had said. I told myself that her not coming back that night was good news. Her not returning meant that she and Bobby got to celebrating early. It crossed my mind that they had left so quickly that they had forgotten me, but then I remembered my farm, and I didn't think she'd pass that up. Plus, I loved her. Bobby or no Bobby, Abigail would be lonely without me, and I would be lonely without her. She was my friend, and I believed I was her friend, too. She wouldn't leave me here waiting with my baby to be born in a few months' time.

The sun shined through my window and cast a bright stream onto the back of my eyelids. I hadn't realized it, but I must have fallen asleep, despite all that worrying. My breath caught when I looked at Abigail's empty bed, the bedsheet unruffled and the pillow untouched. I remembered then that I had Dr. Fender that day, so I pushed the worries down. My worries were getting so heavy, I realized I'd have to work hard to keep my shoulders from slumping during my doctor's visit.

Breakfast didn't sit well with me. I nibbled on some hard bread and had a few slurps of cornmeal mush, but my stomach had butterflies. I held my breath that Abigail would be at breakfast, sitting in her usual seat, and I'd drop my tray next to hers so we could talk about all the great things Bobby had said. How he couldn't wait to marry her.

How he was excited to be a dad. How he couldn't wait for me to come with them. But she never showed.

When Miss Millie appeared in the doorway, I dropped my spoon. The silver clung on the metal plate, and the lady next to me shot her head towards me and scowled. I screeched my seat back and stood up. Miss Millie waved me to come towards her. I picked up my tray and walked down the aisle between tables and spotted my mama, her ragged hair and sad face, sipping mush from a spoon. I wanted to tell her that I was on my way to see the doctor, but I feared she'd just look at me with the same expression she had at that moment, not caring much one way or the other what happened to me, her grandchild, her other children. My heart ached.

I reminded myself of my promise. Shoulders back, chin high. I was going to walk into that Dr. Fender's office and show him just how capable I was of minding my family and farm. It felt like play pretend, but if I was real good, I figured my lie would have legs.

Miss Millie and I waited outside Dr. Fender's door, and for the first time, I noticed his name on a plaque beside it. My reading must have been getting better because I read the 'ender' part. They had a 'Ph' to start it, and I guessed everyone had trouble with mixing up their letters every now and again.

The door swung open, and out crept an old lady hunched like a cane. She didn't look up at me, just stumbled towards the desk and leaned on it to catch her breath.

Miss Mille moved to put her arm around the lady. "Oh, Gertrude. You mustn't worry yourself. I will take you to your duty in the laundry."

She waved for me to go into the room, and my stomach sank at the thought that she wouldn't be standing on the other side of that door, waiting for me. That thought made my shoulders drop low, but I perked them back up, because now was not the time to change plans.

I did one last check on shoulders and chin, then entered the doctor's office, ready to be whatever it was I had to be to get home. I wasn't one for being something I wasn't, but I wasn't one for spending my life locked away either. I had to give this old doctor what he wanted.

"Hello, Doctor Fender," I said, with a soft voice that sounded more like Helen's.

"Please, have a seat," he said, pointing to the small chair in front of his desk.

It looked to be the size of a child's chair, and I couldn't understand why he hadn't replaced it with the fine, big chair sitting on the other side of the office, if he wanted us to sit so close to him.

I sat down, and he breathed a heavy sigh that smelled of onions and liverwurst. I cupped my hand over my mouth, because I was afraid of offending the doctor with the face one makes when the person across from them has breath that smells like onions and liverwurst. "Thank you, Doctor," I said, still cupping my mouth.

"Miss Wilson, have you traveled much?" he asked.

"No, sir. Never been outside of Pennsylvania."

"Oh, that is a shame. Traveling does offer many advantages." He had grown a beard while he was away, a full beard that blended with his mustache and dripped a few inches below his chin. He scratched it with the tip of a sharp pencil. "Let's get to the subject of schooling. How much have you had?"

I paused a minute to think of what he wanted to hear, but I didn't want to be trapped in a lie. "Enough, sir. I've had enough."

"And how long is that?" he said.

"Some here and there. I can't remember just when I stopped, but I received plenty of schooling." I swallowed the lie.

"It says here you had about four years of schooling. A start of the fifth. Does that sound about right?"

"If you have it there, it must be right." I felt my chin drop an inch, and I flicked it up. He judged me by all the ways I fell short. What about all the ways that raised me up? They didn't seem to count a lick in his mind.

"And your mother and father? Tell me about them."

A lump the size of an egg lodged in my throat. Mama and Papa had nothing to do with where I was going. I knew that now. How could this smart doctor not have figured that out? "My mama and papa don't mind my business much. I've been doing what needs to be done around the farm for a long time now, without so much as a crust of bread from them." I crossed my fingers behind my back, and in my mind, I promised I'd do more when I got back

219

home. I'd see to it that no more horses froze in winter, if I could get my hands on another.

He waved his hand at me as if shooing a fly. "Your mother is an inmate here at Farview?"

My leg jerked so hard that my foot kicked the desk. He had no business asking questions he knew full well the answer to. But I put my hand on my knee and smiled like I knew he wanted me to. "Yes."

"And your father?" He sat back on his chair and crossed his arms, as if he had caught me in some sort of lie.

"I'm not sure, sir. He disappeared some time ago. I sure hope he didn't meet ill-fate. He is a good man." I coughed as the words choked out of my mouth. *Dear Lord, please forgive my lies.*

"Hmmm." The doctor flipped through some papers. "He has a history of inebriation, pauperism, poor temper, no? There have been some arrests in his history."

Again, a question he did not need me to answer. I stayed mum this time. Silence was better than any words that confirmed my poor breeding.

"I see you're still carrying," he said, scoffing and pointing at my belly. He perched his glasses on the tip of his nose, as if to closer inspect. "We hope, in cases like these, the pregnancy mercifully ends before full-term, which is not unlikely in cases of poor stock. But it seems the angels are not looking out for you." His tongue clicked on the roof of his mouth.

No one was looking out for me. All I had in this world was me and Abigail. I balled up my fist, wanting so much to haul off and whack him. I slammed it on the desk instead.

He jumped and his eyes grew wide.

"I never asked for this here baby, but like it or not, we're in this together now."

He straightened in his chair and flattened his coat. "In cases such as yours, Miss Wilson, with your history of pauperism, inebriation, a mother already a ward of the state, we tend to favor the science. You will be comfortable here, continuing your work at Farview." He paused for a moment, as he combed through his notes. "I've heard your contributions to the henhouse reflect a good work ethic for someone of your lot." He stared off as if he were no longer talking to me.

I shook my head, trying to make the words stick. "Excuse me? What are saying?" My voice trailed off at the end, like a rumble of thunder.

He cleared his throat. "I think it best you mind who you are speaking to. I will not have the likes of you raising your voice to me." He leaned forward, resting his elbows on the desk. "You will remain here. We will place your child in the almshouse, where someone of proper character can raise him."

My mouth dropped, and my eyes widened, but I couldn't speak.

He must have seen my surprise because he went on. "You must realize, Miss Wilson, even with your limited

221

intelligence, that anyone is better suited to raise your child. You must recognize you are not equipped economically, morally or intellectually to raise a child, if there be any hope for him to become a proper citizen. We must look out for all of humankind, not only ourselves. We are seeking the betterment of society for all. Isn't that what you want?"

His face blurred as blood rushed to my head. My heart raced so fast that I thought I might keel over. I gripped the arms of the small seat and tried to steady my mind. How dare he think I didn't have a place in this world? When my hands grew too sweaty, I held them out in front of me and spread my fingers wide. My vision swirled so much that it looked like a kaleidoscope of hands forming shape after shape. I had no idea how to convince this man I was worth my salt. I had just as much right to be a part of this world as anyone. Then I remembered.

"What if I had a place to go to raise my child? A job? I could live with a married couple and tend the land. You said yourself that I had the work ethic."

"Oh, that you do, Miss Wilson. But who would take such a burden on as you? And with a child, no less? Who would possibly accept such an impediment as you?"

I felt heat rise up the back of my neck, and soon enough, my hair was on fire. "I'm a hard worker, Dr Fender. I have smarts you ain't seen. I can take care of my own, and I won't be a burden to no one."

He smirked and scratched the tip of his nose. "Well, if that's so, I'd see to considering it. We'd have to put you before the committee panel first. But if such an offer, as unlikely as it seems, comes along, it must do so quickly. You see, we will be seeking placement for your child to see that he has proper care from the day he is born." He clustered his papers together and set them in a pile on the side of his desk. "So, if the heavens plan to grant you a wish, I suggest they act quickly."

Those damn stars.

I kept my shoulders back and chin up all the way as I walked out his door. I smiled at the sight of Miss Millie having gotten back already. Then I heard the doctor call for her from inside his office.

"Stay here," she whispered. "I will be right back."

I stayed proud-looking, in case he peeked his head out the door to spy on me. I figured he'd want as much information on me as he could get, unless he had already made up his mind. But I wasn't going to let that thought cave my shoulders. I held them tall until Miss Millie returned, and I kept them like that all the way out the main door and into the cool air. Once that brisk wind hit me, they sunk like the bruised side of an apple. I looked out at the land before me, for what felt like the first time. I hadn't paid much mind to anything lately, except setting myself up to go home. The leaves on the trees had turned a crisp brown when I wasn't looking and already covered the lawn. It reminded me of the paint we used to chip off the bedroom wall and leave speckling our wood floors. Winters on the farm were grueling. Still, I had never noticed how much dying was happening all around us. There was no way to stop it. It made me think how I'd get that farm up and running in the dead of winter. If my counting was right, in January my little one was due. How could I get an old farm back to good with everything frozen and dead? I felt like the whole world was against me. As if those stars conspired to keep me trapped away. But once I proved that old doctor wrong and told him I had a couple who would take me, I knew I'd figure out a way to make a living somehow.

Miss Millie asked, "How do you feel about the meeting?"

"What's a panel?" I asked.

"Oh, it's a group of trustees and board members—people who oversee Farview."

"Why would I go before them?"

She tucked a stray piece of hair under her hat. "Before they release anyone, they must sit before the Board. They ask questions and decide."

"Decide what?"

"If an inmate should stay. Or if they can be released."

"Do they ever let people out?"

"They can't keep everyone, Anna," she said, but I didn't believe her.

Miss Millie was watching me as thoughts spun in my mind. Finally, she cleared her throat and said, "Have you seen Abigail? She's missing."

I turned to look her straight in the eye. "She hasn't shown?" My hands pulled at my hair. "I need to talk with her." My throat dried up like green grass in a drought. I could hardly speak. "No one has seen her?" I started to run to look for her, but Miss Millie grabbed my apron string and pulled me back.

"Where are you going?"

"To find her. I need to find her. Are you sure no one has seen her?" I leaned over, resting my hands on my knees, trying to catch my breath. It was as if my world had been ripped apart—again.

"No one has seen her since last night. The orderlies are to keep an eye out, but with so few, there is little else we can do."

Even though I knew it might lead to more trouble, I asked, "Have you seen Bobby? Maybe he's seen her?"

She pulled me up by my elbow and leaned towards me. "Bobby? Was there something between Abigail and Bobby?" she asked.

We shuffled off the path towards the coop.

I raised my arms to the heavens, as if they ever heard me, and shouted, "Someone must find her! She can't be gone."

There were too many of us who people wanted to forget. Too many nameless faces. Mama was right. We might as well vanish.

Abigail wasn't a nameless inmate at Farview to me. She was my friend. And without her, I'd have no chance of getting home. "I'm going to find her." I took a giant step that sunk into thick mud. Unable to stand any longer, I collapsed in a heap, sobbing. "We need to find her. She's my only way."

Miss Millie stood in silence, as my wails got trapped in the breeze. The scent of dirt and manure filled my lungs, and I gulped for air. When I had cried myself to exhaustion, she helped me stand, then held my elbow as I drew my boot out of the muck. "I'll look for her. I promise. You get on to the coop. You'll be prepping for winter soon, right? Your hens need you."

Miss Millie sure knew me well. "Already started. Nights are getting cold, and you never know when first frost hits. Mother Nature surprises you sometimes," I said through sniffles. I let the mud cake around the folds of my dress, not caring much about anything with Abigail gone.

"Isn't that the truth? Life is full of surprises," Miss Millie said.

My heart felt so empty that I couldn't find words to reply.

"Wait," Miss Millie called.

I stopped near the well and turned back towards her. The chickens started causing a ruckus, hopping around the pen. I started to think they knew me. They were the only things around here that did.

From a few feet away, she said, "Dr. Fender—"

"Spit it out, Miss Millie." Tears still streamed from my eyes, so I wiped them with the back of my hand.

"He says you'll be dividing your time between the hens and work inside, starting tomorrow. It will be temporary. But there are some important visitors coming, and the ladies inside could use the help."

"What are you saying?"

She fidgeted with her dress and straightened her white cap. "I convinced him you needed a couple of days to prepare for weather turning, but then you will start inside." She placed her hand on my shoulder. "It's temporary, Anna. Don't worry. I know how much you love this work."

"It's not fair. I want to stay here. Only here. He said they sold the eggs at the market. How can he do this?"

"There are important visitors, Anna. I'm sure you'll be full-time in the henhouse after they leave."

"He's a good-for-nothing. This ain't fair."

"I know how hurt you must be."

Miss Millie's hands hung by her side, and she did nothing, just like Pa. I didn't say another word to her, just turned to walk towards my babies and watch them cluck at my feet, wrestling with an ache buried deep in my chest, wondering how much more the world could take away from me. Wasn't much I had left, except my baby, and I never asked for him. For all I knew, he'd have Randolph's eyes, and I'd have to find a way to look into them each day and love him anyway. I hated to admit it, but I wondered sometimes if things might have been different if I had learned to use that old coat hanger. Mama hadn't helped me, one bit, to prepare for the world outside. She was a sorry excuse for a mother. If it weren't for her, none of this would have happened. We might not have ever been rich or powerful, but we'd have been together. And that's all I ever wanted.

Chapter Twenty-Six

Miss Millie stood by the old well. I could feel her watching me, as I stepped into the pen and started kicking at the stones that had blown in from the gusts of wind the night before. I ducked into the house and jumped when I saw another inmate there, an egg in one hand, a hoe in the other.

"What are you doing here?" I asked, reaching out to take the hoe.

She stared blankly at me. "Nurse Gladys. She told me to report here today."

I looked at the floor and saw two cracked eggs, streaks of bright yellow crisscrossing a patch of dirt. "Why'd she send you here?"

"This here is my new duty. I'm going to run the coop."

I wanted to sock her good for taking my job. "You ever run a chicken farm before?"

"No, I can't say I have. I picked apples in the orchard, though. Collecting apples is a lot like collecting eggs."

"This job ain't about collecting eggs. It's not about the eggs. It's the chickens. You don't take care of the hens, you won't be seeing any eggs." I took a dustpan from a hook and grabbed the small broom, so that I could sweep up those broken eggs.

She scratched her head, then reached down, saying, "I'm Nan. Nice to meet you."

It was not nice to meet her, so I said nothing back.

"I think that one's dying," she said, pointing to a chicken whose patchy feathers dropped to the ground.

There were feathers all over the dirt, enough to make a pillow, if you wanted to. I collected them each week and turned in the bag to the orderly who paid mind to us when working outside. He'd tip his hat and smile each time.

"He's molting."

"What molten?"

"Molting," I snapped. "They drop their feathers around this time. Grow new ones. Thicker ones. Ones that'll keep them warm for winter."

She shook her head. "I don't understand."

I stomped my foot so loud that the chickens squawked in their nesting boxes. "Don't you know what shedding is? You ever see a mutt shed? Drop clumps of fur to make room for a new coat?"

She smiled, even though I scowled. "I never had a mutt. Dirty, filthy things. No use for them."

I took a basket from the hook. "Did you check for eggs?" I asked, although I knew the answer, because why else would there be cracked eggs on the floor?

"I sure did. Only but a few."

"You didn't take them all, did you? We need to leave extra nest eggs this time of year. They lay less with the cold weather and all."

"I took them all. We need to eat."

"You ain't eating nothing if your hens stop laying. The nest egg gives them a boost. They see that and they think 'This ain't so hard,' then they're more likely to lay again. You take them all, and they feel like the job is too big. You take everything they have, and they feel like it's too hard to get any of it back, so they give up. The trick is to leave them a reminder of what they can do."

"That don't make sense. Hens lay eggs. What else are they here for?"

"I don't have time for talking. I have work to do. So, you just see to it you always leave a few eggs in the nesting boxes. Promise?"

She shrugged her shoulders and said, "Promise."

But I didn't believe her.

I peeked my head out of the door to see if Miss Millie was still by the well, but she wasn't. The single orderly who usually stood by the water pump wasn't there either.

I turned back towards Nan. "I'll be right back. Don't touch an egg until I get back." I returned with a heap of hay and tossed it onto the floor. "Scatter this. Be sure there's plenty to help hold the heat. If you need more, there are bales by the shed out there."

#

I walked the long way around Farview, through the fields and towards the cottages where I'd seen Bobby smoking Luckies with some other orderlies a few times. When I got there, I spied them standing by the propped open door, cigarettes dripping from their lips, a swirl of smoke clouding them. I didn't see Bobby at first and wondered if I should have checked my dormitory first, because he spent time there, minding the place when we were on assignment for the day. As I was about to turn to leave, I saw him, that hook of a nose, and slicked hair that shined like someone just gave him a good polish.

I fluffed up my dress and tightened my braid in the back, so he'd know I meant business. I stayed behind the cover of a piece of an old fence that leaned against a wall, until I was ready. In my head, I counted all the reasons I needed to find Abigail, and all the reasons I knew he was in on her disappearance. Dr. Fender had made it clear that time was something I didn't have. My baby would be born in a few months, and if they did not set arrangements for us, he'd be ripped from my arms before I nuzzled him to my breast. And Bobby; Bobby was the only one who Abigail would share a secret with, besides me. So, if she didn't let on to me where she was hiding, she had to tell him.

I stepped from behind the fence and stomped my feet right up til my nose was inches from his chest. A tall one, for sure. I made myself as big as I could, by sticking out my chest. I felt like a scared cat who fluffed up when a hound spotted him. All the cat really did was show how scared he was. I imagined my shaking voice would do the same for me.

He was smoking a butt, but he flicked it away when he noticed me coming.

"Where is she?" I said, trying to steady my words. The smell of all that smoke made me rub my eyes raw. After a deep breath, I squinted at Bobby and said, "You know where she is."

"Who?" He held a pack of cigarettes, tapped the bottom, and one popped up. He reached down with his mouth and took it, then lit it with a match. The other orderlies watched me from the corner of their eyes but never looked me dead-on. "Who are you looking for?"

"You know who I'm looking for." I put my hands on my hips and rolled back my shoulders again, just like I had for Dr. Fender.

He shrugged and shook his head but said nothing.

"Abigail. I'm looking for Abigail."

"Oh, that dish. I haven't seen her since yesterday."

"You know where she is. You have to."

"Naw. She is always up to something. I'm sure she just hid away for some time. Isn't the first time." He blew a ring of smoke into my face.

"I never seen her disappear like this." I dug my fists into my sides, stamping down all the madness I felt as I watched him take drags on his smoke.

He laughed. "You haven't been around here as long as me. Or Abigail. She knows this place better than anyone. She wants to disappear—she can do it."

He was right. Abigail knew this place better than any of us. She could tuck herself away into any cranny if she wanted to be left alone. A rush of hope coursed through me at the thought. She's hiding. She had to be. She was angry that I had pushed her to talk to Bobby, and now she was teaching me a lesson. But where?

"Where would she go?"

"Hard to hide if people know where you are," he said, and turned his back towards me.

I took a step closer to him and pulled his shoulder to spin him back towards me. "You don't have any idea where she is?" I grew all hot, and my head spun.

"No, ma'am," he said, chuckling. "Can't say I do."

Anger boiled inside me. Without thinking, I stomped hard on his foot with my work boot then turned to run back the way I came. His voice screeched, and I hoped he'd have a sore toe tomorrow to show for his not talking.

He shouted after me, "Get back here, you looney! Get back here."

I never looked back. I didn't have a minute to give, or he'd catch up to me and I'd be in a heap of trouble.

My mind raced. If he didn't know where Abigail was, who would? Where could she be? My stomach roiled over the thought that he didn't mention them marrying. Didn't mention my farm. Did she tell him? Part of me hoped she ran away because of cold feet, before she told Bobby the news, before he decided our future. Papa used to say your future is written in the stars, but I don't believe a lick of that now. My future was written on the back of Bobby, and it wasn't looking good. More than ever, I had to find Abigail to hear it straight from her.

When I got to the back of the main building, I stopped running. I thought back to the nights I had spent locked up there on the top floor and promised myself that if I made it through that, I was going to make it through this. First, I had to track down Abigail. Nurse Gladys was sure to spy me if I went in the front entrance, so I creeped around the back, towards a row of windows. Whirring and clicking sounds echoed from behind the wall, so I knew I must have reached the sewing room. If she wasn't hiding, that's where she'd be. I crept to the wall and reached up toward the lip of the window. My fingertips grazed it. A few feet away sat bales of hay. I carried one over and tossed it under the window. Standing on it made me tall enough to see into that sewing room. By the door was an empty sewing machine where she should have been. A shaking scream rattled through me so loud that the women stopped the whirring of their machines and stared at my pinched face in the window.

I pushed myself away and thudded both feet onto the ground. I sprinted off as fast as a coyote, towards buildings on the far end of Farview. My legs burned by the time I reached the dormitory. I raced to Abigail's chest and tore through her yellowed aprons and nightdresses, until I found her shiny compact tucked in the back corner. It felt cold in my palm and smelled of talcum powder.

It seemed like I spent my whole life depending on people who weren't worth depending on. I thought of

Papa, who left without so much as a goodbye. And Mama, who found leaving as natural as a rain shower. Now Abigail. I had had no other choice but to trust her. She had been my last hope. How dare she turn on me without looking me in the eye!

I ran my fingertips along the ridges of the beautiful, gilt compact, then I opened it and stared into the tiny, silver mirror. My dirty face was so pale that it almost looked purple. Bluish circles sunk under my eyes. I looked like I had been crying forever. Feeling the blood bubbling up inside me, I slammed the compact onto the floor and smashed it with my dirt-crusted boot. The glass crunched as it shattered. I leaned over to see what I had done and glimpsed myself in the shards, pieces of me splintered and broken.

Chapter Twenty-Seven

The next morning, a pinging sound at my window jarred me from a fitful sleep. The sun hadn't risen yet. Most of the women lay in their beds, not stirring, even the ones whose eyes looked like someone had sealed them open with hoof glue. My heart leapt at the thought that it was Abigail. I clasped my hands together and pressed them to my chest.

"Please, please, please," I said in a hushed voice. A tingle ran along my ears and down my neck, as a smile stretched across my face. She couldn't leave me. She loved me as much as I loved her, and she wouldn't abandon me. Abigail, and Bobby maybe, were planning to leave now, and wanted me to know that they'd return for me once they married. My thoughts drifted to an image of me and her running across my field, our field, in our bare feet, with the wind whipping through our hair, our arms stretched out like we could fly.

I threw off my sheet and hopped up to see them tossing stones. I threw open the shade to find a sideways rain pelting at my window. My eyes searched the scrap of land below my window but saw nothing but a scattered bale of hay. My heart sunk. Thick rain sprayed from the sky in a fury, as if God himself were hurling it from the heavens.

I felt the wetness on my face before I realized I was crying. Tears streamed from my eyes, and I couldn't stop them. My heart sped up so fast that I thought it'd burst. Not only was it not Abigail, but it was to be my last day in the henhouse for a while, and I hated to think the rain would keep me away.

As I sat on my bed, I leaned over to touch Abigail's mattress. I wanted to feel close to her, but I also wanted to feel if it was warm, as if she had snuck in and slept a few hours before disappearing again. But it was as cold as night, and the sheet lay as flat as it was the night before. My love for her lit a fire of rage in my chest; she had left me. I didn't think I could survive in this place without her. I didn't want to try. The fire burning through me settled in my ears and pulsed with each rush of heat. I balled the thin sheet in my hands and squeezed as if I might somehow rid myself of the anger and pain.

But soon those feelings caught a new wind. Fear. Without Abigail, I'd never be free from this dreaded place. I had no hope of returning home and reclaiming my siblings without her help. Panic struck me like a rolling barrel and knocked the wind out of me. My chest ached, and my breath came quick and shallow. I crawled towards the back of the bed and pressed my face against the cold bars of the window. Staring at the outside world, the gale whipping through the pines, the hard, slanted rain pummeling stalks of dried corn, I swallowed the spiny truth that without Abigail, I'd be here forever.

The rain let up by the time the sun rose, and so Miss Millie allowed me to finish getting the henhouse ready for winter. I got there early, beating Nan so that I could have some time alone on my last day. I greeted the hens with my usual cheerful voice I reserved for them, no matter how down I was feeling. They clustered by my feet and let me pat their feathered heads.

As the winter was setting in, I started scattering more hay to keep them warm. I combed through each nesting box to check to see they were sturdy and filled with hay. I filled a few bags with sand and set them around the corners of the floor, in case any drafts blew in from the spider cracks along the walls. This might not have been my job no more, but I cared about it still. These hens would always be mine.

Through the door, I heard the wind whip, driving a cold gust through the coop and swishing the hay towards the back wall. I shivered as I spread it out again across the floor, then I gathered my loose gloves and ran to see if rain was returning. I peeked my head out the door and watched as dark clouds moved across the sky. A wall of rain pressed towards the fields. The smell of fresh showers filled the air. Everyone covered their heads with whatever they could find—newsprint, burlap, their hands—and started racing towards the buildings, but I didn't follow them. I sealed up the cracks in the walls with mud and packed the nesting boxes with hay and feathers, so they wouldn't freeze to death over the winter. A clap of thunder shot through the air as I went back into the chicken house. I ducked my head back out to check for lightning, and that's when I saw her.

Abigail.

My heart lightened with the thought that she had returned for me. She had figured out the plan and was coming to take me with her. Bobby had agreed. We would move to my farm, raise our families on the land and eat all the raspberries we could stomach, just as we had planned all along.

But my heart grew heavy when I noticed her expressionless face. Like a ghost floating across the fields, she seemed to have no sense of the world around her. She moved in the opposite direction of everyone else, away from the buildings, and no one seemed to notice. Her hair down, long and soaked with rain, blew in the wind like stalks of wheat. As she moved closer, I saw she was barefoot, dressed in a torn nightdress, a splotch of blood around her waistline. The phantom glided across the dying grass towards me.

"Abigail!" I shouted, but her gaze never wavered. I couldn't tell what she was looking at, but it was as if she couldn't hear me. Louder, I called, "Abigail!"

As she moved deeper into the fields in the coop's direction, I tossed my gloves and ran towards her. I thought maybe she was coming for me. I opened my arms wide, wanting to wrap her in a hug, and shouted again, "Abigail!"

The rain came down harder. I hoped she was heading towards me, looking for comfort because her wandering looked like grief, so I ran hard to meet her. But I stopped when I realized where she was heading. Drenched, I stood frozen as she moved in the direction of the well. "Abigail! I'm here!"

Rooted with panic, I watched as she placed her hands along the lip of the well. She hoisted herself up and stepped one foot onto the stone wall, then the other. Perched tall on the crumbling well, her gown flapped in the wind as she stretched out her arms. She looked like an angel trapped in a storm.

I rubbed my eyes, squinting to make sure that what I was seeing was real.

I thought back to the last time we stood on that well, planning our future and dreaming of a life where we were free, trying to convince ourselves, each other, that the world held promise for people like us.

I watched her lift one foot and hold it over the mouth of the well.

"Abigail! Don't!" I took a step to run to her but stopped for fear I'd push her to do it. She looked at me, her blond hair tossed around her head like a broken halo. "Please, Abigail. Don't," I whispered.

She offered me one last look—her eyes dark—and I knew. Something had happened. Something between her and Bobby, or maybe… maybe with the baby. My heart seized in my chest as Abigail looked down at the long, dark shaft before her. Time seemed to freeze her, and it froze me too, my breath hitched in my throat.

In an instant, she was gone. And with it, my only friend in the world. My only hope of life after Farview. A pain ripped through me, as if someone had torn me in half. My feral cry cut through the stormy air. All hope slipped down the well with my friend, all promise for a future on my own land, with my own family. I'd be lost here, forever, wandering the fields of Farview like a ghost—like my mother.

I raced over and grabbed the edge of the well and peered over. I heard the rain spray down overhead and watched it fill the well. "Abigail!" I called down, my echo being stolen by the heavy waters. The depth of the well was as black as night, and there was no sign of her.

I dropped to my knees in the mud, wailing for my friend.

Miss Millie appeared by my side, placing her arms around my shoulder and shuffling me towards a building. "Come, come," she said over the driving rain.

I reached back towards the well. "I can't leave her. I won't leave her."

"You must. It's too late, Anna. We can't save her."

We walked a few steps, then I collapsed again, burying my face in my hands. I couldn't breathe from the sadness. "She's not gone. She can't be."

Miss Millie sat beside me on the muddy ground and wrapped her arms around me. "I'm so sorry, Anna."

"She can't be gone," I cried. "She can't leave me all alone."

"Let's go. We need to go in."

Thunder rumbled, and a flash lit up the dark sky.

"She's gone," I said, standing to run back to the well.

Miss Mille took my shoulders and pulled me towards the nearest cottage. I looked out over the rain-soaked fields, the lonely henhouse leaning in the wind, and behind it all, I could make out the specks of stone dotting the graveyard, like scattered seeds that never took root.

Chapter Twenty-Eight

An orderly swung open a steel door in the back of a cottage. Miss Millie and I stumbled inside and collapsed on the cement slab in a heap, water pooling around us. The heavy door slammed shut.

I heard the sloshing of Nurse Gladys' wet, rubber-soled shoes. She ran towards us down the narrow hall, swinging a ring of keys by her side. "What in heaven's name is going on?"

I buried my face in the crook of Miss Millie's arm. I couldn't face anyone, especially not Nurse Gladys.

"It's Abigail. She jumped," Miss Millie said. Her voice sounded distant, like she was a world away and not right there with me.

My heart sped up. I heard Abigail calling to us from the bottom of the well. "We have to go back. We have to get her out!" I shouted.

"Where is she? Where did you say she jumped?" I could hear Nurse Gladys' heavy panting, on account of the running.

"The well," Miss Millie said, clipping each word. "She's down the well."

I grabbed the collar of Miss Millie's shirt and shook her. "She's calling for us to save her. We can't leave her there." I pushed off the floor and ran towards the door.

My hand wrapped around the knob, but Nurse Gladys snatched my shoulder and slammed me down. "You're hysterical, child. Nonsense. There's no use trying to save her now."

"She's calling for me. I can't leave her." I covered my ears to drown out the sound of my wailing. My head grew dizzy, then I collapsed onto Miss Millie.

"That child always was some sort of trouble. Can't help her kind, that's for sure." Nurse Gladys reached down and flung my wet hair in disgust. "You get cleaned up," she said, as she wagged her finger at me. "We'll have none of this nonsense today." Then she stared right at Miss Millie. "We don't have all day. There's work to be done." She shook her head. "No sense coddling the inmates. They'll never learn."

"We need to let her calm down. She's clearly in no—"

Nurse Gladys snapped, "She can get herself cleaned up and back to work, or she can calm down in solitary for a few days."

"She's done nothing wrong."

"Insubordination." Her voice rose over the pounding rain. "She and that Abigail were nothing but trouble together." Nurse Gladys huffed. "See to it that she gets to work in the kitchen as Dr. Fender requested."

My mind flashed to the kitchen, nowhere near my henhouse. My wailing kicked up again, and I fell into a slump as I realized that my whole world, as little as it had become, was being ripped away.

Miss Millie finally pulled me to my feet, so I followed her without saying a word. When we reached the room, I dove onto my bed then crawled, sopping wet with shoes still on, to the head. Miss Millie took the hem of my dress and shimmied it up over my head, then unlaced my boots and pulled them off, one at a time. Even my knickers were soaked clean through, so she took the waistband and tugged them off. Slowly, she slipped off each wet sock, then covered me with the sheet. She sat down next to me in my bed, wrapping her arm around me.

"You don't deserve this, Anna. You don't deserve this." Her voice sounded like a song.

I covered my face with my hands and cried. "Neither did Abigail."

"No. She didn't. But you didn't make that happen."

"What if I did? I pushed her to ask Bobby to marry her." I figured there was no sense lying now. "It was my fault she asked him. Now she's dead."

She patted my leg through the sheet. "It's not your fault. What went on between her and Bobby had nothing to do with you."

My mind rushed to the image of Abigail balancing on the well. I imagined I'd see it forever. "I didn't stop her."

245

"Oh, Anna, you couldn't have stopped her. She made up her mind before she even walked onto the field this morning."

"I'll miss her so much. I thought we'd live forever together. Raise our families together. She and I were going to be like sisters." I breathed a heavy sigh that emptied me.

She held me tighter. "What do you mean?"

"She was my ticket home. Without her, I'll be here forever. And nothing I do can fix this." I swallowed hard, trying to stop the crying. "Abigail didn't deserve this. How could I let her down?" I curled into Miss Millie, our cheeks pressing together. "And now I'll never get home."

Miss Millie said, "You can't save Abigail now. But you have a baby to take care of. And your family. Your sisters and brother are counting on you."

"I'll disappoint them all. I'll never be free. Not without Abigail's help."

Her voice rose. "You don't need Abigail to save you. You can do this yourself."

My voice rose to match hers. "How? There's no way I can pass some stupid test. They'll never let me go. That panel won't even give me a chance."

Miss Millie took my hand and held it tight. "They believe what they're doing is right. They don't want to lock everyone away, but they think that's what's best for all of us."

"What if they're right? Maybe the world is better with me locked away."

"Do you really think that it is? Can you tell me the world is better off without you?"

I took a deep breath and held it until I thought my lungs would burst. "What if it is?"

"What if it's not? What do you think you can do if you're not in here?"

I hated Miss Millie for expecting so much of me. I thought she was giving me too much credit. I shook her arm off me and scooted away, my back pressed to the window, the cold of the glass shivering up my spine.

She moved her face so close to mine that I could feel the warmth of her breath. "What do you think you can do if you're not locked in here?"

In my mind, I saw my home and imagined what'd it be like with me back in it. I knew more now. I'd take better care of it. Of everyone. My heart slowed at the thought. "I'd make my farm the best farm on Shaker Street. We'd grow tomatoes, and corn, and peas. I'd get the chicken coop running again. We'd have some broilers and a brood of hens that will lay more eggs than you've ever seen. My sisters and brother will go to school, and they'll never be hungry. We'll have fresh tomatoes and scrambled eggs for dinner every night. And toast. I'll make my grandma's bread every morning so we can have fresh baked bread with butter." I paused and rubbed my round belly. "And maybe this little one will be all giggles and hiccups. And I'll read a story to him every night." I dropped my eyes, ashamed that my dream had the same chance as roasting snow on a wood stove.

247

Miss Millie lifted my chin and looked into my eyes. "That sounds like a pretty good life you can have for yourself. It doesn't sound like the life of someone who should be locked away."

She was right. But the bars. Being locked away changed a person. Forced them to become what someone else thought they were. I was feebleminded, poor, ill-character. What I thought of myself didn't matter here. Those bars separated me from all the parts of myself I loved. "But what if I can't prove it?" The rain beat on the window like an angry woodpecker. "I don't think I can."

"Believe in yourself, Anna. If you don't believe in you, no one else will."

"You do," I said.

Miss Millie smiled. "Sometimes we need someone else to point out just how much we can do."

"Like the nest egg," I said.

"What's that?" she asked.

"In the coop. How we leave an egg in the nest to remind the hens that they have what it takes to lay an egg."

"You know what I think?" she said. She pointed to my belly. "This little one here. This is your nest egg. When you doubt yourself, you remember him. He'll remind you; you can do it."

I placed my hand on my belly and felt the mound of a heel. It wasn't love I felt, but for the first time I knew he was mine. "Where do I start? How do I show Dr. Fender that I can do it?"

"Do you know what I do when I'm scared? I start right where I am. So just do all the things you know you can do outside of here, while you're here. Do what you can. Start right here, and eventually I bet you'll be doing it in your own home on the farm."

Her words warmed me. "Do you think?"

"I know."

Miss Millie helped me put on dry clothes. She placed her hand on my shoulder and looked me in the eye. "You're going to start in the kitchen today. Do you know what that means?"

"What?" I asked.

"One more chance to prove to everyone you are more than enough."

As we prepared to leave, Miss Millie turned back towards my trunk. "Your letter. Is it still in your trunk?"

"It is," I said.

"Can I have it?"

I stared at her but did not respond.

"I'll return it. I promise. But," she said, looking down at her white shoes, then back up at me, "I can use it to locate your family. You should know where they are."

"You would do that for me?"

"Of course. And in the meantime, I'll try to figure out when Dr. Fender will call on you again. The Board is touring the grounds soon, so that will distract him for now. But I can't imagine it'd be much longer."

I went in my trunk and slid the letter out from my book. "Here," I said, handing it to her. "Please find them."

"I promise I will," she said.
I hoped the stars heard her.

Chapter Twenty-Nine

When I arrived in the kitchen, a girl stooped in the corner scrubbed a yellowish stain with a dingy rag. I watched her, while waiting for instructions from an orderly who was supposed to meet me there. Her thin hair and gray skin made her look like a shadow.

"Hello," I said, but she didn't glance up, so I scanned the room for a hint of where I should start.

Dinner wasn't for a few hours, but I had no idea what kitchen help did, aside from cooking meals and cleaning up afterwards. I had only been in the kitchen once before, to sort the silver with Abigail. My heart grew heavy as I looked at the table where we stood hatching our disastrous plan. I realized now how naïve we were to believe in such dreams. At that moment, it was as if Abigail was standing next to me. I could feel her. I tried so hard to hold onto the feeling, but it vanished, like when waking from a dream, and the more I tried to hold onto the memory of her, the faster it fled. The stars were not aligned for Abigail and me.

I shook the thought from my mind and stared at the girl scrubbing. "Excuse me," I said, but she paid me no mind. "An orderly was supposed to meet me. Have you seen him?"

She shot me a hard look, her wide eyes meeting mine for a second, then returning to whatever it was she was working on.

A broom sat in the corner, next to a dustpan and brush. Not wanting to wait any longer, I got to work. As I walked towards the corner, my boots stuck to the floor. At home, dirt from the farm always worked its way into our kitchen, our most-used room in the house. But this felt different. The film clung to my boots, like static in an apron.

The girl in the corner worked on the same spot. As I neared her, I realized there wasn't any special stain where she worked, yet now she used the edge of her thumbnail to chip away at peeling wood.

"I'm going to sweep," I said, hoping for at least acknowledgment. I was lonely. I missed my friend. And I knew an hour of silent chores would leave my mind to wander, and I wanted nothing less than that.

At one end of the kitchen, a dark, wooden wall cabinet held a large, white, marble stone for bread making. I ran the tips of my fingers along the cold, smooth surface and leaned down to inhale. The scent of yeast and flour brought me back to baking bread with Mama. Before John was born, we'd bake bread almost every day, then eat it warm before the butter melted. She taught me her mama's recipe, who learned it from her mama. For all the mamas in my family, I wished one stuck around. A tear stung the edge of my eye, so I wiped it with the back of my hand then stomped my foot. No crying was going to help me now.

I put the stone out of my mind and went back to sweeping. Underneath the cabinet, piles of rat and mouse droppings littered the edge of the wall. I squatted down to sweep the pellets into a pile. After brushing them into the dustpan, I emptied them into the trash. I jumped when I heard a man's voice boom.

"You're the new kitchen help?"

"Yes, sir." I didn't bother with my name.

"The Board arrives in less than a week. You must clean the kitchen for their visit."

"Yes, sir." I wanted to ask some questions: Where should I start? How will I know when I'm done? But he turned and left before I had a chance. There were so few workers. If it weren't for the inmates, the place would cave in. But then, I figured if it weren't for the inmates, there'd be no need for the place, and either way, we might all be better off if it just caved in.

The girl scraping at the floor kept at it.

"Can you grab a broom? A mop?" I asked. But nothing. My skin suddenly felt covered in spiders. The room spun. "Help me clean up!" I shouted.

I held the broom handle tight in my hands and steadied myself. Looking over again at the counter where Abigail and I worked together, I thought of how angry I was at her for finding me trouble. My stomach twisted. How had I not seen the mess she was in? What a fool I was to think only about saving myself! I believed Abigail was fine, because

I wanted to. Now it had cost her her life. If I had been a better friend, I could have saved her. Her death was on me.

I went back to sweeping, trying hard to block out Abigail's high-pitched voice in my head, her nest of blonde hair that kept creeping into view.

When I finished, I checked a broom closet for a mop and bucket. I hauled the bucket to the sink and half filled it with water, before pouring in a cup of ammonia. It splashed as I set it on the floor, and some sprayed the scraping girl.

I yelled at her again, "Get up! What are you going to do all day? Just sit there?"

She didn't look up, but her nail got to scraping harder, so I knew she heard me.

I sloshed the water onto the floor, then pushed it around with the string mop. As the floor got to shining, my head got to thinking more about the mess I was in. Miss Millie believed in me, but there was no good reason. I didn't have any proof that I could handle any of the life I had said I wanted for myself. We had barely made it through the winter with Mama gone. I liked to think that me and Helen had worked together, but there were nights I'd kick her off the mattress, for a little breathing room. I wasn't even able to keep those poor kittens alive. Who was I to think I could take care of my Helen, John, and Alice? Let alone a baby? Then there's Abigail, who I had already let down in the worst possible way. Maybe Dr. Fender was right. Maybe Mama was right. How could a girl like me take on all those responsibilities?

By the time my mind finished swirling like a tornado, the floor shined. And I had decided Miss Millie was wrong. I still hoped she'd find my siblings, so I'd know where they were in this big world. But they were better off without me. A girl like me had no business minding those three and a baby.

#

By the next morning, my insides felt hollowed out, like a roaster waiting to be stuffed. All my life, I had had enough fight in me to battle a wolf if he wandered into my henhouse, but today I knew that it had up and left. I could barely lift my arms to dress for the morning, and the old dress seemed heavier than a sack of flour. Even my heart weighed as much as concrete. I forced myself to think about Abigail, Helen, Alice, John, my baby, but it didn't skip or thump or nothing. I wondered if Mama's feelings had up and left like mine, before she took off. Abigail? Maybe Papa, too? Do you wake up one day and realize you don't have fight or hope? Without those, I can't see much use for putting on your boots and hauling hay.

I couldn't take breakfast, not wanting any reminders of Abigail. Instead, I headed to the kitchen for work a few minutes early. An orderly told me to report by the dining hall door for a truck delivery. When I got there, four other women waited under the bright morning sun. Two had wide builds and stood almost a foot taller than me. One was about my size, but her gray hair and crinkling skin made her look ancient. And the last was a girl who might have been younger than me. Her skinny arms shook, as we watched the driver fumble with the key and open the tailgate.

Packed inside were more boxes and bags of food than I'd ever laid eyes on. Cereal of all kinds, heavy sacks of white flour, bright-blue tins of Crisco, and alongside them, rows of Fleischmann's yeast tins. I knew them all from Mama.

"Haul these to the basement. Be quick about it," the driver said.

I looked around for an orderly to ask where we unload them, but no one was there. I let the other women go first, hoping they'd worked this duty before. After scooping up what I could handle, I followed the others into the building and down a narrow flight of stairs that wound towards a root cellar. It was a lot bigger than ours on Shaker Street and had shelves lined floor to ceiling. There were cabinets along a far wall, which stretched corner to corner. My mouth dropped wide when I saw the refrigerator tucked towards the back. I'd never seen one so big and imagined it packed full of eggs and milk.

"On the shelves with that," one woman said, as she walloped me on the back. "Stop your gawking."

I stacked the cereal boxes in a row and went back to the truck for more. After five or six trips, we had everything on the shelves orderly.

"So much food," I said out loud, as I admired our work.

The woman who shoved me, who I noticed now had a gaping hole in the center of her mouth where she was missing teeth, said, "Never looks like this. This is for the Board. Will be gone by the end of the week, back to the grocer to sell."

"What?" I asked. "It's not ours?"

"We eat what we grow. And they sell the best of that at the market. This here is to make the Board think we're living the high life."

"Why would they want them to think that?" I asked.

The other tall woman said, "You'll live like royalty these next few days. But don't get used to it." She scratched her head and looked me up and down. "You're a hard worker. I suppose that's why you're in the kitchen. We always serve the Board lunch when they visit. Hope you can cook."

"Oh, I'm not much of a cook. But I've baked a little. With my Mama." The sound of my voice surprised me. I had spoken little the last day, and to hear me, I sounded almost happy. "She and I used to whip up a loaf every day, before my siblings got home from the schoolhouse." I was about to add how much Papa loved our bread, but I stopped myself. I didn't want to poison the memory. The more time passed, the more I realized Papa didn't just leave me. He left Mama, too. He didn't deserve any part of my memory.

"Well, when it comes time for the cooking, you make the bread. Sue, here," she said, pointing to the woman missing teeth, "makes the potatoes and the beets. Nancy," she said, as the young one lifted her head, "will bake a pudding. I'll work on the pot roast and carrots, because that's my specialty, and Gayle," she said, motioning to the older lady slouched by the shelves, "we just going to let her help where she can. She ain't got a lot left in her, and I'll be damned if we're going to let her give it all to the Board."

"I'm happy to do it," I said, "but I haven't baked bread in years. I'm not sure I remember how."

"Haul up a sack a flour and practice tomorrow between meals. Don't make a huge batch. We don't have enough to feed fresh bread to everyone. But a flat loaf of bread will get us all sent to solitary. So best you practice."

"Thank you," I said, pausing for her name.

"Jesse. The name's Jesse."

"Nice to meet you," I said. And I smiled at the thought of baking bread for the first time since I'd been back home and before Mama left.

I flung a sack over my shoulder and brought it back up the narrow steps to the kitchen, then opened a cabinet to hide it there until the next day. In the back of the cabinet, a cluster of bright-white rats huddled in the darkness. I screamed at the sight of them, and they scattered into a hole in the corner. All but one. He stood stark still. His pink eyes glowed in the dark space. They made me think of a dress I had made for Alice once. I fashioned it from a flour sack, and she begged for it to be red. I dyed it using beet skins, but I didn't have enough. The finished dress was a soft pink, not a bright red like she had asked for. But she loved it just the same. And this rat, his eyes, made me see her twirling in the parlor in her prized dress, as if heading to a ball.

I left the cabinet door open and searched the kitchen for a crumb to feed him. On the counter, behind a canister, I found a crust of brown bread. It was hard and crumbled when I picked it up, but I didn't think he'd mind. I ducked back down into the cabinet and set the crumb next to him. He scooped it up with his paws and shoved the entire piece in his mouth, then darted into the hole where the others escaped. I closed the doors and hoped that I'd see him the next day when I came back for the flour.

Chapter Thirty

The rest of the day, I helped prepare the meals and ate with the other helpers in the kitchen once everyone was served. I was glad to not have to sit at the table with everyone else. I didn't even want to see Mama. Now that I gave up getting out, I didn't want to see anyone who would make me rethink my choice. Giving up my family and my farm wasn't going to be easy, but it had to be easier than trying to gain freedom and failing. And there was no way I'd ever succeed.

The next morning after breakfast, Miss Millie found me in the kitchen with my head tucked in the cabinet. I was looking for the rat, whom I named Ralph, when she came up behind me.

"Anna, I have good news," she said.

I jumped at the sound of her voice. "Yes, Miss Millie? What is it?"

She squatted next to me and peeked into the cabinet. She smiled at the little pile of mush in the corner. "Have you made a friend?"

"Trying to," I said.

She patted my head. "So, I spoke with Nurse Gladys. Dr. Fender will assemble a panel to evaluate releases, after the Board visit. So, it won't be much longer now."

"What's that mean?"

"It means you'll go before the committee. They'll hear your case and evaluate you. I think you have a good chance of freedom."

"I'm not doing it."

"What?" Her voice pitched.

I shook my head. "I will not go before no panel. I can't do it."

Her eyes grew wide. "But you can. Are you afraid to go before them?"

"It's not that I'm afraid of them. Even if they let me out, which they won't, I can't take care of my family. My farm. This baby. I can't do it. I'll fail. And I'll let them all down."

"Where is this coming from? I thought we decided you could do it."

"That was you, Miss Millie. I never said I could do that." I checked again for Ralph, then realized he'd never come out with us jabbering. After closing the door, I stood up next to Miss Millie.

"What about all you wanted to do? The farm? Raise your baby? Get your sisters and brother? Learn to read? You were so excited."

I took a deep breath. "I was supposed to do all those things with Abigail. I can't do it alone. I can't. I'm not going before the panel."

"What about Helen, and Alice, and John?"

"I want to know where they are. I will really appreciate if you can find them for me. But…" I paused, not wanting to say the words.

"But what?"

"They're better off without me. Dr. Fender is right. Mama is right. They have a much better chance with anyone else but me. I can't give them what they need."

"Don't say that. You are enough. You can do this."

"I'm sorry to let you know. But I made up my mind."

With that, I turned from her and walked out of the kitchen, even though my shift wasn't over. I snuck out the back door and ran as fast as I could to the dormitory. I didn't want to see anyone or hear anyone. In all my life, I'd never felt more lonesome, yet all I wanted was to be alone.

#

When I reached the empty dormitory, my racing heart kept pace with a red fox. Quiet rarely visited this madhouse, so when it did, it made my jitters worse. I walked between the row of beds, until I reached Abigail's. I touched the stiff mattress and coarse blanket, imagined her lying there, waiting for me to lie with her, her curled like a tulip. Once I climbed onto her bed, I placed her pillow between my arms, against my swollen belly. Hugging it, I tucked my knees close to me and cried. The tears came easily and soon turned to sobs.

Wiping my wet face on her pillow, I whispered, "I'm so sorry, Abigail. I never realized how much you meant to me." I struggled to catch my breath.

I lay there in the quiet, trying to feel her next to me. I wished so much for one last chance to watch her eyes glow with the hint of trouble. Suddenly, the faint sound of shoes squeaking down the hall cut the silence, so I wiped my face and listened harder. The sound grew closer. A girl's voice hit a high-pitched giggle, and a deeper voice shushed her. Afraid of being caught, I rolled off the bed and slipped underneath, careful not to smash my baby belly against the bed. I shifted sideways to squeeze myself into the tight space. Layers of dust itched my nose. I held it tight to keep a sneeze from coming. That's when I heard his voice. Clear as a full moon in the night sky. Bobby.

"No, baby, you're my girl. There's no one else," he said.

From under the bed, I couldn't see who the girl was, but her laugh shot through the room like a strike of thunder.

"Oh, Bobby," she said, and I watched from under the bed, her feet shuffling to catch up with his.

They moved further into the room towards where I hid—Abigail's bed. Inches from where I lay were this girl's worn boots and his scuffed, white, work shoes.

He took a few more steps towards the bed of the girl he had once loved. Or so I thought. His feet were so close that I could smell the manure. I cupped my hand over my face and breathed slowly through my mouth.

Bobby sat down on the bed, pressing it closer towards where I lay trapped, and said, "Come on, baby. You know you can trust me."

I imagined him doing this for the first time with Abigail. My friend had had no one in the world who had loved her. Her father had dumped her here and never looked back. She would have fallen for the first person who smiled at her. How many others were before her? How many would be after? Blood flooded my head at the thought. I tried to breathe slowly to stop the dizziness, careful to keep my breath low so I wouldn't give myself away.

The girl jumped onto the bed with Bobby, and it nearly smashed the baby in my belly. My heart sunk at the thought that he chose Abigail's bed for his deed. From under the bed, I saw her apron drop to the floor, then her dress, then her knickers. His shirt dropped next, then his white pants, then stained briefs. I stared at the pile of clothes and tried not to listen to the sound of their breath growing louder and louder.

She giggled again. Then he grunted like a workhorse. The bed rocked, and I feared the thin metal frame would collapse on top of me. I sucked in my breath to make myself even smaller, wrapped my hands around my belly, closed my eyes, and tried not to listen. When I couldn't hold my breath any longer, I sighed too loudly and then figured I had to pace my breath with the rhythm of their pounding, so they wouldn't hear me. I swore over the noise of their carrying on, and I heard Abigail's voice echo in my right ear: 'Pinky swear.' The sound of her made me flinch, and my heel banged into the leg of the bed.

The thrashing stopped as fast as a wheelbarrow striking a ditch.

"What was that?" the girl asked.

"What? I didn't hear anything." He moved again.

"I heard something," she said.

"It isn't anything. Come on. We're almost finished. Let's be quick before someone comes 'round."

"I thought you said no one was going to catch us," she shouted.

"Shh. Stop shouting," Bobby said.

She said, "I'm not shouting. I'm talking. You said no one would be here."

He sighed. "Look. Do you see anyone? No one's here." There was a pause, then he said, "Let's not fight. We don't have much time."

Their bodies moved again. I held my mouth to silence myself. I wanted to scream and call attention to what they were doing, but I didn't trust Bobby. If no one came running in when I called, I'd be a sitting duck. There was no telling what his kind would do. For a few more minutes, the two bounced on the thin pad, then he let out a high-pitched squeak before thumping onto the mattress.

"Is that it?" she asked. "Are we done?"

"Yeah, baby. Isn't that nice?" he said in a weak voice.

She turned and placed her feet on the floor. Her boots were still laced. She reached down to the floor to pick up the clothes, and I prayed she wouldn't notice me.

"Here," she said, laughing.

I wondered what she found so funny about Bobby. I imagined her finding out a few months from now how she wasn't Bobby's only girl, and she wouldn't be laughing so hard then. I wondered if Abigail found out before she jumped down the well, if her jumping had anything to do with this girl who now shared Abigail's bed with the person that she thought would marry her and take her away from all this sadness.

I knew then I couldn't let Bobby slide. He deserved to hear how much pain he had caused Abigail, and I wanted him to know that I knew what type of man he was. All Abigail had wanted was to be his wife and raise their baby. She had loved Bobby and believed in him. Why was no one trustworthy in the world?

I realized then that I wasn't being so trustworthy myself. As I listened to Bobby and the girl get dressed, I thought about how I was giving up on myself. And if I did that, I'd be letting everyone I loved down. I was no better than Bobby. Being there for someone, being the person that they needed you to be, was hard. Giving up was easy. My family, this baby, deserved better than that. They deserved someone who would do everything she could to be there for them. I decided that even if I failed, I would not fail without giving it my all. I'd be there for them, and I'd show Dr. Fender, the panel, Mama, myself, that Anna Wilson wasn't the kind of person who would let someone who loved her down.

Bobby and I were nothing alike. He wasn't there for Abigail when she had needed him. She deserved better, and I'd make sure he knew it. He had no right to live some happily-ever-after when Abigail didn't get hers. But I did. And my family sure did. I needed to get back on track to doing right by my people. Bobby would have to wait.

Chapter Thirty-One

After I heard Bobby and the girl's footsteps move further away, and the heavy door to outside bang closed, I slipped from under Abigail's bed and dug through my trunk to find my book. A shock of nerves hit me when I didn't see the letter tucked inside, but then I remembered that Miss Millie took it. I was glad I told her I still wanted to know where they were, because there was no time to spare. I may have lost my faith in myself, but I knew Miss Millie's faith was as reliable as the sun.

Afraid someone might discover me in the dormitory instead of the kitchen, I took the book and returned to under the bed. The light was meager in the room, but enough streamed in from the window behind Abigail's bed that I could read my book. I read the rest of the day until nightfall, when the light faded, and the other women returned for bed. I blended in with the others, sliding out from under the bed and dressing in my bedclothes. We paced down to the washroom, where I waited in line to clean my face and teeth before returning to bed. My stomach rumbled as I had skipped the full day of meals, but losing Abigail made my stomach queasy, and I doubted I'd have been able to keep much down, anyway.

That night I couldn't sleep. I tossed and turned, my thoughts drifting, from the fear of going before the panel, to my heartbreak over losing Abigail. To distract myself, I replayed the times that Mama and I had baked bread while Helen and Alice played in the fields. I pictured the tin measuring cup filled twice to the rim with flour. I remembered heating the water in a pot over the wood stove, then letting it sit until it was cool enough to touch. We'd pour some into a smaller measuring cup and mix in a cake of yeast and some sugar. It smelled warm, no matter how cold it was outside. Then we'd mix that together with half the flour and just enough Crisco to make it moist. We'd use our hands to blend it all together and sprinkle in some salt and the rest of the flour. When we first started, we formed loaves in tins. After the holes took over the roof in the kitchen, we used the tins to catch the drips. Eventually they rusted out too much to bake with, so we started molding the dough into mounds we had baked on a stone.

Thinking about baking the bread made me feel better about the week ahead. I hadn't looked forward to anything in a long time, and I couldn't wait to get my hands sticky with dough.

Morning came, and I don't think I slept a wink. They did not permit me in the kitchen until the breakfast crew finished cleaning up, so I ate my mush real slow while I watched the other inmates set off to their duties. Everyone seemed busier than they ever had before, and I imagined it was on account of the Board coming for the visit in less than a week. That meant my panel visit would come soon too, and the thought stirred up butterflies in my belly.

#

In the kitchen, I went into the cabinet to take out the flour and check for Ralph. The mush I set out was gone, but there was no trace of him. I hauled the heavy sack onto the counter and dug through a cupboard for some measuring spoons and cups. I found salt, sugar, and yeast cakes, and I set them out. The only thing I couldn't find was Crisco, but I knew there were plenty of tubs in the basement.

"Look who's here early," a voice said from the doorway.

I looked to see Jesse standing there, with her hair pulled up in a tight bun. She walked towards me and yanked on my braid.

"You better get that hair up before someone sees you. Hair needs to be up in the kitchen." She fumbled through a drawer by the door, found a hair tie, and pulled my braid up in a high bun on top of my head. "Now you're ready."

I said, "Thank you."

She pointed to the ingredients on the counter. "You're practicing your bread recipe. Good girl."

"I am," I said. "I think I remember most of it, too." A smile crossed my face. Gayle walked in and nodded hello before washing dishes. I thought for a moment, then said, "I'm going to make two separate loaves, to see which way it comes out best. I'll try to figure out how much sugar, salt and water to use. Those I don't remember so much." I stopped and scratched my head.

"What's that? What are you thinking?" Jesse said.

"I… I need the Crisco."

"What's that Crisco? I never heard of it."

"It's the grease. We unloaded it from the trucks. Those blue tins. They're the grease I need for my bread. Do you think we can use a can?" I asked.

"We sure can. I'm in charge of the kitchen after breakfast, and I say you can use it." She stood a little straighter when she spoke. "I'll even go fetch it for you. You get to work, because we have people to impress."

I laughed, as I filled a pot with water and set it on the wood stove. The kitchen was more like the Monroe's than mine, so I knew how to turn on the fire with no help.

The water simmered by the time Jesse returned. I turned it off and moved the pot to a hot plate to cool before adding the yeast. We didn't always have yeast at home, so sometimes we made do without. But since they had it here, I figured I'd have a fuller loaf if I used it.

I set to work making the first batch, then set it aside in a metal bowl rubbed with Crisco like Mama used to do. Then I went on and made the second batch, adding a little more salt and a bit more water to this one, to make the dough stickier. Both needed time to rise, so I set them near the stove where it was warm and covered them with yellow tea towels.

As I was cleaning up the counters, Miss Millie came in to see me. I was wondering why she had such a frown on her face, until I remembered that I had told her I had done given up getting out of here, the last time we spoke.

"I need to tell you something," I said, as I wiped up specks of flour.

"What's that?" she said.

I looked around and saw that Jesse and Gayle were busy in the corner, working on something for lunch. "I decided I'm going to try. I'll go before that panel if that's what Dr. Fender wants me to do. I'm not saying I'll like it. But I'll do it if it means I might get my farm and family back." I pointed to my belly that was flush against the counter. "And that I can keep the baby."

"Oh, Anna, I'm so happy. You're making a good decision."

She hugged me, and I didn't push away, even though I wanted to. I needed to let people in if I was going to be ready to have a family again.

"What's that smell?"

"That's the yeast, probably."

"Are you baking?" Miss Millie said.

Jessie piped up from across the kitchen. "She sure is. She's in charge of the bread. Going to be a showstopper when the Board visits." She smiled. "You know that lunch is the best we've got to offer around here. Our laundry and dressmaking," she said, pulling on the crooked hem of her apron, "isn't going to impress anyone."

"What a great idea!" Miss Millie said. "And it smells delicious already."

"Few more hours before I can bake it. But it'll be ready to try around dinnertime. I'll sneak you a piece."

Miss Millie smiled and said, "I'd love that." She walked over to the bowls and peeked under the towels. "I can't wait."

I slipped off my kitchen apron and hung it on a hook by the ice chest. As I turned, she took my arm and pulled me close to her.

"Come with me. I have my lunch now, and I think we can spend some time preparing for Friday."

"Friday? What's Friday?" I asked.

"The panel will see you. I confirmed with Nurse Gladys this morning. She was reluctant to add you to the list, but I convinced her. The Board tour will be Wednesday and Thursday. They will hold panels on Friday."

"What's today?" I asked.

"It's Monday."

I counted on my fingers. Two days until they'd be here. Only four days before the panel. "I can't do it." The room started spinning. I leaned my hands on my knees to help steady myself.

"You can. Let's go practice reading a bit. You are ready for this."

I swallowed hard and stood straight. I thought back to lying under that bed and listening to Bobby and that girl. Mama told me I should listen to Dr. Fender and let someone else take care of my family. Papa didn't so much as say goodbye when he left. Anger boiled inside me. I would not let down the people who were counting on me. Everyone around me seemed to do it so easily, but that wasn't Anna Wilson. If anyone was going to keep me from my people, they'd have to do it with me booting them in the belly.

Chapter Thirty-Two

We walked outside into the crisp air. The leaves glowed red, orange, and yellow. Even the brown leaves scattered on the ground seemed to glow. The wind whipped along the trail.

Shivering, I said to Miss Millie, "I hadn't been paying much attention to time. Is it October yet?"

"Just turned. Won't be long, and winter will set in."

My belly felt heavy from the weight of my growing baby. I'd been wishing that time would stand still until I could get myself out of here. I didn't keep track, because every day seemed one day closer until this baby was born, and the thought of meeting him tied my stomach in knots, but the thought of losing him made me as scared as a mouse stuck in a trap. Now the time was coming, and my feelings about laying eyes on this child weren't any more sorted out than when I had started.

I gazed up at the colorful tree line and said, "Only three months until he's born."

"And he's going to stay with you." Her voice sounded so sure that I almost believed her.

"I feel awfully big for three more months to go." My belly had been poking out more and more each day. I couldn't imagine it growing much bigger. I'd hardly eaten since I'd been at Farview, but this little one seemed to take every scrap I managed to keep down.

Miss Millie laughed. "Oh, it'll get bigger. But you're going to be home by then."

"What about my sisters? And John?" I was afraid to ask, but the thought had been nagging at me. "Have you found them?"

Miss Millie's eyes looked at the ground, then up towards the trees. "Not yet. But I just started looking. I'll find them. We have the letter, so we know they're accounted for. It might take a little time, but before long, you'll know where they are. And we'll start seeing about getting them back to your farm with you and your little one."

A cool gust swept through the trees. I felt alive and hopeful for the first time, like the shock of wind woke me from a deep sleep. "Why do you want to help me so much?" I asked. I hadn't trusted Miss Millie in the beginning, but as time passed, I saw she wasn't quick to give up on me. But I couldn't understand why she wanted to help me. There were so many of us locked away for no good reason. Why me?

Miss Millie reached for my hand. "Oh, it's ancient history. Sometimes we can't let things go."

"Let what go?"

She sighed. I could tell she didn't want to talk, by the way she kept looking out into the sky, as if it were the breeze asking about her story.

Finally, she inhaled a deep breath, then exhaled, her breath so warm that it turned to mist. "My mother, I guess," she said. A gale swept her voice away. I leaned in to better hear. "She suffered a terrible childbirth with my younger sister. My mother survived, but the child didn't make it."

"She died?" I gasped.

"Yes. She was born dead. The doctors swear they never even had a chance to save her. But I was young. I really don't know what happened." She squeezed my hand. "We never talked about it, except once, when I asked my father why my mother was going away. I was probably ten years old."

I thought it rude to ask too many questions about something that made Miss Millie's voice shake, but I couldn't help it. "Where'd she go?"

"My father said she was never the same after the baby died. He swore he sent her here for her own good. But—" She stopped walking but still held my hand. She looked up at the trees, then turned towards the fields.

My eyes followed her gaze, and I think she was looking toward the graveyard. I thought of Abigail and how, if her body was taken from the well, they'd bury her there. I think she'd have preferred the well.

"But what?" I asked.

She started walking again, and I stayed in step with her, our hands linked. "He married someone else just a few weeks after he brought her here. He never brought me to visit her, even though I missed her so much. By the time I was twelve, he forbade me to speak of her."

"I'm sorry." My heart ached for Miss Millie. I knew what it was like to miss your mama. "That wasn't fair."

As we approached my dormitory, she slowed down. "I came here to work as soon as they would hire me. But I was too late."

"Too late? What do you mean?"

"She died before I got here. I never got to say goodbye." She sighed. "It didn't change my mind. I still wanted to work here, even if I wasn't able to be here with my mother."

My heart broke for her. I thought about how I was here with my Mama; yet it brought us no closer. Mama wouldn't last long here. This place could never take care of her. Glancing at Miss Millie, I asked, "How'd your mama die?" I felt a tear trickle down my cheek. I wiped it with my free hand and held hers a little tighter.

"I don't know. They never said. When I asked, I was told it was better that way."

"Better she died?"

"In their minds, it was better she wasn't suffering anymore. Better she wasn't a burden to anyone. But I never saw why we couldn't help her not suffer when she was alive. She had a lot to give the world—me—even if she was heartbroken. Even if she was mad."

"I don't see why they couldn't fix her," I said. Then I remembered the way Miss Millie looked out at the burial ground and asked, "Is she buried here?"

She laughed a sad laugh that made me know she didn't understand this place much better than I. "They say she is. But I searched those headstones and markers over and over and couldn't find so much as her inmate number, let alone her name."

"How awful!" I pictured Miss Millie walking around the graveyard alone, the sweet scent of honeysuckles all around, and her bending over each stone in search of some proof her mother was there.

We began walking up the steps to the dormitory, when she let go of my hand and turned to look at me. "That's why I can't let them keep you here. You don't deserve to be here any more than she did. I was too late to save her. But not you. I will do everything I can to save as many of you as I can."

I replayed her words in my head. "Have there been others? Have you saved others?"

"Let's just say my work will never be done. For every person I help, there are countless others whom I can't. But that won't stop me from helping the ones I can."

"Like me?" I asked.

She opened the dormitory door for me. "You don't really need me, Anna. You're going to save yourself."

#

After Miss Millie and I practiced my reading, I returned to the kitchen to check my dough. I peeked under the towels to see that both batches had doubled in size. Jesse and Gayle worked by the trash bin, skinning potatoes for lunch.

I uncovered the bowls and pushed them towards the women. "Jesse, do these look right?"

She squinted and smiled. "Sure do. And I have these for you." She reached into a cabinet and took out a stack of bread molds.

"Thank you. If I remember right, they'll need to do another rise, then we can bake them off," I said.

"I haven't had good bread since before I came here." Jesse rubbed her tummy.

I laid out the molds and sprinkled my hands in flour. "Me neither. But I don't think it's been as long as you."

"I've been here so long that I can't remember not being here. So, I guess I have little memory of fresh bread." Jesse skinned a potato so fast that I was afraid she'd slice her finger.

"I sure hope it's good," I said. "Gayle, you're welcome to a slice, too."

Gayle didn't look up from her potato, but I saw a smile cross her lips.

I punched down the dough and then set it on the stone. I rolled it a bit, not sure how Mama used to do it, then pushed it into the mold. I repeated with the second loaf. They looked the same, except the one with less water had some cracks along the top.

I set them to the side, covered with the cloths again, and went about helping Jesse prepare for lunch. Lunch didn't take much work. We usually had leftover breakfast porridge and some stale bread. On good days, we'd have butter beans and collards.

I turned to Jesse. "Why is the bread always stale? Where's it come from?"

She shook her head. "We sell off the eggs and vegetables. And when they go out to the market, the grocers donate the goods they can't sell. Old cereals, day-old breads and such. That's why it always looks different. Can never tell what the markets will send."

"Mystery bread."

"What's a mystery is why we don't keep more eggs for ourselves. I could whip up a scramble for lunch, in no time. But they don't give me enough, except on holidays."

I thought of saying those eggs were my doing, but I stopped myself. It was time for me to move on. "How can I help?"

She turned to Gayle, who was finishing up the last of the potatoes, and said, "Look at her. She's going to help us. I'll be damned."

"I have another hour before the bread goes in. They don't want me in the field no more, so I'm supposed to stay in the kitchen. Should I find someplace else to work?"

Jesse smacked her hand on her knee. "We're just kidding you. We have more work than we can handle. I'll tell you what. How good are you with arithmetic?"

It felt like a trick. "I never had much schooling."

"Well, can you figure out how many cans of tuna we need for dinner tonight? Unloaded a heap today off the truck, and they're just sitting down there in the cellar.

Figure out how much we need and haul them up here." She pointed at my belly, as if she had just noticed I was carrying. "Can you haul a load up the steps in your condition?"

"Yes. I can do anything."

She glanced at Gayle. "Look at her. She can do anything." She turned back towards me and pointed to the counter by the door. "I tell you what. I need someone who can do anything. You head down to the cellar; figure we feed ten ladies per can. Two-hundred and fifty a night, give or take a few. Figure out how many tuna cans we'll need, bring them up, and set them on that counter."

"Yes, ma'am."

"No one calls me ma'am. Jesse will do just fine."

"Yes, Jesse."

The dark cellar smelled of onions and potatoes. I could hardly see my own two hands, so I felt around for a light. I found a kerosene lamp on a small table and turned it on. The bronze handle was just like the lanterns we had at home. I swung it around, as I walked deeper into the cellar until I spied the tuna. The green cans sat piled high like a tower. My stomach dropped at the thought of figuring out how many we'd need for supper. I went slow. I could count up to how many I could carry each trip. I took five cans the first time. And I counted that as fifty. Then I brought up five more cans and knew that was a hundred. If I did that two more times, I'd be at two hundred. Then one more would be fifty. If I added all that together, I'd have tuna for two hundred and fifty people.

As I was bringing up the last of the tuna, I couldn't help but feel a little bubble of pride roll up in my chest. I forgot all about that Dr. Fender and his panel. I knew then that I could take care of myself, and everyone else, if I had to.

Chapter Thirty-Three

With only two days before the Board visit, everyone in Farview busied themselves with preparations. I barely had time to get my bread out of the oven before Jesse placed the tuna casseroles in. We tidied up while we waited for the bread to cool.

"Don't forget the butter," said Miss Millie, as she bounced into the kitchen.

"You came to try it," I said. "I hope you like it."

"If it tastes close to as good as it smells, we're all in for a treat." Miss Millie set a stick of butter on the counter and set out some plates.

I slid my knife around the sides of the bread to loosen it from the walls of the tins, then popped the bread out and onto the counter. After I sliced it, I placed one from each loaf onto plates, with pads of butter. "I have to figure out which one is better," I said. "So, try both."

"Anna, it's delicious. I've never had such moist bread," Miss Millie said.

Jesse snatched her plate. "I'll be the judge of that." She took a large bite from each slice, then placed her plate on the counter. "This one," she said, pointing to the slice from the loaf with more water. "Definitely this one."

"Really?" Miss Millie said. "I can't tell a difference."

Jesse stood a little straighter. "All I have is this here kitchen. It might not seem like much when you look at the meals here, but I know cooking. If they gave me some decent ingredients to work with, we'd eat like kings." She ripped off a part of the bread dripping with butter and popped it into her mouth. "This here is the bread."

Miss Millie didn't argue. She gave me a hug and thanked me. "Good work," she said, then she left us to finish preparing dinner.

Jesse said, "We might just sneak away some of what you need to make that bread, so that we can have it after the Board visit. Can be our treat for putting up with stale loaves all this time."

I twisted a tea towel in my hands and said, "Oh, I hope I won't be here much longer. I'm going before the panel on Friday after the visit. Hoping they send me home."

Jesse laughed. "Send you home? You think we'd be here if they just willy-nilly let us out? That's not how this works."

"But. Miss Millie said—"

"Miss Millie is a sweet lady who knows what a god-awful place this is. She likes to think we're all biding our time until something better comes along." She huffed and finished the last of her bread. "But there's nothing else for us out there. Once you come here, you can kiss the world outside goodbye. Why do you think I put so much into stale bread and bland potato stew?"

I knew she expected me to know the answer, but I didn't. "Why?" I asked.

"Why? Because it's all I have. It's all I'll ever have."

I asked Jesse what I'd been wanting to know since I started in this kitchen. "If there isn't a chance for you to get out of here, why do you care so much about making this lunch special for the Board? Shouldn't you show them what we really eat?" I regretted it as soon as I saw her expression fall. She always put on such a brave face, and now I thought I saw tears welling up. I looked away.

"What about you?"

"What?" I asked.

"I know you were the one in the henhouse. Turned out more eggs since you came here than we'd ever seen. Why work so hard for something you never got to benefit from?"

"Because that's who I am. I care about my work. And I'm proud of how I got those hens laying."

"Well, I'm proud, too. I'm not giving up who I am just because they locked me away. No, sir. And if I get one chance a year to make a meal that'll knock the socks off someone, I'll be damned if I don't take it."

"Same goes for the panel," I said. "If I get the chance to get out of here, even if it's a far-fetched chance, I'm going to take it. I got too many people counting on me to pass up something like that."

"Good luck to you, then. They must let someone out every now and again. Might as well be you."

#

I couldn't stop Jesse's words from running through my mind. By Wednesday, the day the Board came to visit, I had exhausted myself with worry. My hands shook as I prepared the dough in the morning. For it to be freshly baked by noon, I woke before dawn. I had set out my ingredients the night before and went right to business.

The quiet of the kitchen gave me the creepy crawlies. I remembered the days on the farm when Helen, Alice and John went to school, and I worked alone in the field, planting and sowing until they came home to help. I enjoyed the quiet, knowing they'd be back, chirping about their days, the games they played in the schoolyard and the learning they did. Those days seemed so far away now. I could hardly hear the high pitch of their voices, which got me to wondering how much they'd grown since I'd seen them. I hoped they had someone to love them over this past year and that they were together. If I couldn't be with them, I hoped they had one another. But most of all, I hoped they knew I was looking for them. I wondered sometimes if they thought I forgot all about them. I couldn't bear it.

By lunchtime, I'd changed into another dress and apron, which was the same gray as our usual clothes but scratched a lot less. Everyone had a new dress that day, and I wondered if we would get to keep them after the visit, or if they'd collect them and return our old ones.

I had practiced baking the bread all week. I got so good that I could tell when it was finished by how the kitchen smelled. Just as the crust browned, I pulled out the five loaves I made for the Board and set them on the counter. Then I fanned them with a tea towel, hoping they'd cool fast, so they wouldn't crumble when I cut them.

Each slice turned out moist and delicious. I leaned over the steam and inhaled a deep breath to enjoy the scent of the yeast and salt. Jesse found little china plates, eight of them, so we could serve each member of the Board a proper bread plate. I set a large slice on each, with a pad of butter in the corner.

"All set," I said to Jesse.

"Go on now," she said, waving towards the door, "you serve them. They don't bite."

"Me?"

Jesse smiled and winked. "Why not you? They should get to meet the baker." She handed me a large wooden tray.

"Are you sure?" I asked.

Jesse nodded. "You might see a few of them at your meeting on Friday. Can't hurt to start off with a little gift."

"I'm too scared. I can't." I took a step away from the plates I'd prepared and put my hands on my head to stop the room from spinning.

Jesse took a step towards me and placed her hand on my shoulder. She looked me in the eye and said, "Get on out there. They're across the hall in the parlor room. You baked it. You should serve it." She turned back towards the counter to slice her roast. "I'll be over once I get this on the plates. And be sure to bring back that tray. I'm going to need it for these dishes."

I set the bread plates onto the serving tray. My hands shook as I hoisted the tray onto my shoulder. The dishes rattled. I breathed long, slow breaths as I crossed the kitchen into the hall and the tray stilled. "You can do this, Anna Wilson," I said to myself.

The door across the hall was closed. It was always closed, so I'd never stepped foot into the room until now. I opened the door and noticed that right beside the doorway was a hat rack. Men's hats hung from the hooks, all different shades of brown and one gray. I looked out at the oval wooden table and saw the eight men dressed in neatly pressed suits, all brown and one gray. Each of their ties matched their suits, and I glanced back at the hats and could guess whose hat was whose. I'd never seen men looking so dapper.

When I heard the dishes rattling again, I realized I'd started back shaking.

A cupboard, with only a tiny flower vase, sat beside the table, so I set the tray on it and turned to the gentlemen. I didn't know what to say, so I said, "Good evening, gentlemen," and curtsied, raising my apron and dress a bit, like I'd seen Alice do when she was playing dress-up.

The man in the gray suit laughed. "A little early for evening, isn't it?"

The other men laughed with him, and my face reddened.

I stood there, unable to move for a moment. I don't know what came over me, but my hands and feet would not cooperate.

A man in a brown suit said, "Are you going to serve the bread?"

"Yes, sir," I said. I picked up two plates of bread and set them before two members of the Board. They clunk their glasses as I set them down.

A man scoffed. "Don't you know you should serve from the left?"

"Excuse me, sir?"

"Never mind. I suppose we can only expect so much. Just serve the bread."

"Yes, sir," I said. After I set the rest of the plates down, I shuffled towards the door. Then I remembered I had to bring back the tray for Jesse, so I returned for it. I picked it up in such a hurry that I knocked over the vase, sending water spraying onto me, and goldenrods tumbling onto the floor. "Oh, excuse me," I said. I set the tray back to clean up the vase and flower. After I finished, I took my tray back and walked towards the door. I didn't look behind me to see their faces, but I heard the chattering rise as I left the room.

Someone said, "We can't expect much."

Then I heard them humming. One said, "This is delicious bread. What a treat!"

Another added, "Quite good. Quite good, indeed."

I grew lighter as I walked through the door, as if I could dance my way back to the kitchen. They liked it.

Chapter Thirty-Four

My mind buzzed with fear, as my day before the panel loomed. Preparations for the Board visit busied me, but thoughts of my fate after they left, floated all around me like the scent of dandelions in an early spring meadow. An unfamiliar quiet set over Farview those two days. I wasn't sure where they stored them, but the jumpiest inmates were gone. I imagined a tall man, dressed in white, dangling a loaf of bread and a jug of fresh milk to lure them away from the only place they knew, only to return them once the visitors had left, like sheep returning to the flock, only to be slaughtered.

They set my appointment before the panel for early morning. Just as I finished my cereal, Miss Millie appeared at the doorway and waved. I hopped up, slipped on my worn coat, emptied my tray, and trudged over to her. As we were about to leave the dining hall, I turned back to take one last look at my empty seat and the seat next to mine that was once Abigail's. A few women had tried to sit there since she'd gone, but I shooed them away. The empty seat reminded me of the time we had together. I may have lost my friend, but I couldn't risk losing hope, too. It was all I had left.

I turned to Miss Millie and said, "Are they ready for me?" I straightened my bun, then brushed crumbs from my apron. They should have allowed us to dress up for the meeting. I wanted them to see me as someone who'd blend in on the outside. But I decided to be grateful for the softer dress with no wear in the hem, and an apron with no stains.

We walked down the pathway for a half-mile, towards a cottage set far back, out of view of the graveyard, the well, the henhouse. The building looked like a home, with ivy-wrapped trellises and window boxes dripping with chrysanthemums. I never saw the place before, set off from the rest of Farview on a patch of land with a stream snaking behind it. As we walked up the steppingstones towards the door, I saw where the bed of the stream folded in towards the water, bright moss framing the edges.

Miss Millie reached for my hand. "Are you ready?"

I shook my head. "No. Not ready at all. But I don't think I have much choice about it."

She sighed. "Not if you want to get home." She opened the door, and I followed her. We entered a dark foyer with a round, woven rug and a desk in the center. To one side was a doorway with no door, just a thick, wooden trim and a tall grandfather clock beside it. On the other side was a closed door with an iron knocker.

My mouth dropped open when I realized that Nurse Gladys was standing by a desk, holding a clipboard, a pencil tucked behind her ear. "You're next," she said, making a mark on her paper. "You can hang your coat on the rack." She pointed the pencil towards a curving, wooden coat rack next to me. She didn't say one more word to me after that. I didn't know why, but I hoped she'd wish me luck. But she just worked like I wasn't there.

After I hung my coat, Miss Millie walked me towards the closed door and banged the knocker three times. The sound echoed through the foyer, making the hair on my arms stand up. I pushed my chest out, raised my chin, and took a deep breath.

A man called from inside, "You may enter."

Miss Millie opened the heavy door and stepped aside so that I could walk in. My shoulders drooped as I entered the room, but I quickly pushed them back again.

Eight men sat at a long, rectangular table. One was Dr. Fender, and the others were from the lunch. I remembered their fancy suits and curious eyes, which made me feel more like a wild dog than an eighteen-year-old farmgirl. I looked in the corner and saw a hat rack filled with hats, just like the one from the room where I had served them bread. My heart raced. I hoped they'd remembered me. And if they didn't, if I had the opportunity, I'd remind them who I was and be sure they knew that I had baked that bread. I hoped it would count for something.

"Please, have a seat," Dr. Fender said, pointing to a chair across from the table.

It was bigger than the one from his office. When I sat, it swallowed me. All the men faced me. I straightened my dress, played with my bun, then jutted out my chin again. I didn't want them smelling fear.

"Name?" Dr. Fender said.

I squinted my eyes as if that'd help me think better, then said, "Sir?" Suddenly, I heard a loud ticking that rose louder than my own thoughts. I shot a look behind me to see a tall, wooden clock.

"Name?" he asked again.

A man at the end of the table laughed and said, "He's asking your name. Do you know your name?"

My blood boiled hot, but suddenly I felt my baby kick, and my heart nearly jumped out of my chest. I placed my hand on my belly, felt the roundness of his heel, and told them my name, even though I knew full well that they knew it already. "Anna Wilson."

Each picked up his clipboard and pencil and wrote something down. I imagined they had a list of questions for me, running down their page, and each time I answered, they'd make a tick mark. In the end, my fate rested on how many tallies were for me, or against.

One man, whose mustache curved towards his nose, removed his glasses and asked, "Are you ready?"

The words lodged in my throat. "I am ready," I uttered, then heard the words echo in the room as if someone else were saying them.

Dr. Fender said, "Read these words." He flipped a row of cards onto the edge of the desk, each with large, black lettering.

I scooted forward and almost fell off my seat waiting for my feet to hit the floor. I glanced behind me at the grandfather clock, its bright face almost looking back. Then I returned my attention to the words. "Breathe.

Living. Left. Window. Sold." My eyes grew wide. I looked back at the first card and wasn't sure. Was it breathe or breath?

Each man scratched a small mark on their paper.

For or against? I wondered.

"Moving on." He glanced down at his clipboard, then nodded to the man to his left.

The man reached into his blazer pocket and took out a pouch. He dumped the contents onto the table. I moved forward again in my chair, trying to examine the coins, as he lined them along the edge of the desk. I knew coins. We never had many, but we pinched every cent when we traveled to market.

There were quarters in the bunch, which we didn't have much reason to learn. I didn't remember having a quarter before. Mostly dimes, nickels, and pennies, but we managed. I did my best to count up the amount and said seventy-three cents, like I was as certain as I was scared. If I was sure enough, maybe I'd fool them into thinking I knew more than I did. I watched each of the men make a tick mark, but no one said which way they were leaning. I put my hand behind my back and crossed my fingers that at least a few were on my side.

I glanced up at Dr. Fender, looking for a sign if I was right or not, but his glassy eyes were staring like they didn't see me. I dotted sweat, beading around my brows, with my apron, then wrapped the edges of it around my shaking hands. I clenched the scratchy fabric so tightly that my fingers went numb. It felt like hours before the next man wagered a move.

I thought he might be the gray suit at lunch when he stood and walked over to the front of the table. He set out a row of white, neatly cut circles. They stretched from one side of the table to the next. It took him a few minutes to set them straight, during which time my heart beat in my ears. I prayed I'd be able to hear the directions over all that pounding.

Finally, the man, still standing, turned to me and said, "Count these." Then he sat himself back down like he done pulled a plum from a pie.

I tried counting those circles in my head from my seat, but they got swirly from my nerves, and I lost track after twelve. I didn't want to do it, thought my wobbly knees might give me away, but I stood and pointed at each one, as I counted in rhythm to the ticking of the clock. My head grew woozy, and my knees bent under the weight of me. I leaned on the table to steady myself and took a slow breath to make that darn room stand still. As I exhaled, I blew those pretty circles around the table like a hiccup of snowflakes. "Sorry," I said, gathering them and placing them back into a neat row.

With my heart still thumping in my ears, I counted under my breath so I wouldn't lose track in my head. When I finished, I straightened up, puffed out my chest, and said, "Forty-two." And hot dog, I knew I was right. I used to count the eggs at the henhouse and on my farm, and forty-two was a good day, but I'd gotten better.

They each marked their paper, then looked at me as if they were waiting on me to do something. I wondered if they were as distracted by the ticking as I was. I fidgeted a bit and tried to steady my chair again, but then scolded myself. Showing my nerves would not help me. They needed to believe I knew what I was doing, even if I didn't.

The man on the other end of the table stood up and took out a stack of notecards. Each had a word written on it. He placed the stack on the desk and returned to his seat.

Dr. Fender did the speaking. "Put these words in order."

I scooted forward and set the cards out so that I could read them, then realized I didn't understand the question. I weighed if whether asking would look bad, or if not knowing what I was supposed to do would look worse. A bead of sweat dripped from the back of my ear. Finally, I said, "Doctor, what order do you want?"

The men chuckled.

Dr. Fender said, "In a sentence. Put them in the order of a sentence."

I was in some trouble here, because there were two words I'd never seen before. I must have been taking too long because, after some time, Dr. Fender said, "You have one more minute."

The clock ticked behind me. I watched the face of the tall clock standing, as the second hand measured each moment. The ticking grew louder than my heart, making my skin itch and crawl as if the sound had spider legs. When I didn't think I could take it anymore, I said,

"Finished," and I sighed loud enough for the gray-suited man to shoot me a bewildered look.

They put marks on their papers, and then Dr. Fender said, "Next."

The man to his right stood, leaned over the desk and placed two cards in front of me. "For each set of pictures, you are to identify which is absurd."

The first showed a man with a black mask, holding bags of money. The other a boy shoveling snow. I pointed to the man stealing. The next showed a bear wearing overalls, and a woman sweeping a kitchen, so I pointed to the bear. The next showed a man high in the air after having jumped from a tree. The other showed a man tossing bruised tomatoes in a trash bin. I thought of Abigail and all her reasons for jumping. I thought of how I'd gotten to this point of trying to prove I was worthy of living my own life and taking care of my baby. I looked again at the pictures and the man jumping. His face had dotted eyes and a round circle for his mouth. I pointed to the man with the tomatoes. We could use those for stew.

Dr. Fender spun his pencil between his fingers then made a tick mark. I had stopped watching the other men and kept my eyes on the doctor. He scratched his mustache with the tip of the pencil, then let out a loud sigh.

"Where do you live?" he asked.

"12 Shaker Street," I said.

He shook his head. "You haven't lived there for quite some time, according to our records."

"It's still my farm. It's where I'll go when I leave here," I said.

A loud laugh shot from a man on the end. "You are alone. How would you keep up a farm?"

I rubbed my belly. My thoughts were drifting to my baby, as I heard the men talking. I remembered when I wished to be rid of him. I couldn't see beyond the walls of the Monroe house, couldn't see him as anything but Randolph's. But I was wrong. This baby is no one but himself. He would be his own past, his own present, his own future. Just like I was for myself. It'd be a mistake to think that just because we came from somewhere, it made us who we are. We make ourselves who we are. If anyone knew that, it should be these men, who seemed to have made quite a prize of themselves.

"I kept that farm going, on my own, before the authorities came. I'm eighteen now. I can keep it running and make an income from it."

"How do you plan to do that?" another man asked.

I thought for a moment. "My hens. I sold off my hens before winter last year, but I can get some more on loan, or barter for some of my farming equipment. I'd done it before. And Dr. Fender here knows I'm mighty good at getting hens to lay. I'll sell them at the market and the road stand."

"That's a lot of eggs you'll need to sell." The voice came from the end of the table, but I didn't see who spoke.

My heart raced and sweat pooled around the neck of my dress. "I can get by. When the weather turns, I'll get my crops going again. I've got a nice patch of the land, and it won't be no problem getting broccoli and beets growing for early spring." I glanced behind me at the ticking clock. The air in the room grew thick. I worked to breathe.

The men talked amongst themselves again, and I tried to hear. Then one said, "You are expecting, no?"

Of course I was expecting, I wanted to say. My belly was as round as a watermelon. But I stayed patient. "Yes, sir. I'm expecting this January."

Dr. Fender spoke. "We are aware of your genealogy. You have a history of inebriation, pauperism, feeblemindedness, and ill morality."

"No, Doctor. That's not my history."

"Excuse me," he said. "I have it right here."

I scooted forward and felt the giant chair pulling me back as if it had arms. I wanted to set things straight. "That's not my history. That's my mother's and my father's. But not mine. I worked real hard on the farm. I took care of my siblings, and we might not have had a great feast most nights, but we didn't starve. I made sure they got schooling, and I made their dresses out of flour sacks, even dyed them fancy colors. That is not my history."

"And the illegitimate child?"

Wrapping my arms around my belly, I said, "I am mighty glad for this here baby. I didn't ask for what got him here, but he's all I got now. And my history, it ain't his either. He's going to make his own history. You wait and see."

The men turned to one another and talked again. Their deep voices blended in a low hum. I couldn't make out a word they were saying.

After some time passed, they straightened up in their chairs and looked at me. I crossed my hands on my lap and swallowed bile that rose in the back of my throat.

"We have come to a determination," Dr. Fender said, his hands gripping his papers tightly. "It is our recommendation that you stay here at Farview. We have much to offer you here. And your child, it will be sent to the almshouse."

I jumped from my chair and leaned over the desk. "No!" I shouted. "You can't make me."

"We can, Miss Wilson. It is for your own good."

I slammed my hands on the desk and shouted louder. "My own good? How can this help me or my child?"

Dr. Fender pushed his chair back but stayed seated. "Someone will care well for your child. Someone of better means will take him in. And you can live at Farview and continue the work you do here."

"No. I deserve to leave," I said, pounding my fist on the desk.

A man at the far end of the table tripped over his words as he said, "According to your test today, you are borderline. That gives us pause to whether you'd be capable of living on your own, let alone with a child."

"Borderline? What's that mean?" I asked. My face must have been redder than a beet.

Dr. Fender's face narrowed as he said, "It means you're on the edge of moron."

"What side of it am I on?" I asked, showing my teeth. I had nothing to lose by forcing them to see my way. I wasn't going to stay without a fight.

The man on the end straightened his tie and said, "You pass slightly. A low enough score that we have pause."

"I've had no choices in my life, but I done the best I could. You know I don't belong here." My back arched as I leaned towards the men, pointing a finger at each one. "You know it."

"We are happy to see you have land to return to. But we must consider how you'd keep it. We don't believe you'd sustain yourself with hens alone. And in winter? What would you do?"

Then I remembered their smiles as I left them the other day. "The bread," I said.

"Excuse us?" a man said.

"The bread. You liked the bread at lunch, didn't you?"

"Well, yes, it was delicious."

"I made it. And I can make more. The market, the road stands. They'll sell my bread, too. Until my hens get going, I can sell bread. Then I can do both, once the weather breaks. Everyone likes bread. I can make other things, too, in time."

The men started murmuring to one another, and this time I tried to listen better. I couldn't make out their words, but they grinned and nodded a lot.

"Please, take a seat," Dr. Fender said to me.

I sat back on the chair and planted my feet, ready to jump up screaming again, if they refused to let me go.

"We will prepare for your release. Given you have a means of earning and a residence, we will permit your release in one month's time, so long as you can get your farm in order by then. Conditionally. We will check on your progress periodically, and if we deem necessary, we will commit you back to Farview and relocate the baby."

I heard nothing that they said after they announced I'd be released. I jumped from my chair and let out the sweetest cry I'd ever heard come from my lungs.

Chapter Thirty-Five

I ran out of the room, afraid that if I stayed too long, they'd change their minds. Miss Millie was startled at the sight of me busting through the door.

"They're letting me go!" I shouted.

"What?" she said, looking like she forgot what I went in there for. "What are you saying?"

"They're releasing me. One month I got to get myself in order. That's all the time in the world." I hugged her so tight that I could hear her struggle to breathe, but I didn't let go. I could feel her heart beat as strong as mine, with our bodies pressed together. "Thank you so much. I couldn't have done it without you."

She patted my head and stepped back to look me in the eye. "You did this yourself, Anna. I had nothing to do with it."

"If you didn't believe me, I never would have gone through with this meeting." I leaned over and put my hands on my knees to catch my breath. The scent of pine filled the room, and I noticed a pretty wreath on the inside of the door. Pine and acorns. *When I'm back home, I'll fancy it up just like that.* I stood straight, my breathing steady, and said to Miss Millie, "I was too afraid. I wouldn't have been able to do it without you."

She smiled, as a tear sprung from her eye. "I'm so proud of you. You did it. You really did it."

Nurse Gladys waited in the back of the foyer, busying herself with writing something down on the clipboard, then looked at me and said, "Well, son of a gun, you're going home. When you came to us, I thought for sure you were staying." She went back to writing, but I noticed a grin creep across her lips.

I took Miss Millie's hand, pulled her ear close to my mouth and whispered, "What's conditionally mean?"

"Conditionally?" she asked, her brows knitting.

"Dr. Fender. He said I can get out. Conditionally." I sounded the word out slowly so I was sure I got it right.

"Oh, he means that if you're not successful, you'll have to return."

My head dropped, and my smile vanished.

She placed her hand on my shoulder. "But there's no reason to fret over that. You'll find your way. I know it."

My mouth flooded with saliva, and I thought I might gag. I put my hand to my mouth and swallowed hard. I watched Nurse Gladys in the corner, too busy to notice me. "What if they bring me back?"

"We can't think about things like that. You have a long road ahead of you to prepare to go home. We shouldn't waste any time in getting your farm ready for you," Miss Millie said.

"We?" I asked.

"I have off in a few days. I can see about taking you out to work on the farm. They'll give you leave if you're working to prepare a place to stay for your release."

My heart filled my chest. "Do you mean it? You'll help me?"

"Of course, I'll help you."

#

Miss Millie and I walked back towards the dining hall in silence. My excitement turned to worry and sadness, as we walked the long path back. A chilly breeze whipped through the air, reminding me of the day I watched Abigail walk through the storm towards the well. My stomach lurched. I wished I could share this celebration with her.

The land was quiet. The fields were dotted with a few inmates, but most were empty, already having been prepared for winter. The scent of burning leaves floated through the skies. The smell of home.

Finally, I broke the silence. "Where is everyone?" I asked. "Why aren't they working?"

Miss Mille pulled her coat tighter. "The weather is turning. There's a lot to do inside. Sewing. Laundry. Soap-making. It won't be long and they'll be outside again in the fields."

I stopped walking to look out over the land. I always thought of my farm as big. It was my whole world. But compared to Farview, it was small and shabby. My stomach clenched at the thought of fixing it up, making my way by myself. Doubt nudged me.

When I started walking again, I said, "What if I can't do it? What if I can't get the hens to lay enough eggs to keep the farm going? What if no one wants to buy my bread? What if I'm not conditional?"

"Is that how you told them you'd make your way?" she asked. Her voice rang like a melody.

"Yes. That's all I could think of. I don't know how to do anything else."

"I think it's a clever idea."

By the time we arrived at the dining hall, the women had finished lunch. A few sat scattered at tables. My stomach gnawed from the excitement, so I had no appetite.

"I have to attend to other duties. But we will plan to work on your farm early next week." She took my hands in hers and leaned close. "I'm so happy for you, Anna."

The sound of my name on her lips made my soul bubble up. I smiled and said, "Thank you, Miss Millie."

When I was about to leave the dining room, wild gray hair caught my eye. It was Mama. My blood ran cold, as I realized I needed to tell her. I hoped she'd be happy for me, for Helen, Alice, and John, but I was afraid of what she might say. Miss Millie might have believed in me, but I wasn't so sure about Mama.

I walked up behind her and saw that her lunch was hardly eaten. The stew meat floated in the pale broth and a few potatoes clumped together by her spoon. Even the nub of brown bread lay untouched.

When I brushed her shoulder, she turned around. Her eyes grew wide. "Anna, I forgot you were here."

I slumped into the chair next to her. "How'd you forget, Mama?"

She held my chin in her coarse hands. "You look like your grandma." She smelled of acrid soap and urine.

"Mama, I'm getting out. Dr. Fender said I can go home to the farm."

Her forehead tensed. "Oh, Dr. Fender is a good man."

I didn't want to fight with her. I wasn't sure how much more time we'd have together. "He says I can go home. Do you know what that means?"

She shook her head.

"It means I can see about getting back the young'uns. We can live on the farm again."

She smiled, but it never reached her eyes. "You'll do right by them?" It was a simple question, not an order. She wasn't sure.

I clasped her hands. They were paper-thin and cold as rain. "You, too. I'm coming back for you."

"You'll do right by them," she said. "Go on. Go on." She patted my shoulder and shooed me towards the door.

I wondered whether Mama needed more help than she let on. She seemed strong and brave when I was younger. I never realized how hard raising us, on her own, must have been. How lonely she must have been. Did she think we were better off without her? That she was better off here, wasting away without a life of her own? I vowed that

once I settled myself in and the baby came, I'd come back
for her.

Chapter Thirty-Six

My heart rose the day I finally got to prepare my home for my return, as if each day that my release grew closer, the weight that held me down lightened. After an hour's drive, in what looked like the same automobile that brought me to Farview months earlier, we turned onto Shaker Street, as the sky shifted from dawn to daytime. The air seeping around the windows was brisk, but the sun shone so brightly that you'd think it was the height of summer. As we pulled onto the dirt driveway, I looked out my window at the overgrown vines wrapping themselves around the sides of our shack and climbing the peeling white beams on the porch. The rich scent of wood burning filled the air.

Miss Millie sat quietly next to me. Neither of us said a word during the drive. She arranged the ride for us, but she didn't speak to our driver as if she knew him. Once he stopped in front of the porch and opened our door, I felt relieved. I looked at Miss Millie's face and saw her mouth drop open and her eyes grow wide as plum pits. I imagined she thought my house was in better shape, but I was happy it looked very much the same as it did when we left.

We took our lunch sacks and a bag of tools Miss Millie brought and walked towards the steps. The wheels kicked up the orange dirt as the auto pulled away, leaving us alone at my home. My home. It was a shack, not much to look at and leaning a bit to one side, but it was enough for me. I touched my belly to feel the swirling life under my palm. We were home. And soon, we'd be there for good.

We stepped onto the creaking porch and looked through the paned windows.

"Do you have a key?" Miss Millie asked.

"We never had use for a key."

"Then I guess we can go right in," she said, her voice raising with excitement.

"I guess so," I said, reaching for the knob. As I walked through the doorway, my heart felt heavier than I expected. I thought this moment would make me as happy as a stray cat who wandered home, but the weight of what I'd lost since I was last there pressed on my chest. The chair I sat in, that day Mama left, still had the fraying arms. All I thought was, *How did we lose it all?* I had no idea our lives would fall apart once Mama walked out that door. And now here I was, fixing to put it all back together.

I jumped when I heard Miss Millie's voice.

"It's cold in here. Should we start a fire?"

I almost forgot she was here with me. "Yes. We've got the fireplace in here," I said, pointing to the one in the front room, "or we can use the wood stove in the kitchen. That one'll heat the whole house, if we get it going well enough."

311

I followed Miss Millie into the kitchen. We hadn't known when we left that we would be gone long. It was untouched. Had we had dinner in the icebox or the cereal in the pantry, mice and the stink of rot might have covered the place, but we didn't have food to speak of. I had fretted that morning over how to get us enough for supper.

Miss Millie bent towards one bucket set in the center of the kitchen, a thin layer of ice forming on top. "Are these for leaks? Good thing you had them set up when you left. I'm surprised they're not fuller." She picked up the bucket and walked out the back door, to dump it over the railing.

I looked down at the cracking wood floor and puddles splashed around the buckets. I swallowed the memory. "It rained just as the authorities came. We were setting up the buckets when we heard them pull up." The image of Helen, Alice, and John, that day almost a year ago, popped in my mind, their scrappy bodies bony like barn cats. "Have you found them?"

She set back the bucket and looked at me, pursing her lips. "I will. It will take time. I have a new person to speak to at the Children's Aid Society. I'm hoping that will help."

"Miss Atkinson," I said.

"Who?"

"She's the woman who took us away."

"Miss Atkinson," she said. "It can't hurt. I will try to reach her tomorrow. Today, let's see about getting this place in shape for you to come home."

I smiled at the thought of it, then looked around the room at the puddles, the dusty furniture, the rusted coffee mill. "It needs a lot of work. I don't know where to start."

"Best to think little at first. What can we do right now?"

I shivered and looked at the stove. "We can get the fire going. There's wood stacked out the back door."

I passed Miss Millie as she reached over the railing to grab a few logs, and I went down the steps towards the field and sheds. We had sold off any livestock that didn't die after Mama left, so the barns were empty, but the roofs looked to be in fine shape. We'd have to mend the roof of the house before I moved in and make sure we got the house warm enough for a baby. The old coop we used before we sold off the last of the chickens looked rickety, so it'd need some fixing up. I'd fix it with what I already had around the farm. I had a way of making do.

I walked across what used to be the patch of land we used for our winter crops, towards our storage shed. Weeds tangled around the chicken wire and stakes, like angry fingers. It was small but allowed for enough broccoli, cabbage and turnips to feed us, as well as some extra for selling at market. The land was overgrown now and needed tilling before I could plant anything, but once I settled, I could turn it around.

I rummaged through the shed for something to patch the roof. A barrel of roofing cement sat on top of a few tarps. I collected the tarps and the barrel and brought them towards the back of the house. I left the barrel by the steps and went into the kitchen to find Miss Millie lighting the fire.

I held up the tarps and said, "We can use these to close off the upstairs. That way, the wood stove will just need to heat the kitchen and the front room."

Miss Millie smiled. "What a great idea! That will make it easier for you once the baby comes."

"There's twine in that drawer," I said, pointing to one in the Hoosier cabinet next to the stove. "We can use that to fasten the tarps."

"I have a hammer and nails in my bag," Miss Millie said.

By afternoon, we had finished hanging the tarps, and the place grew warm and cozy. Miss Millie took a towel and wiped down the table and set out our lunches.

"Peanut butter. My favorite," I said. "And a Coca-Cola."

I had only drunk a Coca-Cola one other time, at a picnic at the end of Shaker Street. The people who lived there had moved years ago, but that day was filled with hopscotch and jump rope. It was sad to think of how much had changed, and I wished to get my siblings back, so I could see to it they were safe and happy.

"Do you think you'll find them?" I asked.

"Your sisters and brother?" She took a bite of her sandwich, then said, "I do. I promise I will find them soon. Miss Atkinson can help, I'm sure."

"Now you just need to find her."

"I will. I will," she said, as she drained her Coca-Cola.

We finished the day with dusting and sweeping. By the time we finished, we had a load of dirty towels, but the front room and kitchen were the cleanest I'd ever seen them.

"I'll take home these towels and clean them for next time. Is there anything else we should plan for the next time?"

"The roof. I found some roofing cement, so maybe we could patch it. And the henhouse."

Miss Mille placed the dirty towels in a laundry sack as she said, "Good ideas. Anything else?"

"We have plenty to do. But I'd like to see about getting some hens again."

"That would be great. Do you know where you'd get them?"

I helped her hoist the heavy bag of towels onto her shoulder, and we walked towards the front door. I pushed aside the tarpaulin and opened the door. We stepped onto the porch, and she dropped the bag with a thud.

"My neighbor's, right there." I pointed to the Joneses' house. "We're mighty close with them. I imagine they wonder where we up and went. I bet if I ask them, they'll let me trade with them some loaves of bread or some farm work for a few hens, to get me started."

"Oh, that's lovely."

I reached down and squeezed her hand. "Out on the farms, we have to stick together. But I guess it's not just farms?"

She squeezed mine back. "We all need to help one another sometimes. And I'm glad to be here, helping you get your home back."

"I'm glad you're here, too."

#

When we returned to the farm a week later, the Joneses ran to meet us as we stepped out of the automobile. I was grateful for the opportunity to introduce Miss Millie to them and hear they'd been well while we were gone. They never knew what had happened to us, but they tended the house during storms when we were away, by emptying the buckets. It felt good to know someone had been looking out for me when I wasn't there. All this time, I'd been looking out for so many people. I never realized someone had been doing the same for me.

When I told of our plan to restore the henhouse, they brought over extra planks they'd had from a shed they took down a few weeks ago. They piled it by the coop and offered help. I appreciated their kindness, but this was something I wanted to do alone; with the help of Miss Millie. I had come so far and wanted this handiwork to be my own.

We carried a toolbox and walked along the back property line towards an old garden shed with a caving roof. As we neared it, the scent of mold and rotting wood hung in the air. I walked around the structure to examine the damage of neglect and rain. Most of the wallboards were decayed, but I figured there'd be enough salvageable pieces to rebuild the coop.

"If we pull off the good boards, put those together with the healthy ones already on the coop, and add in the boards from the Joneses, I think we'll have enough to make it sturdy," I said to Miss Millie.

A stiff wind swept through the farm. She pulled her jacket tighter and slipped her hood over her head. "Whatever you say. I've never done this type of labor before."

"On a farm, you do what needs getting done." I reached into the toolbox and took out two hammers. "This is for you," I said.

We pried nails from the healthier boards which were towards the center of the roofline. Rusted nails made for easy work pulling the planks apart. I squatted to work on the bottom of the frame, wiggling the hammer claw to loosen the nails. The board popped off when I repeated the same thing for the top. I tossed it in a pile of healthier wood. We kept the scraps in a separate pile for kindling and firewood. As we tore off the walls of the shed, the roof sagged more and more. The smell of soot and mold grew thick. By the time we finished, only the outline of the shed remained. We heard rumbling overhead and jumped back as the roof gave way.

We carried the heavy stacks to where the chicken run used to be. Only a few boards remained.

"This isn't sturdy enough. Let's take it down and start over with longer boards. We can use these shorter pieces to make new nesting boxes."

"How long should we make it?" asked Miss Millie.

I sat down the piece of wood I'd been holding and thought a minute. I walked the length of the old run, then walked it again. "Twenty paces if I want to raise a proper amount of hens. Enough to see to it that we have eggs for eating and selling."

"That's a fine idea."

Within a few hours, we had the coop looking proper enough to raise hens and keep them dry and warm in the cooler months. All we had left to do was run chicken wire. I thought back to when I started in the coop at Farview. I remembered those poor chickens working themselves into such a tizzy that they couldn't lay. As Miss Millie started unrolling the wire to attach to the old metal stakes in the ground, I stopped her.

"Wait. If we want to keep them safe, we need to dig a foot-long trench along the outside, so the wire is deep enough underground that no foxes can dig under it."

It was mid-afternoon by the time we finished, and we hadn't even had our lunch yet.

As we dragged the scraps to place into the woodpile for the stove, Miss Millie said, "You never practiced making your bread."

I rubbed my hands together to warm them, then dropped them by my side. I looked out at the fields, barren and frozen—but mine. Turning towards the house, I saw my home again. "That's OK. It's all coming back to me now. I think I'm going to be OK."

Chapter Thirty-Seven

For the next week, I felt like I was living someone else's life; it was as if my spirit had already left Farview, but my body remained. The time I wasn't in the henhouse, I spent in the kitchen, yet I hadn't brought myself to tell the others I was leaving. Part of me believed that once I said it, I risked having it taken away. Another part of me feared that my good fortune might make them feel sad about their bad. The more I thought about the women at Farview, the more I realized that so much of what brought us here was luck. These were good women who, if given the chance, would find lives of their own and something to be proud of. None of us were likely to become wealthy or famous, but we could make a life for ourselves through hard work. Wasn't that enough?

A week before my release, I started tying up loose ends. They had been tugging at me for weeks, but I couldn't bring myself to bind them. That meant I really was moving on, and as much as I wanted to go home, there was a lump in my chest that kept growing the closer that day came.

In the kitchen, alone with Jesse, while chopping celery for a potato-soup dinner, I turned to her and said, "They let me out."

"Son of a gun," she said. "I was going to ask, but I figured you'd tell me if there was something to tell." She took a fresh stalk of celery and carried on chopping. "Didn't know you had it in you."

I laughed. "Neither did I. At least, I didn't think I could convince them I did."

She nudged me with her elbow. "It was the bread that convinced them."

"I don't think it hurt," I said. I chopped for a few minutes, then stopped. "Why are you here? How'd someone like you end up here?"

Without looking up, she said, "Ain't no more good a reason than you're here. There're a few ladies here that might need looking after, but most of us—" She set her knife down and turned to rest her back on the counter. "Most of us had someone who thought we were more trouble than we were worth. I have a loud mouth, and I'm not afraid to use it." She turned back towards the celery, and chopping, said, "My story isn't any different from anyone else's. We all have a tale to tell, if anyone will listen." She wiped her brow with the back of her hand. "Problem is, nobody will." She looked at me and smiled. "But I'm happy for you, kid. You deserve it. You and that little one of yours. You're going to be OK."

"Thanks, Jesse."

#

I had one last thing to do before I left Farview. The day before I was leaving, I found Bobby walking the halls of my dormitory. He stood, toe tapping, over a gray-haired woman who mopped the floors with a shredded rag. I choked on the smell of ammonia as I walked towards him. He turned to look at me. He must have seen the fire in me, because his eyes bulged, and he tried to turn away. I grabbed his shoulder and turned him back to look at me.

"You're going to listen to what I have to say." My face was so close to his that I could smell stale smoke on his breath.

He laughed. "What are you talking about?"

"Abigail." The sound of her name made my vision swirl and my head fuzzy. I shouted at him. "You didn't do right by her! She trusted you!"

"You loon. What do you know?"

"I know she was having your baby. And you were running around."

I heard a bang and turned to see an inmate toting a bucket of water. She moved past us and stopped by the older lady. She replaced the old bucket with the new one, then passed us again.

I lowered my voice. "She trusted you."

He shrugged his shoulders and rolled his eyes. "She was a loon, too. I never promised her anything."

"She was having your baby."

He scoffed. "No proof it was mine. Could've been anyone's. You know that's why she was in here."

"I saw you with the other girl. I know there must have been others."

"So what? Abigail was crazy."

"She thought you two would marry. You were supposed to take her away from here."

He huffed and kicked at the bucket. Water splashed where the woman scrubbed. "She told me all about that plan you two came up with. That was crazy talk. I thought she lost her mind when she told me about it. I laughed at her—"

"You laughed at her?"

He held up his hand and turned away from me. "You two were a perfect match. Living in some dream world," he said. He started walking down the hall but turned back one last time and said, "She got what she wanted. She's out of here."

"She deserved to live!" I shouted at him.

He stopped, turned towards me, and straight-faced, said, "She had nothing to live for." He walked away.

I raced after him. When I caught up to him, I shoved him hard, and he flew into the bare wall. "She was a better person than you'll ever be. You didn't deserve her. No one did. She was too good for Farview. Too good for the world. I only wish she saw you for what you are."

He shrugged his shoulders and laughed. "Oh, yeah, what am I?"

"Some no-good rat who's afraid to look in the mirror to see who he really is. You think you're high and mighty because you get to boss all these lost women around. But out in the real world, I bet you're as chicken and feeble as the rest of us."

I dragged myself into the dormitory and slumped onto my bed. The next day, I'd be home with so much to live for that it scared me. I questioned how much I could have counted on Abigail from the start, but she had offered me hope. I was grateful for that. But hope was a tricky thing. It made you believe in something that wasn't yours—maybe never would be. If you leaned too far into hope, you got sucked in like a twister. You believed the impossible. I think that's what happened to Abigail. She had so much hope that once she lost it, she lost everything.

I like to think that if I knew how lost she was, I'd have been the one trying to save her. I could have gotten us out, and we could have left Bobby behind. We could have raised our babies as sisters or brothers, with no fathers to speak of, no past to speak of, just a future that was all theirs. But it was too late for that now.

I left the dormitory and walked outside in the brisk air. The bare trees stood tall all around Farview, like tall fence posts trapping us. When I came to the well, I placed my hands along the lip and stared to the bottom, hoping to see a glimpse of Abigail, some last image to leave me with— even though I knew it'd haunt me forever. There was nothing but darkness, the kind that burrows itself in the pit of your stomach and stays with you long after you've left a place. I leaned down and picked a handful of dying wildflowers. They had suffered the cold yet still maintained a bit of their colors: yellow, orange, purple. I dropped them into the well, hoping they'd make their way to my friend.

I moved towards the coop and saw a few hens in the front pen, pecking for feed. In the corner, farthest from the group, sat Queenie, one eye now missing, and a patch of feathers ripped from her wing. I stepped into the pen and walked towards her. She didn't scurry; she remembered me.

"Hi Miss Queenie," I said, squatting and patting her head. She let out a rumble that sounded like purring. "You're going to make it. Just keep fighting. Show them you're better than they think you are."

As I sat there, rubbing the hole where her eye was, I wondered what would happen to Queenie. The pecking order was set. The others would always see her as less than them. I wanted to tuck her under my arm and bring her with me.

"I'll come back for you, too," I whispered to her. And I vowed then that I would. I leaned towards her, "You deserve better." I made a promise to myself that when I had the chance, I'd help those who needed it. Queenie would be my first, but she wouldn't be the last. Life was hard, I learned, and we needed to help one another when we could. I was glad that Miss Millie had learned that a long time ago.

I stepped out of the pen and headed towards the dining hall to start my last duty in the kitchen. When I turned the corner into the hall, I saw Miss Millie standing outside the kitchen door, holding a book.

"I couldn't wait to tell you," she said.

My heart raced, and I leaned towards her. "Did you find them?"

"I did. They are together. The three of them. In the home of a couple who has three other children. I don't know how well cared for they are, but I thought you'd want to know they are at least together."

My shoulders dropped, losing the weight I'd been carrying. "Thank you. When can they come home?"

She glanced towards the floor, then back at me. "It won't be that simple. But I'm sure they'll allow a visit. I will see to it."

My vision grew blurry, and my breath quickened.

"You'll see them again, Anna. They'll be so happy to see that you're home."

I sighed. "But I want to have them home. Forever."

"We know it won't be that easy. Start small. A visit. Once you settle, you can see about getting them back."

"What about my mother?" I asked. It surprised me that I said that. From the way Miss Millie's eyes widened, it surprised her, too.

"What about her?" she asked.

I shook my head and put my hands in my apron skirt. Words lodged in my throat.

"What about her?" she asked again.

An emptiness filled me. "I can't leave her here. Can I bring her home?"

"Does she want to come home?" Miss Millie asked, placing a hand on my shoulder.

Jesse called from the kitchen, "You out there? We could use some help in here."

"I should go," I said. As I walked away, she reached for my hand.

"Take care of you and your baby, for now. You'll reach your Mama when the time's right. For now, you'll have a hard enough road ahead." She held up the book she was holding. "This is for you. It's a journal. Write every day about all you learn, all you overcome. This little one," she said, pointing to my belly, "will want to know how brave his mama is."

"Thank you," I said, taking the book. I held it tight to my chest as I walked in to make my last meal at Farview.

Chapter Thirty-Eight

On the day I was leaving, I woke early. I packed up the few things that were mine, my pillowcase stuffed with the book I stole from the Monroes, my comb, the doll Alice made me, and the pair of tights that were now too rotted for wearing. While the others were stuck in fitful sleep, I set these things, that had once seemed so important to me, on my bed. I had hardly taken them out since I'd been at Farview. I touched them, remembering why they had meant so much to me when I rushed out of my home that day. But I wasn't the same girl who packed these up. The hidden girl, whose only goal was survival, no longer existed. Now I wanted to make a life for myself, my baby, my family. I hankered for a life of my own, and I wouldn't concern myself with people who thought ill of my kind. I knew I had as much right to a proper life as anyone. Bobby, Dr. Fender, Randolph, Ma; they had all tried to convince me I wasn't enough. But I knew better now.

Somewhere, somehow, people like that convinced Mama that she couldn't live a life of her own. That thought weighed heavy on my chest as I picked up my pillowcase and held it close to me. I crawled in a ball by the window, looking at the stars as the sun rose. Within moments, they'd be gone, outshined by the sun. But for now, I watched them sparkle, as if their shine would never burn out.

I looked at Abigail's old bed. Someone had moved in there a few nights before. An older woman whose hair was as gray as ash. I looked back at the stars and wondered, if Abigail were watching me, if she'd be smiling.

As everyone woke, I dressed quickly so I could sneak out to the henhouse before anyone else set to work. On my way, I stopped by the kitchen to grab an empty box used to store potatoes. I snuck into the coop and found Queenie pecking away at the dirt, not a speck of feed in sight.

I bent down to pet a tuft of feathers on her head. "You're coming with me, girl. I'm taking you home." I scooped her up and placed her into the box, then sprinkled feed onto the floor of the box. I closed the top loosely then snuck back up to my room to put it with my pillowcase. I knew no one would miss poor Queenie.

Then I darted to breakfast. I didn't want to miss Mama, and I knew she was an early riser. I sat in a chair by the door, holding the pillowcase on my lap. When she walked in, I jumped.

"Mama," I said, realizing I hadn't planned what to say, only that I knew I couldn't leave without seeing her one last time.

She looked surprised to see me. "Anna, is that you?"

"Yes, Mama, it's me. I wanted to see you before I go." I reached out my arms to hug her, but she took a step back.

"Where are you going, dear?" Her eyes looked cloudy, like a fogged mirror.

"Home. Remember? I told you Dr. Fender was letting me go home."

"Oh, Dr. Fender is a good man."

"He is, Mama. And he's letting me go home."

"That's right. I remember now." She pressed her hand on my belly. "You're having a baby, too."

"I am. I'll be home before he's born. He'll get to live at the farm." I paused a moment, then said, "One day, I want you to come back to the farm to live with us, too."

She smiled and opened her mouth, but no words came out.

"I'll come back for you. I promise."

"You just see about the others. You take care of them. You hear?"

I reached in to hug her, and this time she didn't step away. She leaned in to hug me back.

"I will. I promise." The words felt like vinegar on my tongue. I hoped I wasn't lying. I would do everything I could to see about getting them home. "I love you, Mama."

"I love you, too."

#

The ending always feels fast, like a twister whipping through your days, picking you up in one place, dropping you in another. I landed at my farm in what felt like a moment, even though I'd spent a year fighting to get back. The driver pulled up my dirt drive, then walked around to open my door. I stared out the window, seeing my house as if for the first time. This time, it was mine to keep, or to lose, and the thought rattled around my head as I stepped my booted feet on the cold, orange dirt. My shaking hands gripped the box, and I set my pillowcase on top.

"Thank you," I said.

The driver tipped his hat and drove off in an instant.

For the first time in a long time, I was alone at my home. My body felt lighter than it had in ages, and I spun around the front yard, holding the box with Queenie high over my head. "We did it, girl!" I shouted. Then, because I could shout now, as loud as I wanted, I screamed it again. "We did it!"

I trekked to the coop and opened Queenie's box. She looked up at me with her single eye and let out a loud-pitched cluck.

"You're home," I said. I hoisted her up and set her in the pen. She hopped and flapped her wings, enjoying her freedom. "Nobody's going to hurt you again. I'll see to it." The sight of her in her new home warmed me, despite the frigid air. She looked happy.

I scattered a little feed for her then walked back to the front of the house and up the steps. Their creaking pounded in my ears, and my heart raced. I pulled back the tarp and stepped into my home. I placed the box and bag on the floor next to me and dropped into the chair, just as the tears started falling. They shifted into heaving sobs, shaking my insides. Tears of happiness, I knew, because with each drop a weight lifted from my body, and my muscles grew less tense. I'd been prepared for a fight for so long, and this was the end of it. Now I had a safe place of my own again. And I wasn't letting anyone take that away.

I made a fire in the wood stove and prepared some bread with the ingredients Miss Millie got me. I trudged to the well for water and poured a glass to drink, as I mixed the dough. As my hands pounded the dough, I felt a little lighter, grateful that this was the beginning of a new life, and the end of an old one.

I set out the dough for its first rising and strolled outside to check the coop. It looked sturdy and beautiful, and I imagined it full of hens to keep Queenie company, their feathers dotting the run and tiny feet leaving imprints in the mud. I wouldn't allow any of them to treat each other like Queenie was treated. That I swore.

I rummaged through the shed in search of anything to trade for a few chickens, and I stacked the items. When I found little, I searched the house for furniture, pictures, mirrors, or vases. Anything of value. I put on a coat and climbed the stairs, where it felt near freezing. Our bed we had shared remained the same, a few quilts, flattened pillows crumbling from dry rot, and a patched mattress. In the corner, I found a coat rack we used to hang our night dresses on and hauled it downstairs to add to my pile for bartering.

When I checked on the dough, it had doubled its size. After kneading it a second time, I placed it in the bread tins that were stored in the Hoosier cabinet. I covered them with the towels that Miss Millie had cleaned, and suddenly a warmness overtook me. I was doing all this for myself and the people I loved. No one would steal the life I wanted to live. Exhaustion settled into my bones, the kind that hits after you realize a fight is over, win or lose. I tucked the bread by the stove for warmth, covered them, and rested on the chair with a quilt.

I awoke from a nap, with a crick in my neck and legs tingling. I gazed around the room, and it looked fuzzy and out of focus, like I was looking through the surface of a lake. I felt like a mixture of myself and a stranger. The Anna who had left this farm a year ago had returned as someone else. But a piece of her had survived under the layers of who I was now. It was like she was the seed that brought me here. Now I could bloom. I thought I'd want to leave her behind when I came back here, thinking there was something terribly wrong with her. But now that I got to thinking, if it wasn't for her, I'd never be back here, earning my keep and making myself proud.

I set an empty bread tin upside down onto the wood stove and set the one filled with the dough on top, then covered them with an upside-down stockpot. As I shifted the pot to make sure the bread was centered on the hot surface, I heard the crumbling of stone on the drive. I jumped and ran to see who was visiting me already. My heart sank at the memory of Miss Atkinson coming here to take us away.

A long, black auto stopped in front of the porch, but I couldn't see inside. Then Miss Millie stepped out of the passenger side front seat.

"You came!" I shouted.

Then the other doors swung open, and out poured Helen, Alice, and John. I ran down the porch steps shouting, "You're here. You're here!"

They wrapped their arms around me, holding so tight that I could hardly breathe.

Helen stepped back and pulled the others off me. "You're having a baby?" she asked.

"You're here," I said, still unable to believe what I was seeing. "Where have you been?"

She smiled brightly and said, "We've been together. The Hutchinsons out by the county road. We're close to here." Tears welled in her eyes. "I wish they didn't split us apart. They said you were too old to come with us."

"I missed you. I missed you all," I said, reaching towards them.

John, who'd grown the length of a dandelion stalk since I'd last seen him, said, "Why didn't you come with us?"

"They wouldn't let me. I had no idea where you were until Miss Millie found you." I walked towards Miss Millie and hugged her. "Thank you for bringing them to me. I missed them so much."

I looked over to see Alice dancing on the front porch, twirling in her long dress. "We're home."

"Can they stay?" I asked Miss Millie.

"No. They're just here for a visit."

My smile fell. "Do you think I can ever have them back here with me?"

Helen interrupted. "Yes. We are coming home now. We're not going back there," she said.

Miss Millie took a step towards us. "I have to bring you back. Maybe one day you can come home, when Anna gets things in order."

I asked Helen, "How are they treating you there?"

Alice called from the porch, "They have cakes and cookies, and I get to read all the books I want."

"Hush, Alice," Helen said. "They are treating us fine. But it isn't our home. We want to come back. With you." Helen reached down and touched my swollen belly. "Are you really—?"

"I am. Due January. Will be here before I know it." I swallowed my words, knowing what she'd ask next.

"Who's the daddy?"

I shook my head, not wanting to lie to Helen but knowing it wasn't the time for truth-telling. Those truths needed to be peeled back like an onion. One day. "That's no matter. He's all mine." I laughed. "You're going to be an auntie."

"Oh, an auntie. I can't wait." She bent down and kissed my belly.

John ran and gave me one last hug before he took off into the fields.

Helen and I watched him as he hopped through the dirt, kicking his heels.

"He misses the farm terribly," Helen said. "We've all missed you."

"We'll be back together. I promise." I put my hand on her shoulder, and suddenly a whiff of yeast struck me. I said, "Oh no, come inside."

We raced inside, past the tarp and into the kitchen, the house filled with the scent of freshly baked bread. I took the tea towels and covered my hands to lift the stockpot, then placed the browned bread on the counter. I rummaged through a drawer to find a knife.

"It looks delicious. Remember when you and Mama used to bake bread?" Helen said.

I looked around to be sure that Alice and John were not around. "I found her."

"You what?" Helen asked.

"I found Mama," I said, in a voice a hair louder than a whisper.

Helen shook her head, and her eyes grew wide. "Well, where is she? Is she coming home?"

"I can't talk about it now. But someday I'll tell you everything. For now, we have to work on getting you home. Then we need to work on getting Mama home." I loosened the bread from the pan, then said, "Now let's just enjoy that we found each other."

Miss Millie called from outside the house. "We'll have to be going soon."

I cut the bread into thick slices, while Alice called for John and Helen out the back door. They raced in.

"Bread," John said. He took a slice and inhaled the scent in a deep breath. He took a big bite. "Delicious."

Alice did the same.

As they finished their bread, I said, "You'll have to go back now. But you can come visit me again. And I'll see about getting you back home." I paused, realizing they had more at their new home than I could give them. "That is, if you want to."

"Oh, I want to be home," said Alice. "More than anything."

John, a big ball of bread in his mouth, said, "Me, too. I want to be back home."

The four of us hugged, then I scooted them towards the door. "Go on, now. And I'll see you soon."

The younger two darted. John got trapped in the tarp for a moment, but Alice unraveled him.

When they were gone, Helen said, "I love you. I've missed you so much."

"I've missed you, too. We'll be together soon."

"I know," she said, giving me one last hug before following the young'uns out the front door.

I trailed behind them and stood on the front porch, waving as they loaded themselves into the car.

Miss Millie walked onto the porch and held my hand. "I will be back to visit soon. Good luck here. You should be very proud of yourself."

"Thank you," I said. "I couldn't have done it without you."

Miss Millie smiled. "Anna Wilson, I think you can do just about anything."

As they drove away, I placed one hand on my belly and waved with the other. "We're going to be OK, little one."

I looked up at the setting sun. Dim stars peeked out from behind its fading rays. When the wind died down, I heard them call to me. *You're not invisible.* And they were right. And for the first time in my life, I was glad to be seen.

Printed in the USA
CPSIA information can be obtained
at www.ICGtesting.com
LVHW090752060524
779415LV00003B/191

9 781837 940103